To everyone who grew up in Evergreen, or a town similar.

Thanks to my family for always being there. And thanks to the BFVC for keeping me connected, and for spending countless hours discussing all the irrelevant shit that totally matters.

BAD COP WORSE COP

A BLACK FOREST NOVEL–BOOK 2

J. SCOTT BOYD

Published in the United States by Deadese Publishing

ISBN: 979-8-218-51478-5

Book design by Jelena Gajic, @coverbookdesigns

Second Paperback Edition

PROLOGUE

TREES HAVE GROWN SO CLOSE TO THE cabin over the years, that it's difficult to tell where the forest ends and the dwelling begins. The wood exterior has darkened with age to the point it looks burnt. A single window on the ground floor sits propped open with a stick. The pine scent entering through the opening is no match for the sour stench of unwashed men. The cabin, and the three men who wait inside, aren't all that far from Black Forest High School—where, just yesterday, Jack Larson and Cash McDermid endured their final day of tenth grade.

The town of Black Forest sits nestled in a sprawling, hundred-square-mile forest, more than a mile above sea level. Despite being twice the size of San Francisco, its population is less than 15,000—no density issues here. Even though it feels like it's in the middle of nowhere, Black Forest is only a forty-minute drive from a major city, so most of its inhabitants make the daily trek down the mountain for work. Many of the residents are the type who will grab a shovel and help you free your car from a ditch in the winter, or they'll wave as you drive by, even if they don't know you. "Black Forest is Beautiful" is written on the sign leading into town, and it's true. Huge pine forests, a big lake at the center—fishing and boating in the summer, ice skating in the winter. A mostly ideal place to raise a family.

A *mostly* ideal place because it also attracts a less savory sort. It's as if the isolation Black Forest affords emits a dog whistle specifically tuned for the maladjusted—the fuck-ups, druggies, drug dealers, criminals, white supremacists, and the occasional dirty cop (or two, or three).

Damon Storey is the tallest of the three present in the cabin. He's also the baldest. He currently occupies a folding chair positioned in the middle of the floor. His unusual height, shiny head, and severely pocked face stand out in equal measure. His flat eyes focus on the nail of his left ring finger. He snips the tiniest fragment using small nail scissors. Each fingernail is devoid of even the slightest trace of white. There will be no removing stickers from the skins of supermarket produce with those nails.

To Damon's right, standing in front of the open window,

is Charlie Murray. Medium height, medium build, and middle-aged, unremarkable in every way except one—the missing chunk from the bottom of his left ear. The wound is red, inflamed, and no doubt hurts like a motherfucker. It looks like it was done with someone's teeth—and not done well. Like they failed to make a clean bite and then just tore the rest off. He raises his left hand to his injured ear, his movement delicate. Even so, he winces in pain.

A faint squeak escapes the sink located at the back of the room. Buck Carter, the third individual present, short but compensating with a massive, bushy beard, has turned on the water and is filling a fast-food cup. He takes a cautious sip, pauses, then spits the water into the sink. He throws the cup to the ground, where it lands with unsatisfying silence atop a pile of trash.

"Fucking tastes like blood," he whispers.

Charlie pivots from the window and addresses the room. "We can't stay here forever, you know."

Damon laughs. "Not like you have a job to go back to." The focus on his nails remains unbroken.

"I'm just saying I don't think he's gonna give it to us..." Charlie looks at Buck for support, but Buck heard the edge in Damon's voice and wants no part of it.

"Well, maybe you should have considered that before you fucked up so badly," Damon says, snipping another microscopic piece of fingernail.

Without his usual caution, Charlie turns to Damon. "I fucked up? How the fuck did I fuck up? Wheels is *your* guy."

Damon ignores him.

Charlie tilts his head to the left, rubbing his ear against his shoulder, sending a jolt of pain through his body.

"God damn it, my fucking ear!" he yells.

"Whaaa, my baby ear, it hurts so bad, mommy," Damon taunts.

"You said baby ear," Buck laughs, but also takes several steps back, distancing himself from Damon.

"Fuck you guys. Who the hell bites off someone's ear, anyway? A fucking psycho, that's who," Charlie meant to say the last part under his breath, but he's a little drunk, so...

Damon stands so quickly the folding chair skids across the room and crashes into Buck's legs. "What did you say?" he demands.

Here we go, Buck thinks. He knew this was coming, even discussed it with Damon. He just thought they had more time.

"I asked, who bites off someone's ear," Charlie says quietly.

"It was only part of your ear. And after that?" Damon's voice is measured, but his body is tight like a spring.

"That's it, that's all I said." Then Charlie throws up his hands in exasperation. "You know what, fuck it. My ear's infected, like one-hundred-percent infected. I'm going to get something for it."

Charlie retrieves his keys from his jacket. He's surprised it's taken him this long to realize that he needs to get the fuck out of here. For good. He pats his back pocket to ensure he has his wallet, then steps to the front door. Charlie most definitely needs something for his ear, but first and foremost, he needs more vodka. In fact, there's probably not enough vodka in this entire weird fucking town for what he needs. And that's fine with him because he wants to get the fuck out of Black Forest. He wants to get the fuck away from Damon, from his pervy little pet Buck, and this whole fucking mess.

"Let me take a look first," Damon offers calmly. "If it's infected, absolutely, get something for it."

"I know it's fucking infected," Charlie murmurs, his hand continuing toward the door. *Run*, something screams in his head, *just fucking run.*

"It's fine, man. We're good. I'm sure you're right. And by all means, you should go. Actually, I'll have you grab me some new scissors while you're out. Just let me take a look first." *I am the pinnacle of reasonableness*, that voice says.

"Don't be a pussy," Buck adds from the corner, "and grab me the new *Kinda Legal* while you're there. The service up here is for shit." Buck's pretty sure he's gonna have to wait on that magazine, though, because he doesn't think Charlie's going anywhere.

Buck's and Damon's words don't entirely alleviate Charlie's apprehension, but they're enough for him to lower his hand from the knob and tilt his head toward Damon. It's as much of an invitation as he can muster.

Damon approaches slowly. "Turn around," he instructs.

Charlie looks at the lower half of Damon's face and finds solace in the softening of his mouth. He complies. If he had the courage to look Damon in the eyes... well, he doesn't, so no matter.

Damon reaches out and cradles Charlie's chin in his hand and turns his head, revealing the ghastly state of the injury up close—fire-engine red and oozing a mixture of pus and blood. *Is part of it green? No, it can't be; must just be the light.* Even so, a child could see there's something seriously wrong with that ear.

"Yeah, that's not good," Damon remarks, clucking his tongue. He moves his left hand to the earlobe, causing Charlie to flinch. "Not. Good. At. All."

Charlie begins to fidget. "Chill, I'm just examining," and as Damon says this, a quiet moan escapes his lips. Charlie tells himself it's just some odd throat clearing. But if he were to look down and to his left, he would understand what the moan was about, and he might still have a chance. Because if he did, he would see Damon doing what the kids call *pitching a tent*. And then, he'd run for all he was worth. But he does not see, because he does not look. Therefore, he does not run. And he absolutely would have run because he knows how turned on Damon gets from violence.

One late night, when Damon was black-out drunk (and for this, Charlie is eternally grateful, because he doesn't think he'd still be alive otherwise), Damon shared the story of his first orgasm. It wasn't from a wet dream, or from masturbating under the covers thinking about some classmate—sex has never done much for Damon. It happened when Damon was twelve years old, and he stabbed a sharpened stick through the neck of a neighbor's cat. As Damon marveled at the cat pinned to the soft earth, its back leg contracting in the occasional spasm, fighting against the end, desire overcame him, and before he knew it, his pants were down around his ankles and with no more than three strokes of his hand, he was cumming. His seed landed on the top of his sneaker. Only then did he remember he was not alone. He looked over at Bill Colliers, and before Damon could threaten him with the same sharpened stick piercing Patches' furry neck, Bill said, "I will never say a fucking thing. I swear to fucking God. I swear to fucking God on Barry Gladstone's grave." And Damon knew he meant it. Bill idolized Barry Gladstone, felt he was the greatest player to ever pick up a mitt.

Although interesting, these reminiscences of Damon's youth are not particularly helpful to Charlie at the moment, because he neither sees Damon's dead eyes nor his ever-hardening cock pushing against the fabric of his jeans—all he sees is the smile.

Charlie clenches his jaw as Damon gently grabs the top of his ear, pulling it away from his head, but he doesn't move.

"Yeah, definitely infected. I guess I need to take better care of my oral hygiene," Damon says with a hollow chuckle.

"Just one thing before you go, though," Damon quickly moves his thumb and forefinger from the top of the earlobe to the damaged area and squeezes as hard as he can.

"Owww, owww! What the fuck, Oh my God!" Charlie screams. His knees buckle as Damon pulls him to the ground by his mangled ear. Fresh blood runs through Damon's fingers and splashes on the dusty floor. Damon's right hand comes into view, revealing the nail scissors.

"Hold still, you fucking baby. It's just a little prick," Damon spits, and with swift expertise, he stabs Charlie's neck several times on each side of his trachea. He finishes the act and stands before Charlie has much of a chance to react.

"What the fuck?" Charlie exclaims in horror. He scoots away on his butt until his back rests against the wall. He instinctively reaches for his neck, like a man choking himself. He brings his hands to his face. His look is confused, like he's trying to remember how he got so covered in red paint. A weak cough pushes significant amounts of blood from his wounds.

Damon stares at him like a child might a broken toy he has recently tired of—*Fuck that toy anyway.*

"What the fuck?" Charlie repeats in what now sounds like a gargle.

"I don't appreciate being called a psycho," Damon states calmly.

Charlie manages to push himself to a standing position, his hands still covering the wounds on his neck. He gazes at the doorknob, releases his right hand, which allows a stream of blood to shoot across the room. He readjusts his left hand, so his index finger does a manageable job covering the wounds on the right side of his neck, and his thumb attempts to cover them on the left. With determination, he opens the door and stumbles out. The door swings wide, revealing the outside world—dry heat, bright sunlight, air hazy with dust and pollen. This level of violence feels out of place in the full light of day. He stumbles across a small porch and manages to descend the three steps into the dirt yard before falling. Drops of blood release pillows of dust into the air as they hit the dirt. He rights himself, his eyes focusing weakly on the path leading to a gate and the forest beyond. With slow, awkward steps, he continues across the front of the property. As he moves farther away, the cabin door closes behind him in the gentle breeze.

Damon brushes past Buck and proceeds to scrub his fingers—and the scissors—free of blood at the sink.

"Well, that escalated quickly," Buck says in an attempt to lower the tension.

"How far until he bleeds out?" Damon asks flatly.

"You got both of them?" Buck asks, his voice part awe, part terror.

"Of course I got them both. What kind of question is that?"

"It all happened so fast," Buck says again, but thinks to himself, *not near fast enough. And fuck, someday that's gonna be me if I don't get clear of this psycho.* Even thinking the word *psycho* sends a jolt of fear through him, as if Damon can hear his thoughts. He knows just up and leaving isn't possible. Because

Buck has his own, let's call them enjoyments, that society frowns upon. And Damon knows all about them—has them on video, even.

"Same as cats, but easier. Humans have larger arteries," Damon explains, his voice husky with what Buck fears is lust.

"Yeah, looks like he had them covered pretty well, but he sure was stumbling," Buck says, his stomach uneasy. Then he thinks, *What if I puke right here and now? He'll fucking kill me for sure.* He manages to take several panicked breaths, each one slightly deeper than the one before. *I'm not gonna puke. I'm not gonna puke*, he tells himself. Mercifully, it passes.

Then Damon starts laughing. He tries to form a sentence numerous times, but can't. Eventually, he manages to say, "He looked like a drunken toddler," and then loses it in hysterics.

"Oh my God, he did," Buck agrees, forcing his own laughter.

Damon grabs the chair he sent flying across the room and sets it back upright. He sits down. From behind, Buck watches Damon's right hand move between his legs. Buck was hoping this time would be different, but he knew better.

"Use your shoe," Damon says in a child-like voice.

"Of course. Of course," Buck says, removing his shoe and holding it in his left hand. His right hand moves to the gun holstered behind his back, but he knows he's not going to use it. Not yet, anyway.

As Buck approaches, Damon says, "Catch it all." Each word is spaced so that it sounds like its own sentence. His hand moves so violently between his legs, the words come out jerky. Damon's gaze is fixed on the puddles of blood gathered near the front door, their coppery scent dominating the room.

"I will, I will, I swear," Buck says, looking at the ground.

"Watch, goddamnit," Damon says, his breathing now punctuated with moans of pleasure.

"Tell me, tell me," Damon struggles to get this out between his ragged breathing, his moans, and what now sounds suspiciously like sobs. It's clear enough to Buck, though. He's been here before.

Buck watches as Damon nears; he won't turn away again. He won't get a third chance. Damon's hand moves with such speed, it's blurred. Damon's "thing" is so small, he only uses his thumb and first two fingers. The act looks more painful than pleasurable. Buck holds the shoe in what he prays is the right spot—far enough away that none will shoot past, but close enough to catch everything.

Buck says, "I swear I won't say anything. I swear to fucking God. I fucking swear on Barry Gladstone's grave. I'll never say anything, I promise, I fucking promise." The moment Barry Gladstone's name exits Buck's mouth, a primal grunt exits Damon's, and he finishes all over the shoe. Luckily, not a single drop hits the dirty floor. Buck, on one knee, head bent, cum-covered shoe in hand, looks as if he's offering a gift to royalty. The smell of blood and Damon's emissions turn Buck's stomach again. He gags, and with the position of his head, he's confident Damon doesn't notice. He prays the nausea passes. But it does not. It builds and it roils and it threatens. *Please God no, please God no, please God no.* He speeds the words in his mind in hopes it will increase their efficacy. It's not so much the pleading that keeps the chewed-up and partially digested Kum Quick breakfast sandwich and the now flat and warm sixteen ounces of Kola Kountry from defying gravity and exiting through his mouth— and, knowing his luck, his nose. It's the knowing that he can pass on whatever it is that's below the nausea. Like a game of hot potato no one asked to play. And he knows who he needs to pass it to. And how. He thinks about the room upstairs. He knows he's not gonna puke now. His thoughts of being upstairs and relieving the pressure that pushes against his bones and skin are so consuming, it takes him a moment to come back to the present when Damon says, "God, you're dirty. Look at you on your knees in that filth. And your shoe." Damon notices a small amount of cum touching Buck's thumb and has never wanted to kill him more.

"I'll never say anything, I swear," Buck has learned his assurances of silence need to continue until Damon says otherwise. Sometimes this takes minutes; luckily, today it's quick.

"Oh, I know you won't. Clean that up," Damon says, staring at the shoe in Buck's hand.

As Buck stands to wash his shoe—and hands—what sounds like a gunshot can be heard from outside. They both turn and stare out the open window. Moments later, a second sound can be heard, and there is no doubt it's a gunshot. It came from the direction Charlie was stumbling toward. Damon sprints for the door. Buck puts the cum-covered shoe back on his foot and follows after.

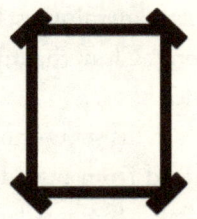

ONE DAY EARLIER

IT'S THE LAST DAY OF SCHOOL, AND AS KIDS flow into the building, the animation and energy teachers have begged for all year is finally present. Two giant walls of windows flank both sides of Black Forest High's front doors. The windows, which are normally pristine—washed multiple times a day by kids in detention—are currently almost entirely covered in missing flyers. It's the same flyer repeated over and over. It's actually a pretty dumb place to put them; everyone here knows she's missing. She went to school here, after all. The text at the top of the flyer says: *Have You Seen Her?* Below that is a picture of Casey West. The photo shows her standing at an angle, her head turned over her shoulder toward the camera, her eyes focused to the left of where the camera would have been. A small, fading smile rests on her face, like whatever she saw killed it, and the camera caught it mid-death. A single phone number for the Black Forest Police Department sits at the bottom of the flyer. Someone scrawled in red pen across one of the flyers: *She ran the fuck away.* Then, below that, in blue pen, it says: *As we all should, lol.* Another defaced flyer originally said: send tips to BlackForestPI. Someone took a marker to it, added arrows and other words, so now it reads: *Send your dick tips to Black Forest Hair Pie.* Clever.

For some statistically improbable reason, I had six classes with Casey this year—four the first semester and two the second. We were friendly, almost friends even. This was her second year in Black Forest; she told me she moved around a lot. She has darkish skin, and at first, I didn't know what her racial make-up was, but I have since learned her mom is Black and her dad is white. Her hair is curly and stops just above her shoulders. She isn't tall, but her thin arms and long legs made her seem so. She's also one of the few kids in our school with a visible tattoo. She has the back of a muscle car tattooed on her forearm. The license plate says *Wheels.* She'd spend a good chunk of class staring at it. I always wanted to ask her about it, but I never did.

Casey was quiet, but we'd chat some, and initially, we'd walk to our next class together. I passively put an end to that when I could tell it bothered Hailey. Not that Hailey is the jealous type, but Casey was a flirt. The handful of times she and I passed Hailey in the hall, Casey would lean in close and whisper something in my ear or put her hand on my arm. I didn't feel like I knew her well enough to tell her to cut it out, so I just started taking longer and longer to get my books together at the end of class. Eventually, she got the message. Pretty cowardly of me.

"Jack Motherfucking Larson!" I look up and see Cash, Kelly, and Hailey walking toward me down the hall. Cash McDermid and I have been inseparable since middle school. He's tall and has wavy red hair. Today, he has on Converse low-tops, jeans, and a plain black T-shirt. He's hand-in-hand with Kelly Stokes, who's also tall and lanky. She has choppy brown hair and wears a gigantic smile. Hailey's last name is Culver, and we've been going out almost a year—the same as Kelly and Cash. Hailey has shortish black hair, a swimmer's body, and olive skin. Her dad is white, but her mom is Middle Eastern. Well, American, but her grandparents—or maybe it was her great-grandparents—were from there. So far, it probably sounds like Black Forest is relatively diverse. It's not. You could drive around town for an entire day and see nothing but white people.

"Finally," I say as they approach. We move to the side of the hall to make way for the kids rushing to class. I grab Hailey's hand.

"Barnes' party tonight? We've got to make the most of the next week or so before we become working men," Cash says, rubbing his hands together in anticipation.

Cash and I got jobs working construction this summer, even though neither of us has any skills that would qualify us. My stepdad was more of an academic, so he didn't teach me much on the building front. Cash's dad is more of a drug dealer, so same. But Cash's brother's friend offered us jobs, so we took them.

Before I can answer Cash's question about the party tonight, the three of them turn and stare at a girl opening her locker down the hall.

"What?" I ask. The girl's name is Maggie. The first several years I knew her, I knew her as Matt. But the last couple of years, she has been Maggie.

"You of all people haven't heard?" Hailey asks.

I shake my head.

"Maggie Parsons is BlackForestPI," Kelly says.

"Absolutely no," I laugh.

A week ago, when Casey first went missing, it seemed everyone in town was talking about her and looking for her. The local weekly paper put out a special edition mid-week. But a few days ago, the police department released a statement saying she's not missing, she ran away. Right after that, the rumors about there being trouble at home started. BFPD stated that a number of witnesses came forward telling them they frequently overheard Casey and her mom fighting. One person said they saw Casey leave her house with a suitcase. The whole statement struck me as odd, especially the fighting part, because Casey, on the handful of occasions she mentioned her parents, had nothing but good things to say about them. Casey's mom posted a video the day she went missing asking for help finding her daughter. The day BFPD released their statement saying Casey ran away, her mom posted a second, and final, video saying Casey absolutely did not run away and for people to please keep looking.

Most people in town are divided between those who believe Casey ran away and those who believe Casey was kidnapped. A few think she ran away and then got kidnapped. I'm unequivocally in the kidnapped-from-the-start camp. For two years, I had to listen to people tell me my dad just up and left me when I knew there was no way that was true. I heard similar conviction in Casey's mom's voice when she put out that second video. I haven't shared this with anyone, not even Cash, but I don't think Casey would have left without saying goodbye. I know that sounds egotistical, and I know I just said we weren't even really friends. But, whatever, there's just something about her—about us—even though there wasn't an "us," that makes me believe she would have at least said goodbye. It doesn't help that Hailey, Kelly, and Cash are all in the Casey-ran-away camp.

Anyway, BlackForestPI is the name of someone obsessed with the Casey West disappearance. They use the username online and on social media. BlackForestPI is one-hundred-percent convinced Casey was kidnapped. There's a Casey West-specific online thread where people post questions and theories, and BlackForestPI is the de facto leader. Some of the stuff they say is way off base— they went down an organ-harvesting rabbit hole right after Casey disappeared—but they're also the only person actively looking into this. They said they've repeatedly asked BFPD to give them the names of the witnesses who said Casey ran away, and the cops haven't responded. They also complained about receiving a number of parking tickets after making the requests. I'm not sure those are related, but you never know. In the beginning, they were in contact with Casey's mom, but that's since stopped. Casey's mom doesn't seem to be talking to anyone now. BlackForestPI says that's because she's been silenced. Everyone else says it's because she knows Casey ran away.

"Absolutely yes," Kelly says. "She posted a video. You know how she does it—she used the pixelation on her face, but partway through the video, the voice-changing filter she used cut out, and you can tell it's her."

"Come on? Her? She's so, I don't know, quiet. BlackForestPI is pissed," I say.

"Maggie is pissed. Trust me, she grew up in Inwood, a couple of streets over from me. In fourth grade, she—well, he at that time—threw a miniature garden shovel at me for zero reason. Hit me right above the eye. I dropped to the ground crying. He walked over, stared at me, didn't say a thing, grabbed the little shovel, and left."

"I remember that story. I didn't know that was her. She just seems so normal now," I say.

"Okay, how about this? She dated Wilkinson for a year. A full fucking year. How normal is that?" Cash asks, shaking his head.

"Say no more," Hailey says.

"She dated him as Maggie or as Matt?" I ask.

"Does it matter? She fucking dated Wilkinson. That's the takeaway," Kelly says.

Cash was born and raised in Inwood, the undisputed hood of Black Forest. There's not a nice house in the entire area. Every yard is littered with broken-down cars, refrigerators, couches, fucking toilets even. There's this kid, Miles Baker, who lives in Inwood. He goes to our school, chews tobacco all day in class, and just spits into the inside of his jacket. He may have a cup or something in there, but there's no way spit isn't getting all over him. Anyway, his parents parked a trailer in Inwood before he was born and never left. Not like they bought a piece of land or rented it—just parked it in the woods there. No idea what they use for a bathroom, because it definitely doesn't have plumbing. He's also one of the few people who showers after gym class, which might explain some things. They cook everything on a barbecue outside the trailer. The population of Inwood is one hundred percent white and two hundred percent white trash. It's the exact opposite of Aspen Springs, where Hailey lives, where the houses are all custom and super far apart. Cash and I know Wilkinson, the guy Maggie dated, but we do our best to steer clear of him. He split town last summer after he stabbed a skinhead, and we haven't seen him since.

The tardy bell rings, and Hailey says, "Shit, Jack, we gotta go. I don't wanna get lectured in front of the class again."

"See you guys tonight. Just meet at Barnes'?" I ask.

"Yep, see you there," Cash says, and he and Kelly wave goodbye.

Hailey and I hustle down the hall to our class. It's History, and it's taught by the wrestling coach. To his face, people refer to him as Coach Mike. Behind his back, most of us call him Cock Mike. And he is a cock, but he earned the nickname because he drives a bright green muscle car with a vanity license plate that reads: COCH-MYK. Just a terrible decision on his part.

We try to sneak in the door as Cock Mike writes on the board, and just when I think we're home free, he says, "Oh, look, the two lovebirds grace us with their presence." A number of his wrestlers sitting in the back corner erupt in laughter.

One of them says, "Yeah, lovebirds, grace us with your presence." Cock Mike gives him an annoyed look. Ninety percent of what that kid says is exactly what Cock Mike just said.

"Yeah, sorry, Coach," Hailey says and sits.

"Sorry, Coach," I say and take my seat next to Hailey.

"Actually, I'm tired of writing. Hailey, come up here and finish this for me," he says.

Hailey gives me a *what the fuck* look before heading up. Cock Mike hands her a sheet of paper and says, "Just write this up there," and then he leans on the edge of his desk with his back to the class. Everyone else projects lessons on a screen from a computer—not Cock Mike. Hailey starts transcribing some dumb sports analogy that barely makes sense. I can't tell exactly where Cock Mike is staring, because all I can see is the back of his head, but it looks like he's focused on Hailey's ass. As she moves to the other side of the board, she has to pass in front of him—squeeze past him, really—and as she does, it's clear he moves closer to her, rubbing himself against her.

I can't take it anymore and blurt out, "Isn't that your job?"

The class, which was kind of murmuring amongst themselves, goes silent. Cock Mike stiffens. Without turning around, he gives me a hard look and says, "Excuse me?"

After a moment, I realize he's waiting for me to respond, so I say, "I mean, how's she going to take notes if she's up there writing on the board?" I try to recover from my outburst, but I can't remove all of the disdain from my voice.

"Well, I'd say she could copy from you, but you're gonna spend the final class in the hallway." This is followed by a collective "oooh" from the students. Some "Yeah, Coach Mike's" are shouted from the wrestlers' corner.

"Come on, really, Coc—" and I almost call him Cock Mike, but I manage to stammer out, "Coach Mike?" The class catches it, though, and a number of them snicker.

He stands, turns, and stares at me. His face throbbing. I think he's flexing his muscles, but he's the kind of guy that is both muscular and fat at the same time, so it's hard to tell. He took a leave of absence a couple of years ago after a student complained that he slammed him up against the lockers. He's that kind of guy.

"What did you say?"

"I said really? You're kicking me—" but he cuts me off before I can finish.

"Out. Get out!" he yells.

I stand, grab my bag, shake my head, and walk toward the door. I make eye contact with Hailey, and she mouths, "Thank you." I take a seat in the hall with my back to the lockers.

I look at my phone. Forty minutes left in class. This school year can't end soon enough.

HAILEY AND I HAVEN'T EVEN MADE IT around the final curve to Barnes' house when we come to the end of a long line of parked cars. I think they call where he lives "golf course adjacent." The neighborhood is about as close to suburbia as we get up here in the mountains. Scanning the line of cars, I see a few kids pounding beers and sharing joints before they head up. Barnes was peripherally involved in the shitshow that was last summer. He has taken on a kind of hero status after he beat the living shit out of a skinhead. It's what inspired him to start training in mixed martial arts. His opponents have fared better than the skinhead did, but not much. I haven't spoken to him since his last fight, but I heard he hit a kid so hard he put him in the hospital.

"I guess we park here?" Hailey asks.

"Looks like the entire school showed up," I say as Hailey stops at the end of the line.

We get out and walk toward the sounds and lights. I pass a kid, who I think is named Corey and is a year younger than us, puking into the ditch on the side of the road. A friend stands beside him sipping a beer and shaking his head.

"Early start?" Hailey asks as we walk past.

The kid sipping the beer says, "No, literally, he took one shot. Just now. Fucking lightweight."

"Fuck y—" the kid almost gets out but is thwarted by another stream of vomit.

Hailey and I laugh and continue toward the house.

I know Cash and Kelly are here, but we don't see them in the yard with the other kids. Once inside, we do a quick pass on the first floor. In one room, kids huddle around the pool table and a handful take part in what looks like a modified game of beer pong that somehow involves a bong. We don't see Cash or Kelly, so we head downstairs. Barnes' parents seem to be out of town every month or so, and we end up over here a lot. Never this many kids, though. In the corner of the basement, I spot Kelly, Cash, and Barnes.

"What's up, player?" I ask Barnes and give him a hug. I can tell he's put on a bunch of muscle. "Jesus, dude, you're huge," I say. Barnes laughs off the comment. Girls love him. He's broody and mysterious and has a chiseled face. Although at the moment, the yellow and green remnants of a shiner encircle his left eye.

"Welcome to summer," Barnes says without enthusiasm. "You guys want a beer or something?"

"That'd be great. Thanks," Hailey says.

He walks toward the fridge on the other side of the room. His gait lumbering, his head hung low.

"He get that shiner from a match or just a fight?" I ask Cash when Barnes walks away.

"A match. From the kid he put in the hospital," Cash says.

"The kid okay?" I ask.

"Decidedly not okay. Has a traumatic brain injury. They did some kind of scan; he can barely talk," Kelly says.

"Oh my God, that's terrible," Hailey says, and her eyes well up.

Barnes gets held up in a conversation at the fridge, so Cash is able to tell us the whole story. Apparently, Barnes knocked the kid out in the second round. Said he didn't even hit him as hard as he could—just in the perfect spot. Or not perfect spot. Barnes tried to go see the kid, but the kid's parents wouldn't let him. Apparently, Barnes has sworn off his training. I don't blame him.

Eventually, Barnes makes his way back with a couple of beers and hands them to Hailey and me.

"Shit man, sorry to hear about that kid," I say.

"Thanks, it's fucked," and right then we hear a crash from upstairs. I really hope that wasn't the bong.

"Fucking idiots," Barnes says and takes off in pursuit.

"God, I feel terrible for him," Kelly says. "The other kid too, of course." The thought of someone our age suffering that kind of injury silences us for a spell.

Cash claps his hands together and says, "I'm ready to get high." Kelly gives him a look.

"I know, I know. Really sucks for that kid," Cash says. "But it's the last day of school, and we only have a week before Jack and I have to become master builders, two weeks before Hailey leaves to tour the world and, well, Kelly, you'll be high."

"Fuck you," Kelly says and hits Cash in the arm. "You know I have a job. And you're the one that mentioned getting high."

We walk outside so Kelly and Cash can smoke and take a seat on a bench overlooking a small slope that leads into the trees. The sun, more red than orange, resembles a blood clot as it slides behind the mountains.

Halfway down the hill, a girl types into her phone; the light from the screen illuminates her face.

"Is that Maggie?" I ask.

The three of them look, and Cash says, "Yeah, I think so."

I want to ask her about being BlackForestPI, so I yell, "Hey Maggie!"

She looks up, squints, flips me off, and goes back to her phone.

"Told you. Real sweetheart, that one," Cash says.

"You gonna team up with her for Operation Casey?" Hailey teases.

"Maybe. I mean, she actually seems to know some stuff," I say.

"Like how Casey was taken because someone needed an appendix," Kelly says, and the three of them laugh.

"Ha ha. She was actually communicating with Casey's mom before she was silenced," I say.

"Oh my God, Jack. Come on. All those witnesses?" Kelly says.

"Yeah, but do you know who they are? No names, no nothing," I say, and hear Hailey sigh.

"Right, right. It's a conspiracy. Let's not go with the simplest answer or anything," Cash says.

"Let's not go with any answer, actually. Or any question. For tonight at least, okay? She's not here. We are. No missing kids, no brain injuries, okay?" Hailey says, her voice hitching as if she's holding back tears.

"Okay, okay. Sorry. Absolutely," I say and put my arm around her. She doesn't pull away.

"Change of subject then," Kelly says with a big grin on her face. She turns to Cash and says, "When do I get my graduation present?"

Cash raises an eyebrow and says, "Now? I'm sure there's an empty room or shed around here."

"Gross," Hailey says, laughing.

"Don't be crude. And I said present. As in something I want," Kelly says, but quickly follows with, "Kidding, kidding."

"You're mean," Cash says, pulling her into a hug.

"My real present. When we gonna 'pop the Glock?'" Kelly asks, and although she tries to say it with a straight face, she can't.

"You don't get a present for 'graduating' from tenth grade," Cash says.

"Hailey did," Kelly says.

"Well, of course Hailey did," Cash says, rolling his eyes.

"Would you mind telling us what you're getting?" Kelly asks, but it's clear she already knows.

Hailey answers so quietly, it takes three times for us to make out that she said, "A new car."

"Are you fucking kidding me? You already have a new car," Cash says.

"Cash, that old thing? It's like ten months old. And has like three thousand miles on it," I say.

"Ha ha. You guys are funny. I didn't ask for it," Hailey says sheepishly.

"If it starts smoking and making weird noises, take it in for service, okay?" Cash says and looks at me.

"Funny. But true, do that," I say. Right now, my car's in the shop because I did not.

"Princess Hailey, can we get back to me for a minute?" Kelly asks.

"Pretty sure you started it, but yes, of course," Hailey says and curtsies.

"When are you going to teach me to shoot a gun?" Kelly asks, dead serious.

"Fuck, really? I thought you were kidding," Cash says.

"Yeah, really. When Jack said he wanted to check out the area by the shooting range, I told you and you agreed," Kelly says.

Both Hailey and Cash stare daggers at me.

"I mean, yeah, I did mention that. It's just, I read about someone seeing a teenage girl and two guys in a car near there. They said it looked like Casey. There's good hiking over there too," I say nonchalantly.

"Oh my God, Jack, when was the last time you went hiking?" Hailey scoffs.

"Well, true, yeah, it's been a while, but I like nature," I say.

"You like video games. And you like obsessing over Casey

West." Hailey sticks her hands in her pockets and moves a step away from me.

"Okay, fine, fuck," Cash says, defeated.

"Yay!" Kelly says, jumping up and down in excitement.

We spend the next fifteen minutes figuring out when to go shooting. Cash does his best to put it off, but eventually decides it's better to just get it over with, so we settle on tomorrow. No doubt the last way Cash wants to spend his first day of summer vacation. The rest of the night, we cruise around the party, catching up with different people. Cash and I make a pretty good run on the pool table until Kelly and Hailey decide they want to play and destroy us. We bet that the loser had to wear the sunglasses Barnes' sister wore last week when she had pink eye. We know the story because she spent most of the night drunkenly trying to touch people with them, before forgetting about them and leaving them on the pool table. Thankfully, Hailey let me off by allowing me to *wear* them on my shirt and not on my face.

Around midnight, we decide to call it. We say bye to Barnes, who is now in a much better, albeit drunker, mood. As we walk to our cars, a group of five guys approach us on their way to the party. As we get closer, I can tell they're all kids from the wrestling team. Not all the wrestlers at our school are assholes, but these ones are. Three of them are Cock Mike cronies from my history class.

One of them mad-dogs me as they approach and says, "Time to go night-night?"

"Guess so," I say and continue walking, but they move laterally to block our path. We stop a few feet from them. It's clear they lift a lot of weights, and every one of them wears tight or sleeveless shirts showing off their muscles. One kid has a shirt with a giant chewing tobacco logo on it. Another one has an American flag bandana wrapped around his head in a non-ironic way. Another kid, with a full-on beard, says, "His name's not Cock Mike."

Kelly, clearly confused, says, "Are you really talking about a teacher right now? It's fucking summer."

A fourth one with a tank top cut so severely you can see his nipples says, "He's not just a teacher, he's a leader."

Kelly scoffs, Cash sighs, and Hailey says, "Cool story, yeah, he's the best. Well, have a great one." She attempts to walk past, but they shift again to block her.

"He's a great American, and you shouldn't disrespect him," bandana guy says.

The first guy again, "His name is not Cock Mike," and he looks right at me.

"Fine, got it," I say. "His name is not Cock Mike. We good?"

"Yeah, bro," he says and then pulls back as if he's gonna punch me. I flinch, and when I do, he reaches toward me and removes the sunglasses that I have hanging from my shirt and puts them on his face. A couple of the other kids say, "oooh."

"Really? Those are my sunglasses," I say in disbelief.

"They're mine now," he says, and his pals bust up laughing.

"You want to try and get them back?" he taunts and moves into some kind of three-point wrestling stance.

"Ah, no, man. They look better on you anyway," I say.

"Damn right they do," he says, and they split into two groups, allowing us to walk between. We hear them cheering and chest-bumping as they walk to the party.

"Those fucking guys talk about Cock Mike like he's a cult leader," Cash says.

"His name's not Cock Mike," Kelly says, and we all laugh.

I THOUGHT I WAS DONE WALKING EVERYWHERE, but since my mom is at work and my car is in the shop, I'm hoofing it to Cash's. My mom left me a post-it this morning in the kitchen. It said: "Jack, if someone ever attempts to abduct you—scream, bite, fight, run. It's your single best chance to get away. Love, Mom."

Where to begin regarding my mom? First off, she's fine, I

guess. We get along well enough; it's not like she's neglectful. I just don't think she ever really pictured herself being a mom. I mean, I know she loves me, but my stepdad was the one that was there for me on an emotional level. I think mostly my mom is looking forward to when I'm in my twenties, so she can just see me as a friend. She used to work overnights. I thought it was because she really liked her job, or really needed it. And both of those were true, but I also think she liked not being home. She left that job after all the trouble happened last summer, but it wasn't long before she exchanged the overnight job for staying overnight at her boyfriend's. I'm fine with it. Most of the time we're together, it's one long awkward silence anyway. I saw a documentary once on this group of kangaroos. The people filmed them for a long-ass time. One of the female kangaroos was an objectively bad mother. She'd leave her baby kangaroos alone all the time and they'd end up getting lost or getting eaten or whatever. I'm not saying my mom's like that, but I am saying she's in the same genre. After last summer, my mom got into true crime podcasts; that's when the post-it and text message warnings started. If she's awake, she has her headphones in and she's listening. It's definitely an escape for her, but I also think it gives her a sense of control. Like if something really bad happened—again—she'll know what to do.

The walk to Cash's is hot, like the sun's been filtered through a magnifying glass and now it's doing its best to burn a hole in my shirt. By the time I reach his neighborhood, I'm dripping sweat. Cash's house looks the same as it did last week, last summer, and no doubt twenty years ago. "Ramshackle" is too quaint. More like small, old, and shitty. His dad's car is parked out front. His dad isn't terrible. I mean, yeah, he deals drugs, but he's not scary or anything. He manages to keep the lights on and food in the fridge (most of the time). He's just kind of a dumbshit. Cash's mom died of an overdose when Cash was young. Cash's older brother still lives at home, but he's not around that often.

I walk through the open front door and spot Cash's dad sitting on the couch, smoking a joint.

"Want?" he asks, pushing the half-smoked joint my way.

"Nah, I'm good. Good to see you, though. How have you been?"

He takes a hit and holds up his finger, signaling for me to wait. "I've been better, Jack. I've definitely been better," he says as he blows out his hit.

"Well, um, that's not great."

"No, it's not," he says and puts out the joint. "I'm going on a little trip, Jack. Will you make sure and give this to Cash when you see him?" He reaches into his back pocket and hands me a wad of bills. Not like a roll of cash like you might find on a good drug dealer. He attempts to get the mess of bills to stay in my hand. Some are folded, some crumpled, some permanently rolled into coke straws. There are definitely some twenties in there. I can even make out at least a single hundred, but there are also several ones. Most of the bills fall out of my cupped hands and land on the dirty carpet. As I reach for the bills, Cash's dad heads to the front door.

"Pretty sure Cash is in his room. I mean, you could give him this yourself."

"I wish there was time, Jack. I really do." And with that, he walks outside. His dad is always odd, but this is next-level shit. I head to Cash's room with the money. I find him sitting on the bottom bunk, staring cautiously at two guns on the bed next to him.

"Dude, um, your dad just gave me this to give to you." I set the crumpled bills next to the guns. "He said he was going on a trip."

Cash ignores the money and says, "Trying to repair things with his ex."

"The one that moved to Maine?"

"Maryland, but yeah, that one."

"The one that's only like thirty?"

"The very one."

"He's driving all the way there for the chick that tried to light his car on fire?"

"Yeah, he knows he's an idiot. That's why he didn't say bye. He knows I'd list the reasons it's a bad idea."

"How long's he gonna be gone?"

"Based on how much money he left, I'd guess two weeks."

"And he doesn't say goodbye? Doesn't tell you when he's getting back?"

"Have you met my dad? He's never met a problem he couldn't run from."

"I'm sorry, man. That sucks."

"Yeah, kinda. But I like it just being Wes and me here. So, whatever."

"Your dad is like the criminal version of my mom. I'd suggest he should stay and try and date her, but they'd probably forget to talk to each other."

"Ha."

I watch Cash as he stares at the guns on the bed.

"They don't bite," I say.

"They do though, Jack. That's their whole fucking point." We both instinctively rub the clothing above our scars.

"I can't believe I agreed to this," Cash says, shaking his head. He stands and gives the guns space.

"I can. When was the last time you said no to Kelly?"

"Probably around the same time I said no to you. And you're the fucking start of this, don't forget. You wanting to search for Casey."

"I guess to you, a polite ask from Kelly is the same as a demand," I say and give him my winningest smile. "But fair on my end, sorry."

"Well, whatever. Still. It's fucking nuts. I hate these things."

"We kind of had fun shooting at cans last summer, no?" I ask.

"Shooting at cans is the gateway drug to getting shot. And now, I have for real PTSD."

Before I can put him at ease, a car pulls up out front.

We head to the front door, look out, and see Hailey and Kelly exit a brand new luxury sedan.

"Ta-da!" Hailey says as she stands next to the driver's door and introduces us to her new car. She smiles uncomfortably—her toothpaste-commercial teeth sparkle. Her black hair perfectly messed.

"Beautiful," I say, not taking my eyes off her.

"Well, I finally know what the oft-mentioned new car smell is all about," Kelly says as she hugs Cash. He towers over her, and Kelly is not short. His red hair, just long enough to shade his eyes, blends with hers. They intertwine one another like a pretzel.

"Not quite the same as new bus smell," Cash adds.

"I don't think there's such a thing as new bus smell; like they literally make new buses out of old shit," Kelly says.

"I don't think I've ever been on a bus," Hailey says and winks at me.

"Oh. My. God," Cash says.

"I'm kidding. Kidding."

"I don't think you are," I wink back.

Hailey flips me off and runs inside laughing. We follow.

Hailey throws herself on the couch in the living room. Looks around. The barn she houses her horses in is nicer than Cash's house, bigger too, but she seems comfortable.

"So where are the gats? Where's the iron, man?" Kelly jokes.

"You are way too excited about this. Remember last summer when I almost died," Cash reminds her.

"Oh, come here. I'm so glad you didn't," Kelly pulls Cash into a tight hug.

"Follow me," Cash says and leads us to his room.

We stand near the door, giving his bed, and the guns, a wide berth. The weapons lie on top of an uncomfortable-looking army blanket. They point at one another in some kind of still-life standoff. One flat black, one shiny silver. A semi-automatic and a revolver.

"That's them, huh?" Kelly says with awe in her voice. She walks over and reaches for the black one, the Glock. She grabs it, finger on the trigger.

"Whoa, this thing is heavy," she says as she turns toward us. The barrel sweeps across each of us at eye level. We instinctively duck.

"Jesus. Lady. Are you crazy?" I jump toward her and lower her hand and remove the gun.

"What? I wasn't gonna shoot anyone," she protests.

"No one purposely accidentally shoots anyone," I say.

"Why is it we are doing this again?" Hailey asks with dismay.

"Because I have terrible boundaries," Cash says.

"Right. Kelly's insanity, Cash being a pushover, and Jack being obsessed. Perfect, I'm sure this will end well," Hailey sighs. Before I can make eye contact, she turns away.

I grab both guns and gently place them in the backpack on the floor. I can tell by the weight of the bag Cash has already put the ammo in there.

"Oh my God, I can't wait to shoot those things," Kelly says, running in place, unable to contain her excitement.

"Well, first and foremost, we are going to do some gun safety shit," Cash says.

"Some gun safety shit? Is that what it's called?" Kelly teases as she pretends to try and grab the bag out of my hand.

"That's what I call it," Cash says and places himself between Kelly and me. He grabs the bag from my hand and heads toward the front door, clearly not happy about how his summer is starting.

I sit shotgun, Hailey drives, and Cash and Kelly sit in the back. I rest my hand on Hailey's arm. The car does indeed smell new. My seat is more comfortable than anything in Cash's house, or in my apartment, for that matter. God, I fucking love this car.

Cash shouts directions over the music as we wind through the dirt roads. After about twenty minutes, and a couple of U-turns, Cash tells Hailey to pull to the side of the road. I look out and see the slight trail through the trees with a steep hill behind. A perfect backstop for bullets. It looks the same as the last time we were here. Maybe a few more broken bottles and bullet-riddled cans. We aren't far from where I think the person reported seeing someone that looked like Casey. I turn, taking in as much as I can. As I come almost full circle, I see what may be the edge of a roofline through the tops of distant trees.

"You guys see that?" I say, pointing. Cash, Hailey, and Kelly look in that direction, eyes squinting from the bright sun.

"Trees?" Hailey asks.

"Through the trees," I say. "Follow my hand." I walk behind Hailey and point my arm over her shoulder. Kelly and Jack walk up next to her.

"More trees?" Kelly jokes.

"No, right there," I say, jabbing my finger for emphasis, "like maybe the very tip of a roof. Like a cabin."

"I think you're seeing things," Hailey says.

"Well, I want to check it out," I say, mildly frustrated.

"Whatever, but let's get the gun stuff out of the way first. I want to finish here, then put the guns in the safe and never touch them again," Cash says and looks at his palms. I can tell from here they are shiny with sweat. He wipes them on his pants.

"And after, we'll just take a little hike and see if there is anything over there," I say, trying to sound nonchalant.

"And if we see something, *over there?*" Hailey asks.

"Then we call it in. Simple as that," I say, hoping she'll drop it. I know looking for Casey has more to do with my dad than it does Casey, but it doesn't help that she's gorgeous. The fact that she's a giant flirt helps even less.

"Can you guys just give me a piece already?" Kelly tries to hold a straight face, but can't and ends up laughing and breaking the tension.

I open the bag and grab the guns. I try to remember what we learned about shooting the last time, but can't. We end up searching on our phones for videos on how to load them. After much argument, we get it done.

"One thing I absolutely remember is that the black one doesn't have a safety," I say, still finding it hard to believe.

"And before you say, 'of course it does,' it really does not," Cash jumps in.

"Well, I'm definitely not shooting either of them," Hailey says.

"Baby, give me that thing. I'll shoot all kinds of shit," Kelly reaches for the gun. Cash shakes his head and helps her with her grip. He moves her arm down, pointing the muzzle at the ground. As he walks her through sighting the gun, I grab a handful of not fully destroyed aluminum cans and a few pinecones and set them up about twenty feet from us.

I back up behind, way behind, Kelly and watch.

Cash says, "Close your left eye and get that vertical pin lined up in the gap between the two other parts of the sight. Then line that up where you want the, umm, bullet to go."

"You should be a shooting coach," Hailey teases.

"I wish I didn't even know this much," Cash responds.

"Imma shoot some shit. Cool?" Kelly asks.

"Yeah, just not us. It's all ready to go, all you have to do is pull the trigger," I say.

Kelly tucks the gun in her arm and pulls a joint from her pocket. She holds it to her mouth, lights it, and takes a huge hit. She lets go of the joint, leaving it hanging from her lips and lines up her shot. She takes another big hit and holds it for five, ten seconds, and just as I realize I'm holding my breath as well, I see the smoke slowly flow out of her nose, like some stoner assassin. Then I hear the loud bang and the can in the middle of the group pops backward.

"Oh my God, I hit it. I hit it," Kelly says with genuine excitement.

"Great, can we go now?" Cash asks.

"You're a natural, Kels," Hailey adds.

"It's the weed. I'm telling you, it gives me superpowers."

Then a whole bunch of shit happens in what seems like the same moment. Kelly lines up her next shot and as I see her tensing her right arm, ready to fire, I hear someone to our right whisper-yell, if that's even a thing, "Hey."

Apparently, everyone hears it because we all reflexively turn and see a man leaning against a tree about twenty-five yards away. And just as I focus in on him, I see the blur of Kelly's arm. And then I hear another bang. Immediately followed by a thunk sound and then the guy twenty-five yards away falls to the ground.

Hailey is the first to put two and two together and says, in a disturbingly calm manner, "Huh?"

In a not even remotely calm manner, Kelly follows with, "Fuck! Fuck! Fuck!"

Her arm drops, barely holding the gun. The tiniest bit of smoke escapes the barrel. And then she drops it. The gun lands on a bed of pine needles and thankfully does not go off.

"Did I...did I..." Kelly can't finish the sentence, but she doesn't need to. She's wondering if she just killed someone. We all are.

"I don't know," I say and grab the gun off the ground and tuck it in my waistband. I look at Cash and nod toward where the man lies on the ground. Cash nods back.

"We're gonna go check it out," Cash says.

"I'm going with," Hailey says.

Kelly doesn't move, her eyes have glazed over.

We walk toward the guy as slow as possible, no one wanting to see what we are pretty sure we are going to see. I'm slightly in the lead and I'm the first to get a good look at him. His right arm is pinned behind his back at an unnatural angle. That alone makes me want to puke. I scan the rest of his body. Maybe in his thirties, average looking, green pants, boots, and a plaid shirt. His neck is turned to the side and his head rests on a football-sized rock, which could not have felt good landing on. There is a significant amount of blood on his neck and chest. Like more blood than I think you can survive losing. He's not moving and doesn't look to be breathing. Something is clearly wrong with his ear too.

"Is he dead?" Hailey asks.

No one responds. No one moves. We just stare. We stare at what I have no doubt is a dead person. A person that was very much not dead a few moments ago. And a few moments before that, didn't even exist to us.

I kneel down next to the body. I check for a pulse, and can't find one. His chest is not moving. As I stand, my toe pushes open his unbuttoned outer shirt, making visible the butt of a gun in a holster and something gold and shiny hanging from his neck. A badge.

"Yep," I say, "that cop is super fucking dead."

A FUCKING COP?" KELLY STAMMERS, HER fingers shake in some weird jazz-hands trauma response.

"How?" Hailey wonders aloud.

"Well—" Cash starts.

"Rhetorical, Ca—" but she doesn't finish because we hear what sounds like people running toward us from behind where the body lies. Cash and Kelly freeze as Hailey and I turn, ready to run.

"Dudes, let's fucking go," I say and nudge Kelly and Cash, bringing them back to the present. "People are fucking coming."

"But shouldn't we stay, I mean, we can't leave..." Kelly mumbles.

"Something doesn't feel right. We don't know who this person is, what he was doing here, nor do we know who the people coming are. And you still have a fucking joint in your mouth. We need to go."

Thankfully, that's all it takes, and we sprint to Hailey's car. We pile in, I jump in shotgun, and just as I shut the door, I hear from behind us, "There they are. Go! Go!"

Oh fuck.

"Drive, Hailey!" I yell, but don't need to. She has the car started and slams it into drive. Her wheels spin, spitting rocks, until they catch and we take off. The stretch of road is short before we bank left and will be out of sight. I turn my head as we round the corner and see the two guys stop at the top of the rise, watching us drive off. One is tall and bald, and the other is short with a huge beard. If we were in an older, nondescript car or truck with regular license plates, we might be far enough away that they wouldn't be able to make out any details, because that's what ninety percent of the vehicles up here look like. But alas, we are not. We are in a brand new luxury car with temporary plates, and there are not a lot of those in our town. God, I fucking hate this car.

"Did they see us?" Hailey asks.

"I'm not sure," I respond. But I'm pretty sure they did. And if so, I'm completely sure that's not good.

Cash says, "Guys, that was a fucking cop of some sort. Worse, even. Like a detective."

Kelly emits a low screeching sound and bobs her head up and down.

"Not helping, Cash," I say, directing my look toward Kelly.

Cash puts his arm around her, and she leans into him.

"Sorry, but it's true. That was a dead cop," Hailey states.

We are quiet for the rest of the drive back to Cash's. I keep almost saying something, then don't. It can hold.

We park in front of Cash's and head to his front door. Just as we approach, his brother walks out and has to jump aside to avoid us.

"Hey, Cash, I—" his brother starts.

"Not now, Wes," Cash says as he brushes past.

"Fuck you too then," Wes responds, shaking his head as we hurry by. The long haired part of his mullet flipping from side to side.

Once in Cash's room, we spread out. Cash and Kelly on the bottom bunk and Hailey and I on the bean bag.

Cash turns to me as if he is about to say something. Then stops. Then starts and then stops, like a fish out of water.

"I know, what the fuck?" I say for him.

"Did I really just shoot a cop and then flee the scene?" Kelly asks.

Cash and I both mumble "yes" at the same time.

Then Hailey says, "I don't think so."

"What?" I ask. "Were we not all at the same place a minute ago? The place where Kelly shot a gun at a dude, a cop, and he fell to the ground dead, covered in blood with a bullet hole in his neck?"

I look to Cash for backup. He nods.

I look at Hailey for an explanation, but she's deep in thought.

"No? Like no, she didn't do that?" I ask.

"Well, I don't think she did."

Hailey can tell I am about to interrupt, so she holds up her finger and says, "Just listen. We all agree there was a person. A man. In the woods that was standing, then wasn't, and when we saw him on the ground, he was apparently dead and covered in blood and had a wound in his neck. Right?"

"Um, yeah. A guy who was no longer standing because he got shot. And not just a guy, a cop," Cash states.

"Give me a second here. Back up. Did you see how much blood was on that guy?" she asks.

"I think it would be described as tons," I say.

Cash adds, "Buckets."

"Hailey, no one wants Kelly to have killed him, but come on," I say.

"Jack. Fucking stop. Let Hailey finish. If there is even the slightest chance I didn't just kill that guy, I want to hear about it."

"Fair. Go ahead, Hailey. Sorry," I say.

"Okay. So tons of blood. And how long did it take us to get over there after Kelly shot the gun? Fifteen seconds? Twenty?"

"Wait, I thought I didn't shoot him," Kelly says, fear creeping back in her voice.

"I didn't say you shot him. I said you shot the gun. I don't think that is in question. We heard it. I saw the recoil. You shot once at the can, which you hit. And then a second time after the person yelled," Hailey says.

We all nod in agreement.

"So the gun went off. We heard it hit something. The guy fell.

We got over to him in twenty seconds tops and he is already dead and entirely covered in blood. That doesn't feel right."

I say, "Come to think of it, that does seem a little weird. And it wasn't fresh. I mean, it wasn't dried, but it didn't seem like the massive amount of blood on him was inside his body like literally twenty seconds before."

"Exactly. And then he falls dead. Just like that. By the time we got there, he wasn't gasping, he was *dead*. He wasn't reaching for his neck, like 'oh my God what just happened that's making me die,' he was just dead," Hailey explains.

"Okay, so what happened then?" Cash asks, clearly skeptical.

"Did you guys see his neck? The wound? Did that look like a bullet hole to you?" Hailey asks.

"Well, when I was in bullet hole identification school—"

Hailey cuts me off. "Jack, zip it. To me, it looked like there was more than one wound there. Hard to tell with all the blood, but it looked like two or three punctures at least. I was just too freaked out to focus on it. Let's assume for a second it was a single wound and it was caused by a bullet, well, a bullet that Kelly shot..."

"I thought we were past this," Kelly whines.

"Let me finish. Let's just say it was. Since the guy was farther up the hill from us, Kelly would have had to have been pointing her gun upward at an angle to hit him in the neck. But she wasn't, the gun was level, I definitely remember that. If Kelly shot him from where she was, she probably would have hit him in the knee or thigh. Or the stomach at the absolute highest. There's just no way for her to have shot him from where she was and hit him in the neck," Hailey insists.

"Keep going," Kelly says, her face showing the hint of excitement.

"Okay. Here's what I'm thinking. Whatever caused him to bleed, well, to die, happened before he got to us. Let's say he was stabbed, or his neck was sliced. Somewhere else. Then he escapes, or whatever, and winds up near us. That would explain how he died so fast and the massive amounts of less-than-fresh blood and the wounds on his neck."

"It would also explain the guys who showed up right after," I add, "the ones that may very well now have an interest in us."

Cash says, "Yeah, add that to the list."

What Hailey said actually makes sense. I mean, the guy did die really fast. And the more I think about his neck, the less convinced I am that Kelly's bullet would have hit him there. The hard part to swallow is the timing. How he falls, dies really, right after Kelly shoots. Seems too coincidental, but weirder things have happened, I'm sure.

"How about we put the guns away then make a pact to never take them out again," Cash says, looking exhausted.

"I'm down with that," I say, and Hailey and Kelly nod in agreement.

We get up and put the guns back in Cash's dad's safe next to the drugs, close and lock the door. We stare at the safe for a minute, then Cash puts his hand out. Kelly puts hers on top, and then Hailey and then I follow.

"Umm, two, four, six, eight...guns we don't appreciate," Kelly chants. We pull our hands away. I look at Kelly, like *where did that come from?*

She shrugs. "Well, whatever. I never played team sports," she says.

"I think it was great," Hailey concludes.

"No more guns. Ever. Like ever fucking ever," Cash adds.

I have a strong urge to add "famous last words," but don't.

We pull into the Kum Quick lot and park on the side of the convenience store. We decide to give the talk about the dead guy a rest for the moment. I see Kelly in the rearview. Her eyes are red. More from crying than weed. She's holding Cash's wrist, squeezing it really. Her nails are digging into the veins in his arm.

There's a missing flyer for Casey West taped to the side of an ice cube freezer outside of the Kum. The tape has come off one of the bottom corners. It moves rhythmically in the breeze, like it's breathing. Kelly must see me staring at the flyer because she says, "Allison told me she ran away with her dad."

"Pretty sure her dad lived with her and her mom," Hailey says.

"He did live with them, but last I heard she wasn't sure where her dad was," I say.

"She tell you that?" Cash asks.

"Yeah, but more in an offhand kind of way. It didn't sound like it was that unusual, him going off somewhere."

Hailey gives me an eyebrow raise.

"I bet you tried to track him down, didn't you? What did you find out?" Cash says, laughing.

He knows I can't help myself when it comes to online sleuthing.

"I didn't find out where he was, but I did find out that his name is Reed West, and that he's been arrested a bunch of times for grand theft auto."

"That's insane. A real-life car thief. I can't believe you didn't tell us," Cash says.

Hailey looks at me like, *yeah, I can't believe you didn't tell me.* And in that same look, a*nd I wonder why you didn't tell me?* I really wasn't hiding anything; I just didn't feel like it was my place to share.

"How do you know it's him?" Kelly asks.

"Since he's been arrested so many times, I figured he'd done time, so I typed his name in the Department of Corrections site. One of the photos of him showed a tattoo on his arm that said *Casey.*"

"Her dad Black?" Cash asks.

"Nope. Super white. Like full-on racist-looking white if I didn't know better."

That ends the questions about Casey's dad. At least for now. No one says a thing. We sit in Hailey's car in the parking lot, lost in our own individual thoughts. Our own individual fears mainly.

"Anyone need anything?" Cash asks. We all shake our heads.

"I just wanted to get out of the house," Hailey says. She turns and looks at Kelly and says, "Kelly, I'm positive you didn't kill that guy, and I'm going back there tomorrow to prove it."

Kelly glances at Hailey, her face brightening for the first time since this afternoon and says, "You're the best."

I'm not sure going back there's the greatest idea, but I'm not about to mess with Hailey's look of determination nor with Kelly's smile.

TODAY IS THE THIRD ANNIVERSARY OF MY dad's disappearance. I haven't found out everything about what happened to him, but I know he's not coming back. I think about him and miss him every day. My mom has to work this afternoon, so we decided to commemorate his anniversary by having breakfast. It was his favorite meal of the day, after all. No headphones the entire meal. We shared a few stories about him. I cried after mentioning the time we were halfway through grocery shopping before we realized he wasn't wearing shoes, just socks. My mom stood and walked over to me. I thought she was going to give me a hug. Instead, she gave me a pat on my back and said my father was a good man. Then she started cleaning up. As I was walking out the door, she told me how to break out of zip-ties. Even did a demonstration of sorts.

I watch Hailey drive up, and a jolt of fear runs through me when I realize how much her car stands out next to every other car she passes. I really hope we made it around the bend yesterday before those two guys saw us. I hustle across the grass, open the passenger door, and slide in.

"How was it this morning?" she asks and gives me a quick kiss.

"It was fine. My mom is fucking petrified of emotions. She dodges them like they do bullets in those sci-fi movies. It's remarkable, really."

"Remarkable is one word for it. I'm sorry, babe. Want to cry?" she says, trying to be helpful and humorous at the same time. It works.

"I'm good. Thanks," I say, and I mean it.

"I'll drop you off at Cash's, but I need to go hang with Kelly," she says.

I've been messaging with Cash this morning, so I know Kelly's not doing well. Sounds like she's been having an hours-long panic attack.

"I hope you guys find something definitive out there."

"We'll do our best," I say and give her hand a squeeze as she drives to Cash's.

Hailey pulls into the driveway and stops. I lean over and give her a kiss. We discuss meeting up later depending on how Kelly is doing, and she drives off.

"Red hair, don't care," I say as I walk into Cash's house and see him in the kitchen.

"PB&J?" he asks.

"Don't mind if I do."

I grab some chips and dump them on the paper plates Cash has out for the sandwiches. I search the fridge for Kola Kountrys but don't find any. I settle on pouring two glasses of milk. We walk out back and sit at the picnic table.

When Cash finishes a bite that consists of at least half of his sandwich, he wipes his mouth and says, "I got the bike all gassed up. Thing started on the first kick."

I look at the shed in his backyard where we used to hang out. Only two walls remain standing. The other two walls and the ceiling are flat on the ground—luckily we moved everything important out of there last year. About a month ago we were in Cash's room just hanging out when Cash's brother ran down the hall, opened Cash's room, and yelled, "I'm building a grow house, motherfuckers!" Dude was manic and was talking super fast. Then, just as quickly as he arrived, he slammed the door and took off back down the hall. Cash and I looked at each other like, *What the fuck?* I figured this was some far-off plan he had, but apparently not, because we heard the garage door open, and then we heard Wes wreaking havoc in there. It was quiet for a moment, then we heard a series of super loud bangs. We hustled out back for a look. Wes, in the pitch black, was going to town on one of the walls of the shed with an axe. It was about eleven at night, and the only light out back was like a two-watt bulb next to the door. We could barely see him, but we could damn well hear him.

He was huffing and puffing as his axe crashed again and again against the wood. Cash didn't seem to care that his fort was being destroyed, he was just enjoying the show.

"Dude, what in the fuck are you doing?" he finally asked.

"You deaf? I'm building a grow house. I fucking told you."

"Now? Like literally in the middle of the night," Cash almost gets the question out without laughing.

"What, I should wait to start my future?" Wes asked.

We watched him attack the shed for another fifteen minutes, until he was too winded to go on. He took a seat on the ground next to the shed, trying to catch his breath. He managed to knock two of the walls down, which caused the roof to cave in. It looked then, exactly like it does now. Even the axe is sitting in the same place. Next time his brother does a bunch of meth, he might try and finish it. Until then, I guess his future is on hold.

"You done?" Cash asks, pointing to my plate. I nod, and he tosses it in the trash. We walk to Cash's bike, and he hops on and kicks it to life. I slide on the back and hold on as he takes off.

The trip takes us about fifteen minutes. It's faster to take the trails than it is to drive on the roads. Cash stops a half-mile short of the spot we were shooting and asks, "What do you think?"

"I say we keep going right past it, stash the bike, and then creep back. We know the guys came from the other direction."

Cash agrees, and we start walking. Just past where we were doing target practice, Cash spots a group of trees and pulls over, and we hide the bike. We're on the opposite side of the rocks that served as the backstop we used yesterday. Cash and I head off, and it takes about five minutes to get around them. I search for the tree the guy died under; they all look the same. I realize it's hard to find because the guy is gone.

"Dude's gone," I say to Cash.

"Yes, he is. Those guys take him?" he asks.

"Must have. He wasn't going anywhere on his own."

"There's the tree," he says and points it out.

We walk quietly and stay hidden as much as possible. We stop a couple of feet before the tree. It's a single big-ass pine tree in the middle of a big-ass forest full of big-ass pine trees. Nothing special about it other than the dude dying under it yesterday. The most notable part is the general lack of blood. Because the dude was covered in it.

"So if Kelly shot him, and all that blood poured out of him right then, why isn't any of it on the ground?" I ask.

"Maybe they cleaned it?"

I'm not sure what a forest ground would look like post-being cleaned of blood, but it looks pretty normal here. There are little rocks and plenty of dirt and pine needles, but it looks almost exactly like everywhere else. Not raked or shoveled or whatever they would have done to get rid of the blood.

"So no blood means Kelly didn't shoot him?" Cash asks.

"Maybe. Take into account that right after this, in a mostly deserted forest, two dudes show up and now the dead guy is gone. This just might be the worst coincidence of all time."

Cash and I move from looking down to looking at the tree. He turns back toward where Kelly was standing and then back to the tree. Like he's trying to line up her shot. He starts feeling the tree up and down and then stops about two feet off the ground. He pulls a bit of bark away and calls to me.

"Dude, check this."

I move to the other side of him and look at the spot where he removed the bark. There is clearly a hole there. Not all the way through the tree, but an inch or two deep. If it's a bullet, it went perfectly between two pieces of raised bark. Coincidence upon coincidence. I grab my keys out and whittle away at the hole. My fingers tire after a few minutes, and Cash takes over. It feels like forever, but is probably less than ten minutes, when we get it wide enough that we can see something metal inside. We look at each other in excitement and keep digging. Another few minutes, and Cash is able to pry it out. He holds a small, smashed piece of metal between his thumb and pointer finger.

"This here is a bullet," Cash says, clearly pleased.

"Yes, it is. But are you sure it's Kelly's bullet?" I ask.

"Well, not positive, but come on. Put it together. No blood on the ground. He died within like fifteen seconds of supposedly getting shot. The wound in his neck, according to Hailey, might have been more than one wound. This makes more sense than that."

"How stoked is Kelly gonna be knowing she didn't kill a cop?"

"Dude, you have no idea. She was not doing well this morning. Like not even close to doing well. Luckily, before I headed over, I grabbed a couple Xanax from my dad's stash. She mellowed considerably after that." Talking about Kelly makes Cash realize he needs to update her. He types a message and hits send. He reads her response and a smile spreads across his face. I get a video call from Hailey. She points the camera at Kelly as she jumps up and down, yelling and screaming with joy. Some tears too, but the good kind. I think I'm the only one freaking out about the two guys who saw us drive away. And since Kelly didn't kill the cop, I'm assuming they must have. They didn't have the demeanor of people looking to help the guy. Two people seeing a carload of kids that possibly saw them kill a cop — well, that spells *we're fucked* to me.

"Let's head toward where the guys came from and see what we can find," I say.

"Umm, fuck that. I'm super sure Kelly didn't kill that guy. And I'm even more sure I don't want to get mixed up with who did."

"Cash, we already are mixed up. Those guys saw us in Hailey's brand-new fancy fucking car. You know how many cars there are like that in Black Forest? I bet one. Hers."

"You just want to look for Casey," he says.

"Yes and no. Just a little peek, Cashy," I urge.

Cash looks down. Shakes his head, "Fuck! God damn it!"

"I know. I know. Let's go," I walk past Cash and head toward where the two dudes came from. After a few seconds, he stomps after me. I bet a million dollars he's shaking his head.

We walk for about five minutes. I'm pretty close to giving up when I see a path heading down a slight hill. About twenty feet down that path is a gate. Well, more like part of a metal fence, about three feet high, that sags and is used as a gate. I look back to Cash and nod my head in the direction. He sighs and shakes his head but follows. As we step through, I notice drops of blood on the metal. I point them out to Cash. He takes a deep breath, but before he can try and talk me out of continuing, I start walking. We walk through aspen trees so thick they block the sun and drop the temperature. On the other side, I can just see the edge of a road, actually more like a driveway. Cash sees it too, and this time he leads the way.

At the end of the driveway is an old cabin that you can only see from the front because there are so many trees on the other sides. It's two stories tall and has seen better days. It leans at awkward angles. I'm surprised it's still standing. There are a handful of windows, all of them with closed drapes of different colors. Bedsheets maybe. We duck behind a few chest-high rocks where we can get a good view of the cabin without being exposed.

"Think it means anything?" I ask.

"I don't know. Pretty close to where that guy dropped, and the path he probably walked on leads right here."

There are no cars out front. Next to the porch is a faucet sticking out of the ground about three feet high. They're pretty common for filling up water troughs for horses and livestock. There's a bucket turned on its side next to it. Part of the porch looks wet.

I point toward the deck. "Does it look like that deck was just scrubbed?"

"Yeah, as a matter of fact, it does."

My eyes are drawn to the center window on the second floor above the front porch. I see two fingers pull open the drapes, and farther back from that, a girl's face. It's dark, and the window is crazy dirty, but it looks like Casey West. I turn to Cash, but he's looking down the driveway.

"Dude, the window. Look at the window," I say. By the time Cash turns, the girl is gone. Before I can tell him what I think I saw, we hear a car approaching. It pulls to the side of the cabin where the driveway ends. Two guys get out—it's the same two guys from yesterday. They're in their thirties, maybe. One tall and bald, and one short with a beard. Even from this distance, they look dangerous. They check behind their backs as they get out of the car. Then the bald guy pulls something out of his pocket that looks like a mouse and flings it across the yard. He doesn't even look to see where it lands. They go straight to the front door and unlock the big padlock. They enter the cabin and shut the door behind them.

Before I can tell Cash that we should get the fuck out of here, I get a message on my phone. It's from Hailey, and it says: "Get to Cash's, we got a big fucking problem." There's a photo attached. It takes a second to load, but when it does, I can see it's a picture of Hailey's windshield from the inside. Under the wiper blade is a piece of paper, and on that paper, scrawled in large letters with what looks like blood, it says—*Shhhh*!

THEY KILLED MY SISTER'S GERBIL AND used the little guy's blood to write that note," Hailey says through panicked breaths.

We got to Cash's just before Kelly and Hailey did, and now we're sitting at the picnic table in his backyard. Hailey's voice is as shaky as her hands. I move to her, but she can't keep still and stands.

"They broke into *your house*? Your massive fucking house with all kinds of cameras and shit?" Cash asks in disbelief.

"Yep. I'll show you the video too. They came in through the sliding door on the back deck; I must have left it unlocked. The alarm didn't go off either, because I forgot to set it. A mistake that will not happen again. They walked through a bunch of rooms. My room is downstairs, and my guess is they came across Hazel's room first—maybe thought it was mine. The tall one grabbed Spikey out of his cage, lifted him up in full view of the camera, and snapped her neck." Hailey succumbs to sobs and can't go on. I stand and rub her back.

Eventually, her crying mellows, and she says, "Then he put her in his pocket. He stared directly into the camera, black ski mask on, then he put his finger to his mouth and did the *shhhhh* thing."

"That's so fucked. And, I'm just gonna say, I, for one, am convinced not to say anything. I don't need to say a goddamn thing to anyone," Cash says.

We fill them in with more details on what we found when we looked at the tree. We haven't told them about the path yet; I haven't even told Cash about what, or who, I saw in the window.

"I think I saw Spikey," I say.

"What do you mean?" Hailey asks, confused.

I share how we watched the guys park their car and how we saw one of them throw what looked like a dead mouse out of his pocket.

"Dark green jacket? Tall?" Kelly asks.

"Yep, bald too, but you probably couldn't see that in the video with the ski mask," Cash says.

"The other guy shorter, dark jeans, dark sweatshirt?"

"Yep. Big beard, but again, same thing about the mask," Cash says.

Kelly rests her head in her hands, then lifts it up and says, "We can't just say nothing though, right? I mean, we saw someone die. Then some sketchy dudes show up, and now the body is gone."

"We're not really lying about it though, are we?" Cash asks. "No one's asked us."

"Well, lying by omission. I'm not saying we go to the cops, but let's play it out. We don't do anything, and then we get a knock on one of our doors, a day from now, a week from now, whatever. They have some kind of evidence. Photos of your car, Hailey, heading up the road. Or a witness that saw us shooting and then saw us get into your car. I don't know, but something like that. There's always something like that. My mom tells me all the time—it's the coverup that gets you," I say.

"I don't think there was a witness or photos or whatever," Kelly says.

"At this point, we can say we were scared and freaked out and didn't know what to do, but we thought about it and figured we had to say something. It only happened yesterday. But if we don't do anything at all..." I say, letting the thought hang.

"I'm not going to the cops, fuck that," Cash says. It has been driven into him since birth to never involve the police in anything. A huge part of that has to do with the fact that his dad sells drugs.

"I'm not even saying we go. I'm just saying we should play it out." I look around to see if I'm all alone on this. It kind of feels that way. "The other thing—Cash, remember when I said to look at the upstairs window, right before those two dudes showed up?"

He nods. "Yeah, all I saw were curtains."

I take a deep breath, sigh, and say, "I saw someone inside."

"What window, what do you mean?" Hailey asks.

"So the cabin is two stories. It has a couple of windows on the ground floor and a couple on the second floor, all covered by curtains. Right when we got there, I was scanning the place. I looked up at one of the windows on the second floor and saw movement," I say.

"You saw movement or you saw someone?" Kelly asks.

"Both, I think. I saw a hand pull the curtains to the side. And then, farther back... well, it was darkish in there, but I saw someone. A person. A girl, I think."

"Whoa, whoa, whoa. Hold on just one fucking second. You think you saw a girl in that sketchy-ass cabin?" Cash asks. Not in an *I don't believe you way*, but in a *please tell me you are kidding because I really don't want this to be true* way.

They're staring at me. And fuck, I don't know for a fact. Could I have just been stressed out and imagined it? I guess, but I don't think so.

After a moment, I say, "Yeah, I'm pretty sure I saw a girl in that cabin."

"Jack, are you trying to say you saw Casey West?" Hailey asks, sounding frustrated.

"I'm not saying that exactly," I stammer.

"But you're not *not* saying that?" Kelly presses.

"From what little I saw, yeah, it could have been her."

"So you saw Casey Fucking West in the window of a cabin? Doing what, admiring the view?" Kelly asks.

"I don't know if it was her. And more peeking than admiring."

"Positive?" Hailey asks.

"Positive that I saw something? Almost. Positive that I saw

someone? Kind of. Positive that it was Casey West? No, not at all."

"What in the actual fuck?" Cash says.

"Did the not-positive-you-saw-a-person person look okay?" Hailey asks.

"I couldn't tell, it was brief and they were far away. But Cash, back me up here, there was a big-ass padlock on the *outside* of the front door. Maybe there's a door in the back that's not locked, but if they are holding someone in there, they aren't getting out the front."

"I don't believe for a minute it's Casey in there. No offense, Jack. I think Casey is in California or wherever the fuck she ran away to," Hailey says. "But I believe you saw something. And maybe it's just a friend of theirs, but regardless, I feel like we need to say something to someone. We got a dead guy and a dead Spikey, and it all seems to lead back to this cabin. We don't even need to say we were up there shooting. Jack, you and I can go."

"I'm good with that," I say. I don't feel bad that Hailey doesn't believe it's Casey. Shit, I don't know if I believe it. But I have a feeling that whoever it was, is not there of their own volition. And the fact that I heard the rumor about there being someone that looked like Casey in the back of a car driven by two guys in that same area—well, we don't have to look too far to come up with who the two guys could be.

"Me too," Kelly adds. "I'm not sure I can handle talking to the cops."

"Aren't we forgetting about the warnings to keep our mouths shut, though?" Cash points out. "I'm not saying we don't say anything. But that might just be an issue. Like, those dudes found your house real fast, Hailey? Like, less than a day fast."

"Yeah, they did. But what if someone is in trouble up there?" I'm careful not to say Casey.

"I know, I know. I'm just saying, these guys aren't fucking around. Killing a cop? Kidnapping?" Cash says.

"Killing a fucking gerbil? Don't forget that part," Hailey says.

"And a cop too," Kelly says.

"Well, yeah, I know. A cop. Not great. But also, a gerbil? Who does that?" Hailey says.

"Wanna head down there?" I ask Hailey, and she nods.

Kelly and Cash tell us they're going to hang here until we get back. Instead of going through Cash's house, we walk around the side, and just as we round the corner, I see an unmarked cop car parked out front. It's white and nondescript, but I can see the lightbar on the inside of the roof through the windshield. I raise my arm to stop Hailey. I scoot us back to the edge of the house. She gives me a *what the fuck* look, and I give her the *shhhh* sign. I don't know if the car just pulled up or if it's been there a while. I can't even tell if anyone's inside because of the glare. Hailey clears her throat in irritation. I'm about to tell her what's going on when I see both front doors open. A tall, bald guy gets out of the driver's seat, and a short guy with a beard gets out of the passenger seat. My stomach drops. It's definitely the same guys we saw at the cabin. No doubt the same guys that were on video at Hailey's. The gerbil killers, the potential cop killers, are fucking cops themselves. I lead Hailey and myself behind a tree on the side of Cash's house, and when I do, I step on a branch and it snaps. And then—silence. The two cops have stopped walking.

I hold my breath. I whisper in Hailey's ear as quietly as I can, "Don't move and don't say anything, they're here." Her body tenses. They start walking again. Now it sounds like they're heading toward us instead of the front door. Then—more silence.

I can't see them, but one of them yells, "Freeze!"

They aren't around the corner yet, so I know they haven't seen us. But I freeze nonetheless. If they come this way, we are good and fucked.

The other one says, "Look, the front door's not even closed."

And just then, my phone starts buzzing. The ringer is off, but the vibration alone is loud. I frantically hit buttons trying to stop it.

The first one says with urgency, "Over there, I hear something."

At that, Hailey grabs my arm, and we bolt toward the backyard. We round the corner of the house, and I slam the gate behind me. We see Cash and Kelly making out at the picnic bench. We don't even stop as we approach.

Hailey yells, "Run! Fucking run! It's them."

If we weren't already on edge, they might have been like, *Run? Why? Who?* But thank God they don't, they just pop up and sprint after us. As we run from the house, I hear one of the cops cursing as he tries to unlatch the gate. We continue toward the back corner of Cash's property and into the cover of a handful of trees. We just make it into his neighbor's yard when I hear the gate slam open. We're moving through dense trees in the neighbor's yard when one of them screams, "Fuuuuuuuuuck!" in frustration. We keep running for another quarter mile before we stop behind a shed on yet a different neighbor's land.

Hailey asks, still panting, "The bald guy and the bearded guy?"

I nod because I'm too out of breath to speak.

"They yelled 'freeze' like cops yell 'freeze'," Cash says.

"That's because they are cops. I saw them get out of an unmarked car," I say.

"Beardy and Baldy are cops? No, no, no, no," Cash says in disbelief.

"Exactly," Kelly says.

"You were closer to them just now than we were earlier at the cabin. You recognize either of them?" Cash asks.

"Maybe. Remember that story Barnes told us about that kid getting searched off Black Forest Road? The cops found a bag of weed on him and some coke? And they pocketed it and then let him go?"

"Yeah, I thought it was bullshit."

"Well, Barnes pointed out two cops to me one day, saying it was them. It was from a distance, but it could have been those two."

Kelly keeps repeating, "Oh my God, oh my God, oh my God," until Hailey rubs her back and she stops.

I grab my phone out of habit and see the message that caused the vibrating alert that almost got me killed. It's from my mom and it says, "Jack, just listened to this podcast. An entire family got killed because the dad didn't have his phone on silent and the text message ping led the killer right to them. Always have your phone on silent."

Oh my God. I can't believe her sharing a true crime fact trying to save me from getting killed almost got me killed.

WE HID BEHIND THE SHED IN CASH'S neighbor's yard for about an hour, too scared to check if they had left. Hailey finally said fuck it, and made us move. Luckily they were gone, because as we looked out from the side of Cash's house, my phone buzzed in almost the exact same spot. It was my mom warning me never to agree to a polygraph.

I stand next to Hailey in Cash's side yard. She looks terrified. She was privy to most of what happened last summer, but she wasn't smack dab in the middle of it. This time she is. They broke into her house, fucked with her car, and killed her sister's gerbil. That's about as in the middle as you can get. I want to sleep in my own bed tonight, so I say goodbye to Cash and hitch a ride home with Hailey. She drops Kelly off on the way. When she stops in the parking lot of my apartment, I give her a long hug goodbye. I don't want to let go, but I eventually do. She's going out to eat with her family tonight before they head to the East Coast for a week. Her sister is on a traveling Lacrosse team and her parents are spending the next week at a tournament with her. Hailey's old enough now that she doesn't have to travel with them to these things anymore. When her family gets back all of them are heading to Europe for a month. I really hope everything is fine by then.

I sit on my bed and stare at a photo of the missing flyer for Casey on my phone. Trying to decide if it was her I saw in the cabin window. If it was, I'm assuming she needs help.

I go to the forum dedicated to Casey's disappearance. I start at the beginning. There were a ton of messages posted during the first couple of days of her disappearance. Kids saying they hope she's okay and that she comes home soon. Funny how popular someone becomes when tragedy strikes them. The day the cops came out saying she ran away, the comments about Casey and her mom having a strained relationship started. The people that posted those comments had never posted before and haven't posted since. BlackForestPI replied to the posts, they never responded.

I read through every comment, I guess in hopes I'll find

something helpful. I don't. The most recent comment is from BlackForestPI pleading for more tips. The post contains a link to a video, I click on it, but the video is no longer available. It's probably the one in which she inadvertently shared her identity. I notice there is a blue dot next to her name. I select it. It takes me to the profile page for BlackForestPI, it's blank, other than another request for info and tips. At the bottom of the page it says the blue dot means the person is currently online. I decide to send her a message.

I type: *Did you hear the rumor about Casey being seen in the back of a car with two guys?* I hit send and wait. I stare at my screen for a good ten minutes, but she doesn't reply. When I'm about to give up, I see a yellow dot appear next to my name. I click on it, and it takes me to my profile page, where it says I have a new message. It reads: *Of course I heard that, I look new? Who is this?* I write back: *Jack Larson. I go to Black Forest High. Was the rumor from someone reliable?* I sit at my desk and wait. It doesn't take long for her to respond: *Who the fuck is Jack Larson? Sounds like a made up name. And if you learn one thing in this business it's that no one is reliable.* She thinks she's in a business? I write back: *We had English together fall semester.* She responds: *You don't know me. I'm a fucking mirage.* Great, maybe this was a waste of time. I write back: *Okay, never mind.* Before I click off the page I see a response: *Wait. I wasn't told first hand, but heard the tip came from a park ranger. Why?* Well if that's true, I guess it's pretty reliable. I don't know how much I want to tell her. I'm not sure how she can even help.

I respond: *Just curious. Any description of the two people with her?*

After a moment she writes back: *Just that one had a beard. Again, why?*

Well that fits.

I reply: *I'm not sure how I can help, but it just makes me mad that everyone assumes she ran away.* Feels about as much as I am willing to give her.

She writes back: *I lied. I know who you are. I also saw that you and Casey were friendly. Don't fucking say a word about who you think I am.*

I write back: *I won't. Have you heard anything else helpful?* I don't expect her to have anything to offer, but figure it's worth asking.

She says: *No, but I get a creepy fucking about the two cops that were in charge of her disappearance. They were really eager to convince me Casey ran away.*

I ask: *Do you know their names?*

The blue dot next to her name disappears. I guess that's all I'm gonna get. I can't sleep, so I decide to see what I can find out about Bald Cop and Beard Cop. I click over to the Black Forest Police Department, on the front page are names and photos of their police chief and assistant chief. Neither of them are Bald Cop or Beard Cop. There isn't a search option on the site so I start clicking on random links and going through the pages. I find an *In Memoriam* section. There are only two names listed. The first is, Mike McCarthy, it says he was killed while directing traffic in a storm after an accident. Someone lost control and slid into him. This happened two years ago. The other one is even less helpful. It was a Black Forest Police Officer that died on duty when he was thrown from a horse while searching for a lost hiker in 1963. That pretty much exhausts the site. I leave it and do a search on the Mike McCarthy Memorial and come across a number of photos from the service. I bounce from site to site, but eventually it pays off. I find a picture that has six cops standing next to each other, two of them are Bald Cop and Beard Cop. The caption says *Members of the Black Forest Police Department*, no names given. I keep searching. I find a site called *Black Forest Breaking News 24/7* (it is neither breaking news nor 24/7 in nature). On it is another photo of Bald Cop and Beard Cop. The site hasn't been updated in the past six months, but the photo does list their names. Bald Cop is Damon Storey and Beard Cop is Buck Carter, they're listed as investigators.

The last relevant picture I come across was taken inside what I assume is the police station, because there's an easel with the Black Forest Police Department logo and a DEA logo. Below the logos it says "Operation Engage." I assume it's some kind of training. On the far left of the photo Damon Storey stands next to Buck Carter. Damon is leaning down and whispering into Buck's ear. They look shady. Next to Damon is the chief and next to him is the deputy chief. There are two people to the side of the cops, that don't seem to be aware a photo is being taken. One is a woman of about thirty years of age and the other is a man with a blue windbreaker that says DEA, and although his ear looks perfectly unmangled, it is clearly our dead cop. The cop that Kelly did not kill was a DEA agent. This just keeps getting better.

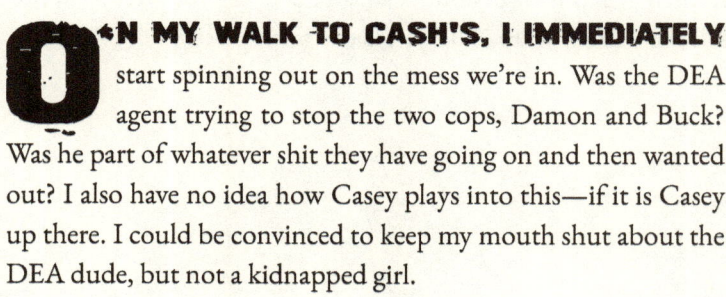

ON MY WALK TO CASH'S, I IMMEDIATELY start spinning out on the mess we're in. Was the DEA agent trying to stop the two cops, Damon and Buck? Was he part of whatever shit they have going on and then wanted out? I also have no idea how Casey plays into this—if it is Casey up there. I could be convinced to keep my mouth shut about the DEA dude, but not a kidnapped girl.

I walk into Cash's house and find his brother, Wes, on the couch, smoking a bong.

"Hit?" he says, holding the three-foot bong toward me as smoke billows from his nose and mouth.

"Thanks, man, I'm good," I respond.

He looks up at me, as if he wants to ask me something, so I stop.

"So, dude, I'm, uhh, taking a poll. Like, I'd say 90-95% of the time after I bang a bitch, she cries. Someone was telling me that's unusual. I was like, yeah, right."

"Is there a question in there?" I ask.

"Nah. Never mind, man. I know what's normal," he says.

I sigh and continue to Cash's room. I'm still undecided if it was easier when we hated Wes and he hated us.

Cash sits on his bed with an open book, scribbling numbers and symbols on a pad of paper. He finishes filling the page with some crazy-looking equations and moves to the next page, filling it as well. I stand watching for a couple of minutes, mesmerized that any of it makes sense to him. He's not just good at math, he is a savant. He's more advanced than any of the teachers at our school. He reaches the bottom of the page with his scrawling and ends with = 0. Only then does he notice I'm in the room.

"They didn't even have a concept of zero in Europe until the 12th century," he says.

"Yeah, super interesting. Can we talk about the fucking DEA agent now?" I ask.

Cash looks wounded but closes his book and says, "Been thinking about it, and my conclusion is we are fucked." He gets up, opens the shades on his window, and looks outside.

"I agree. Not even the Mexican cartels kill DEA agents. I was doing some reading last night, and apparently, one of the cartels killed a DEA agent in the '80s, and the U.S. government went off. Now those guys, who basically kill anyone and everyone—they chop people up, hang them from bridges—well, those guys are like, nope, no way I'm fucking with a DEA agent," I say.

"These two cops, who'd you say they were, Stones and Carter?"

"Damon Storey and Buck Carter," I say.

"Which one is the bald dude? He gives me bad vibes."

"Damon's the bald one. Buck is the one with the beard."

"Well, they're either ruthless as fuck or they're fucking out-of-control crazy to do that."

"Or both," I say. "Either way, back to your original point."

"Fucked, I know." Cash turns from the window, plops down on his bean bag, and buries his head in his hands.

"The way I see it right now, first and foremost, we need to make sure Casey isn't being held there," I say.

"I feel like it's such a long shot that it's her. Even with what Maggie told you. I mean, she's the one that was talking about an organ harvesting crime ring being behind it, after all," Cash says.

"What if we don't do anything, and we hear in a week or a month that Casey was being held up there, or some other poor girl? That they killed her or tortured her and—"

Cash cuts me off, "I get it. Fine, yeah. We go take a look. Just walk right up there and knock on the front door, and be like, you got a kidnapped girl up in here?" he says with a scared laugh.

"I think before we go up there, we try and find Casey's mom," I say. "Maybe she did run off, and she's been in contact with her and is chilling in California or somewhere."

"That's like the most sane thing you've said in a long time. You know where she lives? Her name? Anything?"

"I don't, but I bet Maggie does," I say.

"You and Maggie tight now?"

"Besties, but I think she'll talk to us."

"Whatever, if it means we don't have to go to that scary-ass cabin, I'm in."

"I told Hailey we'd meet her and Kelly at her house this afternoon. It'd be nice to have a little more info before then," I say.

"Well, I know where Maggie lives at least, it's not far from here. She's in Inwood."

"If she's not there, we can go to her work. Guess where she just got a job." I stalked her online last night and found out.

"I don't know, euthanizing cats and dogs that age out at the shelter?"

"Jesus, dude. No. She's really not that bad. She works at Kum Quick. Just started."

"Perfect place for her. I wonder how long before she eats Gordon alive?"

"I'm sure he's terrified. Come on," I say and grab a pillow off the couch and fling it at him. He laughs and easily ducks it.

Maggie's house is less than a half-mile from Cash's, and although hard to believe, hers is more shitty than his. The glass that makes up part of the front door is cracked and poorly repaired with duct tape. The tape is old and yellowed and has lost much of its stick. A few of the taped shards of glass move in the breeze, and pieces clink off one another like a white trash wind chime. Part of the front of the house is painted a different color green from the rest. You can literally see where the brush strokes of the newer, but still old, paint run up against the really old paint. There is a giant pile of clothes in the middle of the yard. It's been there so long weeds are growing up through it. Her dad's, I wonder? Or her boy clothes that she no longer wears? Cash doesn't even notice. Par for the course in Inwood. Cash raps on the front door. Loud enough to be heard, but not loud enough to be the cops.

I walk along the front of the house to a window, and I attempt to peek in, but it's covered on the inside with a blanket or a sheet. Cash knocks on the door again to no avail.

"Maybe she's at work," I say.

"I could use a Slushee Dream anyway."

We leave Maggie's and head to Kum Quick. It's a five-minute walk to the convenience store, and when we are halfway through the parking lot, I see Maggie behind the counter through the big front windows. She's standing next to Gordon. Maybe he's training her, God help them both. Gordon's worked at the Kum for a long-ass time. His older brother worked there before him and their dad before that, so he's kind of Kum royalty.

"Hey Gordon, hey Maggie," I say as we walk through the door. They look up, nod, and go back to inspecting what looks like lotto tickets and scratched-off lottery tickets.

"Whatcha guys doing?" Cash asks.

"Don't worry about it," Maggie says without looking up. Cash gives me an *I told you so* look.

"You'd be surprised how often people throw away winning tickets," Gordon says. He squints and moves the ticket closer to his face, trying to bring it into focus. Then he squints at what I'm guessing are the winning numbers posted next to the register.

"Really?" Cash asks skeptically and makes his way to the Slushee Dream machine and fills two cups.

"Oh yeah, all the time. I'm just kind of teaching Matt here the ropes," Gordon says.

"It's Maggie. I fucking told you."

"How often do you find winning tickets in the trash?" I ask, unable to keep the disbelief out of my voice.

"I found a two-dollar winner in January," Gordon beams.

"So in the past six months, you've done this shit every day for two dollars? What the fuck, man?" Maggie says and drops the lottery ticket she was holding to the floor.

"Whoa. Easy there Magpie, just goes to show the big one is closer today than it was yesterday."

"I won't fucking tell you again. It's Maggie. Fuck this, I'm taking my break."

"What do you mean break?" Gordon asks.

"My break. Like I fucking said. You know, you work like three hours or something, and you get a fifteen-minute break," she says.

"That's not a thing," Gordon says.

"It most definitely is a thing," Maggie says, looking to Cash and me.

"Yeah, dude. It's a thing," Cash agrees as he returns with the two slushees. He hands me one.

"Like a literal law thing," I say.

"Nah, I would've heard about it. I've been working here for six years. "Never got a single break," Gordon says defiantly.

"Well, then you're a dumbshit, because it's a thing. Kind of like when you work more than forty hours in a week, and you get paid time and a half," Maggie says and starts rummaging through her bag.

"Ha, that's not a thing either. I'd know that one for sure

because I've worked sixty hours a week here for the last four years," Gordon says, laughing at Casey's ignorance.

"You make what, like fifteen dollars an hour?" Cash asks Gordon.

"Yeah, kind of. Well, a little less. Closer to nine. Exactly nine, actually."

Cash says, "First, that's illegal. That's not even close to minimum wage."

"Yeah, that's not a thing here. Minimum wage, I mean. They told me since they aren't like a giant company, they don't have to do that. Showed me a piece of paper and everything," Gordon says.

"Okay, sure, that makes sense," Cash says, scoffing, then continues after looking up at the ceiling for a second, "secondly, even based on your illegal wage, this shit place owes you $18,720."

"You guys are the dumbest kids I've ever met," Gordon says and starts laughing so hard he can barely contain himself.

"So, wait a minute. Are you saying they have to pay me more than $7 an hour?" Maggie asks.

"Oh. My. God," Cash says.

"Hey, Maggie, can we talk to you outside for a second?" I ask.

"I'm taking a smoke break, you can do whatever the fuck you want. Fucking off included."

I guess that's kind of an invitation. Or at the very least not a complete denial of an invitation, so we follow her. Gordon probably would have tried to stop her from taking a break, and us from leaving without paying for our slushies, if he wasn't laughing so hard that he didn't notice.

Cash and I stand in the same spot we were parked in the other night. Maggie lights up a homemade-looking brown cigarette and leans back against the ice machine, her body covering Casey's missing flyer. She stares at the mountains and ignores us.

"I was wondering if you could help us track down Casey's mom," I say.

This clearly pisses her off, and she says in a less-than-gentle tone, "I fucking told you last night I'm not the person you think I am." She doesn't realize she just one-hundred-percent confirmed she is the person I think she is.

"Whoa, okay, cool. Just... do you know where Casey lives then?" Cash asks.

"Why the fuck would I know where she lives? Like I've been there? I didn't even like Casey," she's pretty much yelling now.

"I told you, Jack, total waste of time," Cash says, shaking his head.

I see what look like tears welling in Maggie's eyes. I feel like she wants to open up, but her tough-girl shell is preventing it.

"Okay, well, thanks anyway, Maggie. I know you're not BlackForestPI, but whoever it is, is doing great stuff. They're the only person out there supporting Casey," I say and watch a tear escape her left eye and drip down her cheek, taking a streak of mascara along for the ride.

Cash and I turn to walk away, and we don't make it five steps before we hear a choked sob that stops us.

"Fine," she almost screams. We turn around.

"I really do hate her. And I also love her. We kissed. She fucking kissed me. She kissed me. Fucking cast a spell on me she did," and then she takes a huge hit off her homemade cigarette.

I don't know what to say, so I say, "Wow. I'm really sorry."

"What, you just kiss someone and then blow them off? Start

a forest fire of desire in them and then walk right past them in the hall?"

Cash, following my lead, says, "Geez, that sounds so hard."

"It's fucking impossible. And now, what, she's gone? She gets fucking kidnapped? Who fucking does that? Kisses someone and then gets fucking kidnapped? How fucked up is that?"

"So fucked up," I say, thinking that the most fucked up thing is Maggie making Casey's kidnapping about herself.

She takes another huge drag off her cigarette and blows it right in my face. It smells so bad I almost gag.

She sees my reaction and scoffs. She takes the cigarette between her thumb and middle finger in a flicking position, looks me dead in the eye, and says, "Can't handle your sherm, faggot?" and then she flicks the cigarette right at me. It hits me square in the forehead. It doesn't burn, so that's nice, but it does fall off my head and right into my Slushee Dream.

"What the fuck was that for?" I ask.

"I'm sorry, I just miss her, okay?" she says, softening. "She did this to me. She's the only one that can make it better, and she's gone. Sorry about your Slushee Dream," she says and gingerly grabs it from my hand.

"I don't know where she lives. I was never invited over there. I've dreamt about it though. Satin sheets. Blacklight posters. Candles that smell like sex. Whatever, never mind. Her mom works at Bigmart. Maybe try there. If you see her mom and she knows anything, tell her to tell Casey to call me. Tell her to tell that fucking bitch to call me," Maggie says.

The front door to the Kum opens and Gordon pops his head out, still laughing and wiping tears from his eyes. "Magnum, PI. Fake break is over," he says.

"I warned him," Maggie says, balls her fists, turns, and speed-walks to the front door.

I walk backward away from the Kum. "The fuck?"

"I told you, man!"

"What the fuck is sherm?" I ask.

"A cig dipped in embalming fluid," Cash says.

"Like embalming fluid, embalming fluid?"

"Yep, embalming fluid, embalming fluid."

"I can't believe she called me a faggot. I thought she'd be more sensitive to those kinds of insults, you know?"

"Dude. What single thing that came out of her mouth made you think her stance on sexual orientation would be well thought out or rational?"

"That's true. You down for a trip to Bigmart?" I ask. He nods reluctantly.

Bigmart is about a mile from the Kum. It's one of those big-box stores with a grocery store attached. The building itself is a squat, one-story warehouse devoid of a single decoration. Like they went from blueprints to completion and straight forgot about design.

It feels like it takes forever to walk across the parking lot, it's so big. Inside, the fluorescent lights shine as bright as the sun. We head to the customer service counter, where a girl about our age stands staring at her phone. She has shoulder-length yellow hair with the consistency of straw, it could use a good combing. She's wearing a black vest with a name tag that says Veronica. On her face sit bright blue glasses that glow against her pale skin. It's clear that Cash knows her, and he immediately tries to turn away. Too late, she sees him and gives an enthusiastic wave. He stops, and I have to nudge him to keep going.

"Hey Veronica, how are you? Long time," Cash asks.

"Too long, Cash. I'm good. So good, Cash. How are you?" She's practically drooling as she stares into his eyes.

"Good, good. You know Jack?" Cash asks.

She doesn't look my way. She can't take her eyes off Cash.

"How may I be of assistance, Cash?" She draws out the word assistance and lets the s's slide out of her mouth. I think she's trying to sound sexy, but it ends up sounding like she has a lisp.

Her smile is so big it looks uncomfortable, like her lips might rip. Every few seconds she does a weird body shiver. Cash is literally causing this girl to shake.

"I don't even know her name, but Casey West's mom. Is she working today?" Cash asks.

"Classified," Veronica says and tilts her head to the side. Then she tilts it to the other side. I think in an attempt to be coy, but it comes across looking like a tic.

"Sorry?" Cash says.

"Classified, Cashy. Means it's a secret. Means I can't tell you. Well, means I probably can't tell you." She does the head tilt thing again. Now it looks like she's trying to get a kink out of her neck. She is not great at this flirting thing.

"Probably?" he asks.

"Sometimes when I'm completely out of uniform, my lips get a little loose," again with the slippery s's, but this time she licks her lips after. She kind of nails this move.

"I'm not following," Cash says. And I'm not sure if he is playing dumb or literally doesn't get that she wants her some Cash before she tells us anything about Casey's mom.

"You know, the summer between seventh and eighth grade was the best time of my life," she says.

"Yeah, for sure," Cash stammers.

"Really? For you too?" she responds excitedly.

"For sure, yeah, good times," he says, doing his best to match her enthusiasm.

"How about this, give me your phone," she says and waits for him to pass it to her. Cash tentatively hands her his phone. She types in something, and her phone dings on the counter. "Now we've got each other's stuff," she says it like ssssshhhhhtuff, "you can interrogate me when I get off."

Cash cringes but recovers and says, "The thing is, we're kind of in a hurry. Like, we need to talk to Casey's mom now. Can you just tell me if she's here and then I can, uh, probe for other secrets later?"

"Oooh. Cash. You're bad. Come here then," she says and beckons him with her finger. Cash leans in close to her, and I follow. She holds up the pointer finger on her other hand inches from my face. Without taking her eyes off Cash, she says, "Not you."

I back up. Cash leans in, and she whispers in his ear. She takes the other hand, with her finger still extended, and traces it along Cash's other ear. This is the best thing I have ever seen. I'm about to start cracking up, so I back up a few feet. Cash says some awkward goodbyes, and we walk toward the exit. Just before we hit the doors, Veronica yells, "Don't bring him." Cash gives her a thumbs up without turning, and we walk out the door.

CASHEEEEY. WAIT UP. MY GOODNESS, I SAY," sliding my s's. He walks faster.

I catch up to him and say, "Did you find out where Casey's mom is, at least?"

"Veronica said she just stopped showing up for work three days ago. No call, no show, and her phone goes straight to voicemail. I got her address, though." Cash rubs his ear and shudders.

"Nice work, man. You're like a secret agent," I say, laughing.

"She licked my ear, man."

After I stop laughing, I ask, "What did she whisper?"

"If I tell you, you've got to promise that you will never tell anyone. Especially Kelly."

"Fine, fine. Deal." This is gonna be good, I just know it.

"Swear."

"I swear." I even do the cross-my-heart thing.

"During the summer between seventh and eighth grade—"

"The best summer," I tease.

"Yeah, that one. So, this day I was at Brandon's house. I got dropped off, and he wasn't home yet, so I was waiting on the porch. Veronica lived next door, and I guess she saw me and walked over. She had a popsicle in her hand. She didn't even say anything to me, just walked right up next to me and started going to town on the popsicle like she was giving it head. I'm just like, what the fuck. Keep in mind, I am all of twelve years old at the time. And she was like, You like that, huh? You like it? Yeah, you fucking love it. Super aggressive-like, and I was like, Umm, hey, what's going on? And she was like, I'm a woman now, Cash. And then she deep-throats it and full-on gags. She does it again, and yep, gags again. She does it a final time, and pukes over the railing into the bushes. I was like, what in the actual fuck? She wiped her mouth with the back of her hand and said, 'I'll keep practicing.' Thankfully, that's when Brandon pulled up and she went home. That was literally the last time I spoke to her until just now. She went to Wilkinson's school, not ours. Along with Casey's mom's address, she whispered in my ear that she can handle an ear of corn now."

"She did not."

"Swear to God."

"That is the greatest thing I have ever heard."

"Glad you're enjoying it. I feel like I need to beg Kelly for forgiveness."

"You definitely do."

"Actually?" Cash asks, alarmed.

"No, man, I think it's best to keep this one to yourself," I say, appreciating the relief that spreads across his face.

"Maybe Casey's mom left town?"

"Maybe," I say, and an image of Damon and Buck killing the gerbil pops into my head. "But we should check."

We walk the forty-five minutes to Casey's house, seeking as much shade as we can along the way. I crack myself up every five or so minutes thinking about Veronica. By the time we get there, Cash has given up on telling me to shut it.

Casey's house is small but neat. After strolling through half of Inwood earlier, it's a breath of fresh air. No couches in the yard, piles of clothes, or old refrigerators. It's a one-story ranch with a detached garage. We walk down the empty driveway and stop at the front door. I give a quick rap and wait. After thirty seconds or so, I do it again. We peek in the windows, but all the shades are drawn. We walk to the garage and see a car parked inside.

"Mom's car?" I ask.

"Probably. I never saw Casey driving."

We circle around to the back of the house. All the shades are drawn there as well. I try the back door, but it's locked. The door itself is pretty flimsy and has four single-pane windows in the upper half.

Cash sees me inspecting the door and says, "Dude, no way."

I ignore him and start tapping on one of the panes—they seem pretty thin—and say, "You'd rather go to the cabin?"

He rolls his eyes. I take that as him being on board. I turn from the door and hit a pane of glass with my elbow. I don't put enough power behind it, and it doesn't break. All I manage to do is hit my funny bone and send a jolt of electricity through my arm. I pull away and bend over in pain. Cash laughs.

When the pain subsides, I give it another try. This time I put more force behind it, and the glass breaks easily. I knock the remaining shards free. As I reach through the opening to unlock the door, an awful stench hits us, and we recoil.

Cash backpedals a half dozen steps and says, "What the fuck is that?"

"Something dead," I say and shudder.

I've never smelled anything close to this bad. A few years back, a deer died in Cash's yard, and that thing stank, but nothing like this.

"Let's get the fuck out of here," Cash says and steps farther away from the house.

"I'm gonna check it out." It's the last thing I want to do, but I feel like I have to.

"No, you are fucking not. Jesus, dude. Whatever is in there is dead and does not need your help."

I shrug.

"You're on your own then. I'm not gonna end up puking in there and leaving my DNA all over the place," Cash says.

"I'll be right back." I pull my shirt over my nose, stick my hand through the broken pane, and unlock the door. I swing it open, and I'm sure my shirt is helping with the smell, but it can't be much. The house is as clean on the inside as it is on the outside. The back door leads to a living room with the kitchen behind it. A hallway leads off to the right with two doors on either side and one at the end. All three doors are closed. To the left, the hallway has one door midway down on the left and one at the very end, with only the one at the end open. I head toward the open door. I'm not scared anyone's here—no way they'd last in here with the smell—but I am terrified of what I may find. I fear I'm about to see my second dead body in two days.

When I get to the end of the hall, I gently push the door the rest of the way open. The first thing I see, in what is clearly a bathroom, is a significant amount of dark, dried substance on the tan tiled floor. It's more black than red, but I know right away it's blood. And there's a lot of it. I raise my head and see a dark green bathtub. Out of it hangs the left arm of a dead person. A huge cut runs vertically from the wrist to the elbow. I will myself not to look higher, but I do anyway. I follow the arm until I see the rest of the body. It sits in a half-filled tub of bloody water. I assume it's Casey's mom. Under the shower head, written on the tile midway up, in what appears to be blood, it says: I quit. If it's not a suicide, it's certainly meant to look like one. The handwriting, if that's what it's called, does not look remotely feminine. It also looks like there's some bruising on her neck. Not that I'm an expert, but I can picture the scene—Damon yelling at Buck to hold her still while he cuts her arm with some scary-sharp knife. Casey's mom pleading for her life. Buck holds her in place in the tub as her life floods from her arm onto the floor. Maybe they're standing on the edge of the tub or on the toilet to avoid leaving bloody footprints. Then Damon grabs some toilet paper so he doesn't leave fingerprints. He dips it in the blood and uses it as a paintbrush to write the note. Man, these guys love writing in blood. My guess is that when this gets called in to the police, Damon and Buck will take the assignment. They'll quickly determine it's a suicide, have the body cremated, and close the case.

I'm not used to the smell now, but it's not as bad as it was. I feel momentarily removed from the scene, until I see her mouth move. I scream because I think she's come alive. But then I realize it wasn't her mouth moving—it was a dozen or so maggots crawling out of the corner of it. They slowly tumble into the blood-brown water. And now I find the smell worse than ever. I don't think it's gonna be possible to make it outside before I puke. I run out of the bathroom and smack into the half-open door. I manage to get around it and sprint down the hall. I gag the first time before I am halfway to the front door. I actually throw up some as I pass through the door, but manage to keep it in my mouth. Just as I make it beyond the door, I vomit all over one of Casey's mom's flower beds. Bits of half-digested food and yellowish bile splatter a dozen or so purple, pink, and white flowers. I puke again just because my puke is so disgusting. After a few dry heaves, I'm done and turn to find Cash standing behind me. His face, pale to begin with, is now ghost white.

"Dead?" he asks shakily.

"So fucking dead," I manage.

"Her mom?"

"Yeah."

"How?" he asks, barely above a whisper.

"I think it's meant to look like a suicide. In the bathtub, her arm cut."

"Gross?"

"So fucking gross," I say and try to laugh, but it comes out hollow.

All of a sudden, I feel the gravity of our situation. A kidnapped girl, her mom murdered, killer cops, a dead federal agent. The realization of how much shit we're in hits me like a train, and I drop to my knees. My heart pounds so fast it feels like I'm having a heart attack.

"Dude, are you okay?" Cash asks.

I take a number of deep breaths before responding, "I think I'm fine." My shaky hand grabs hold of Cash's shaky hand, and he pulls me up. "Just got overwhelmed for a second. If Casey is in that cabin, we have got to get her away from these motherfuckers, like, now."

"First, I think we need to come up with a plan," Cash says, still holding on to my arm. At this point, I don't know who is reassuring whom.

"As long as that plan gets figured out on the walk back to your house and involves us heading directly to that cabin and getting her the fuck out of there."

THE FEAR HAS SUBSIDED SOME, AND what's left in its wake is a white-hot hatred for these cops. I want to save Casey—or whoever is stuck in that cabin—and I want to make Damon and Buck pay. At the start of the walk from Casey's house to Cash's, we debated the best way to report her mom's death. Cash pulled up the Black Forest Police Department site and found a way to anonymously send a message to report suspicious activity. Cash didn't trust the "anonymous" part, so he opened the site in an encrypted way I didn't understand and sent a message. I spend the remainder of the walk trying not to imagine maggots squeezing their way out of Casey's mom's chapped lips.

As soon as we arrive at Cash's, we head straight for his bike in the backyard. Cash turns it around and kicks it to life. I hop on the back, and we take off. It's hot, but the breeze and the shade from the trees feel nice. Before we approach the spot where we did our target shooting, Cash pulls off the trail. We find a good bush to stash the bike behind and slowly make our way to the cabin.

We post up behind the same rocks and don't see any cars in the driveway. The windows still have the shades drawn tight. We decide our best bet for stealth is running along the line of the fence. As soon as we start, I realize how exposed we are. We plow ahead anyway. Once we reach the side of the house, we squat behind a metal watering trough. It's about fifteen yards from the cabin. No doubt we're still visible, but it's as good as we're going to get. I peek my head toward the cabin. There's a single window in the middle of the second floor. It's not the window where I may have seen Casey, but it's on the same floor. The shades are drawn like all the rest. I grab my phone to send Hailey a quick text, but I don't have service. I show Cash, and he whispers, "Of course."

Before Cash can tell me no, I grab a grape-sized rock and toss it at the window. I miss, and it smacks the metal flashing surrounding it. It seems physically impossible how little sound it makes. Cash shakes his head. At first, I think he's shaking his head because he thinks I'm an idiot for throwing a rock at the window, but then I see him crack his neck and knuckles, and then he grabs a rock himself. He winds up, and I think he's joking because he pulls his arm back like he's going to throw it as hard as he can, but then I see that he's actually going to throw it as hard as he can. Before I can protest, the rock leaves his hand. He should have been a pitcher, because that rock is flying. I'm praying it hits the side of the house and not the window. But, of course, it hits the window and shatters the top-right pane.

"Dude, what the fuck?"

Cash shrugs. "I was aiming for the side of the house, not the window. I've never thrown an accurate rock in my life."

"Then you should have aimed for the window and missed, and hit the house."

He shrugs again as we crouch behind the trough. After a few moments of terror, expecting someone to come charging out of the house, I chance another look. A hand has pulled open the shade on the window Cash just broke. The window's dirty, and the person the hand belongs to is not right up against the glass. All I can really tell is that it's a girl. She inches closer to the window. As she gets right up against it, I am one-hundred-percent certain that it's Casey West.

I poke my head out from behind the trough and say, "Psssst."

She searches, shielding her eyes from the glare with her hand. There's some kind of handcuff or shackle attached to her wrist.

She squints, and then, in disbelief when she sees me, says, "Jack?"

"Yeah. Is there anyone in there with you?"

"No, not now, but they'll be back any minute. I'm fucking chained up in here." She lifts her hand higher to show me the chain attached to the shackle. "You guys got to get me the fuck out of here. You have a saw? Or bolt cutters?"

"What? Of course not," Cash says. "Why are you here?"

"My fucking dad—" Before she can finish her sentence, we hear a car approaching.

"You need to get me out of here. Jack, don't you dare fucking leave me," she says.

"They're coming. We'll be back. I swear."

She starts to panic. "Don't fucking leave me!"

"Casey, we have to. They're here. We'll be back, I swear," I say again.

"When?" she pleads.

"Tonight. We'll come back tonight."

"Oh God, please hurry. And don't go to the cops—they're all fucking cops."

We can't see, but we can hear the car stop and two doors open. We listen as they walk to the house. We make ourselves as small as possible behind the trough, but if they come around this side of the house, we're fucked. Luckily, we hear them fiddling with the padlock, then the front door opens. The moment we hear the door close, I yank Cash to standing, and we take off for the bike. We haul ass up the hill and dive behind some rocks. Just as we do, I hear someone yell from the house, "What the fuck?"

I chance a look and see one of the cops stick his arm out the broken window, like he can't believe the glass is gone. I'm hoping Casey hid the rock and made up a story about how she accidentally broke the window, but then I see a rock—our rock—fly out of the broken windowpane. I plop down next to Cash to catch my breath when one of them yells out the window, "Get them!" That gets us moving. We run as fast as we can for the bike, and by the time we get there, I'm breathing so hard my lungs feel full of splinters. Cash is worse off than me, and he's having a hard time getting the bike started. I finally hear the motor, but it sounds too quiet, too distant. I realize it's not coming from his bike—it's coming from some other motorcycle behind us. Fuck.

"Dude, get that thing started ASAP. They got a fucking motorcycle."

"I'm trying." He jumps down on the kick start a few more times, and it finally turns over. We hop on, and he floors it. The bike fishtails as we take off. I don't want to turn around, but I do. Buck, the bearded cop, is behind us on a motorcycle that is twice as big as Cash's and no doubt twice as fast. I watch as the distance between us shrinks with each second. He's only thirty yards behind us when my head is forced to spin around, because Cash turns the bike hard to the right. So hard that we almost go down. He rights it, and now we're racing along a small path parallel to a steep incline.

"His bike's way faster than ours, he'll be on us in no time," I yell in Cash's ear.

"I know. I can hear him. Hang on," Cash says.

He doesn't have to tell me—I'm probably crushing his ribs, I'm holding on so tight. Thank God Cash is driving and not me. He continues to fly, swerving left and right, catching air as we bounce over rocks and tree roots. He keeps it tight to the edge of the drop-off, and several times I think we're for sure going over. Buck is still gaining on us, less than ten yards back now. Luckily, Cash knows this trail better than he does.

"I got an idea," he says. "When I yell *now*, you lean hard left and do not let go."

I look left just to make sure he doesn't see what I do. Because all I see is a twenty-foot drop into a dry riverbed full of fucking rocks and branches. A riverbed, that if Cash does indeed pull left, will in short order be filled with two teenaged kids with multiple broken bones.

"Get ready," Cash yells.

"Dude, there's nowhere to turn—" I start.

And then Cash yells, "Now! Now!"

I don't even think—I just react and lean left. At the same time I lean left, Cash lets off the gas and downshifts. We go into a semi-controlled skid. When we are just shy of coming to a complete stop, Cash floors it again and pops the clutch. We shoot forward, heading straight for the ravine. I'm fully convinced we're gonna fall to our deaths when I feel us moving forward, not down. I picture a cartoon character running in place, waiting for the knowledge that there is nothing below to catch up with their brain before they start to fall. I open my eyes—we're flying across the ravine on top of a fallen tree that serves as a makeshift bridge. The tree is maybe an inch wider than the tires, and I have no idea how Cash is making this work. It's a miracle, but we make it to the other side without falling. As I feel the ground beneath us, I hear Buck come to a sliding stop on the other side of the ravine. We're headed toward a dense group of trees when I hear five quick gunshots. I feel something whiz under my armpit. The shooting stops as we continue through the trees on what can barely be considered a trail. I hear Buck's motorcycle rev, followed by the sound of cracking wood.

Buck yells, "Fuuuuucccckkk!" Then I hear what I assume is both him and his bike smashing into the bottom of the ravine. The only sound left is Cash's bike and our heavy breathing as we fly through the trees toward his house.

We pull up to Cash's and kill the engine. My entire body is shaking. I take a seat on the picnic bench to get myself under control. Cash sits next to me and points at my left armpit. I raise my arm—there's a hole in my shirt. Below the hole is a small welt on the inside of my arm. How fucking close was that?

"I fucking felt it," I say.

"I can't believe we made it over that log. That thing has been there forever, like as long as I can remember. I've never even walked across it—it's so fucking sketchy."

"You were like a stuntman."

"Pure fear, man. Keeps the senses focused."

"You think that cop's alive?" I ask.

"Of course he's alive. Would be too easy if he wasn't."

I fiddle with the hole in my shirt where the bullet kissed my arm.

"Casey said they're all cops. Do you think she meant more cops are involved in addition to Buck and Damon?" I ask.

"I'm not saying every single cop in Black Forest is dirty, but let's do the math, there's what like ten cops here?"

"There's fifteen. I saw it on the site in a job description for a call center person: 'Join our admin team supporting our twelve officers and three investigators.'"

"Got it. So that leaves thirteen since we know for a fact two of the investigators are dirty. I absolutely do not think we should, but let's say we were like, okay, let's take a shot and reach out to the cops. If we're being kind and assume only one of those cops is in bed with these two dicks, that's a 7.69% chance we happen upon the one who isn't. I don't like those odds."

"Me neither, but we have to do something. She's fucking chained up in there. At the very least, we need to make an anonymous call. There's a chance no one even checks that account we messaged about Casey's mom," I say.

"I'm cool with that," Cash says. "My dad has a stack of burners in his closet."

Cash goes into the house, and comes out with a flip phone in a plastic box. He opens it and powers it up. He reads the instructions, and after a minute of typing in numbers and codes, he hands it to me. I look up the number of the Black Forest Police Station on my phone, punch it into the burner, and hit send.

"Black Forest Police Department, how may I direct your call?" a woman asks after the third ring.

"Ummm, I'd like to report, uh, a kidnapping," I stammer.

The woman sighs and says, "Hold, please." Before I can say no, I hear hold music.

"What did she say?" Cash asks.

"She said to hold. I don't think she believes me. Do I hang up?" I ask, kind of freaking out.

Before Cash can answer, she clicks back on the line and I hold up my finger for him to be quiet.

"I'm reaching out to two of our investigators now. I just need to get some more information from you. First, what's your—"

I hang up before she can finish asking and I power off the burner, and pull out the battery.

"She said she was reaching out to two of their investigators."

"Pretty good chance we know who those two are."

"Fuck," I say, and immediately my phone rings. Not the burner—my phone. The screen says *no number*. I hold it up to Cash. I get spam calls all the time, but one so quick on the heels of the call to the police station... I shrug, looking at Cash to make the decision.

"Might as well," he says.

I hit speaker and hold the phone so Cash can hear. "Hello?"

A gravelly voice says, "I guess you haven't learned how to keep your mouths shut. I think we're gonna have to teach you," and then he hangs up.

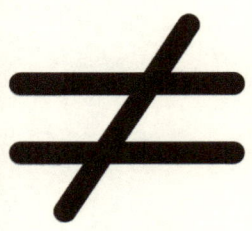

HAILEY AND KELLY PICK US UP AT CASH'S, and then we drop off Cash and Kelly at Kelly's house so she can take care of her dog and do some chores. When we get to Hailey's, I spend thirty minutes filling her in on our crazy day. I start with meeting Maggie, then finding Casey's mom's body, seeing Casey chained up in that cabin, and finally being chased through the woods on a motorcycle (I leave out the getting shot at part). Recounting it made me realize how fucking insane this is. Hailey got more and more scared as the recounting went on.

"How'd he get your number?" Hailey asks.

"He's police. They found out you owned the car they saw pretty fast, or at least that's how I assume they found your house," I say.

Hailey paces the room. "I'm not built for this. What can we do if we can't call the police?"

"That's probably how fifty percent of the population feels every day."

"Not helpful," she says and turns away.

I reach for her. After a moment, she turns. The sunlight from the window hits her back, giving her an ethereal glow. I smile. After a beat, she smiles back.

"I have a plan, okay?" I say, doing my best to sound confident. "In fact, I have two of them."

"You gonna share them with me?" she asks, her hands shaking.

"Can we wait until Cash and Kelly get here?" I ask.

She takes a deep breath, her expression turns playful.

"It's possible there's something that can take my mind off this until they get here," she says, leading me toward her room.

She pulls me down on her bed. Our mouths meet. We kiss hard and quickly remove each other's clothes.

It takes me a bit to catch my breath, but now I'm enjoying Hailey's warm skin against mine. Her hair smells like lemon and coconut. I must have dozed off because I startle when my phone buzzes. It's a message from Cash saying I should get dressed because they're pulling up. At first, I think he must be a mind reader, but then I realize it's probably not that hard to guess what we might be doing. I tell Hailey that Cash and Kelly are almost here. We put on our clothes and meet them at the front door.

"You guys been jogging? Your faces are flushed," Kelly says, laughing. She smooths Hailey's hair, which, in this rare instance, is not perfectly messed, but actually messed.

"Thanks for your concern," Hailey says and messes Kelly's hair in response.

"What in the actual fuck? Cash told me about Casey's mom and the motorcycle chase. Jesus Christ," Kelly says, digging through her pockets. She eventually finds the joint she was searching for.

"Jack has a plan, no scratch that. Jack has two plans," Hailey says with only moderate sarcasm.

"You know what they say," Cash says, sending knowing looks to Kelly and Hailey, "the only thing worse than a single Jack plan is..."

"Two Jack plans," Kelly and Hailey respond in unison. It breaks the tension, and we laugh.

"Haha. But fair. How about we get on our suits, get in the pool, and I'll tell you how I think we can get Casey out of there safely." They look dubious.

"I don't believe you, but okay," Kelly says and hits me softly on the shoulder.

Cash and I run downstairs to one of the guest rooms and put on our trunks. We're back upstairs in a flash. Hailey has a massive indoor-outdoor pool. In order to get outside, you swim under a window that comes flush with the water. Outside, there's a slide that looks like a rock formation and an actual sand beach. The inside half of the pool has a swim-up bar. Cash and I stand about ten feet from the edge of the pool. He looks over and starts counting down from three. As soon as he hits one, we charge at the pool, jump, and in midair yell, "Cannonball!" After we come up, we swim toward the bar. Cash hops on a stool that's part in the water, part out, and I swim under the transparent bar and grab four beers out of the refrigerator. I set two down on the bar, keep one, and hand one to Cash. We pop the tops, clink the bottles, and take long gulps.

The girls enter the room and slip into the water. Hailey goes all the way under and covers the distance gracefully in three strokes. Kelly walks awkwardly through the water, keeping her hands above her head. In one hand, she has her joint, and in the other, a lighter. They sit at the bar. I hand them each a beer. Kelly puts the joint in her mouth, lights it, takes a hit, and passes it to Cash. He takes a hit, looks to Hailey and me, sees us both shake our heads, and passes it back to Kelly.

"I'm high enough to be able to handle your terrible plan now," Kelly says and gives me a wink.

"They're rough, okay. Just want to get that out there," I say.

"Wouldn't expect anything less," Cash says. "As long as it doesn't have us single-handedly breaking Casey out of that cabin that happens to be guarded by two crazy cops that kill other cops, I'm down to hear you out."

I frown and say, "Umm, yeah. That's kind of it."

Kelly says, "Jesus, Jack," and rolls her eyes.

Hailey says, "Jesus Christ, Jack."

I look to Cash for the trifecta, and he does not disappoint: "Jesus fuck, Jack."

"Just hear me out, okay?" They nod.

After Hailey and I, um, went jogging, I started thinking about why this feels so much more fucked than last summer—because our predicament last summer was super fucked on its own. The difference being, last summer we had something the other side wanted. That made us slightly more valuable alive than dead. Right now, we don't have shit. In fact, the sooner we're out of the picture, the better, as far as Damon and Buck are concerned. I keep telling myself these guys won't kill four kids—that would be national news. But Buck shot at us, a bunch of times. And they killed—or at least we assume they killed—the DEA agent. Casey's mom, too. What's four more? So I got to thinking—maybe Casey is the leverage we need. We get her out and get her somewhere safe, then we can find out why they took her. Damon and Buck know we know Casey's at the cabin, which means they probably won't keep her there much longer." I share all of this with Hailey, Cash, and Kelly.

"I think it still sounds about as awful as when Cash described it," Hailey says.

"Same. That's a terrible part of a plan. Like, there are no plans that should be a part of. Unless the plan is suicide by dirty cop. Then yeah, that's a keeper," Kelly says, stubbing out her joint.

"I disagree," I say. "There are four of us. I think we can do this safely."

A laugh escapes Cash. "Shit, sorry, it just came out."

"I'm serious. Just listen. Cash, you and I go to the cabin. Kelly and Hailey, you guys go to the opposite side of town to the Black Forest Bank. You call in a break-in. Use Cash's dad's burner. If it was a break-in at a house, maybe just normal patrol guys go, but I bet if it's a bank, our two cops hightail it over there. If they're at the cabin when we get there, we'll see them leave. If they don't leave, we don't do anything. If they aren't at the cabin when we get there, we don't do anything until you guys confirm you see them at the bank. I repeat, we do not even approach the cabin until you physically see them with your own eyes. If they're at the bank, we know we'll have at least twenty minutes to get in and out of there. It's foolproof," I say.

"It's fool something," Kelly responds, but I can tell she doesn't entirely hate the idea.

"All things considered, it does feel safe-ish. What if the cop that chased you on the motorcycle isn't there? What if he's in the hospital or something?" Hailey asks.

"If you don't ID both of them at the bank, we don't do anything. We call it off and think of another plan."

"What do we do with Casey when we get her out? Her dad's not around, and her mom's... God, I hate to even say it..." Kelly says.

"Dead," I add, and we let that sink in.

"Yeah, that. Well, where does Casey go?" Kelly asks again.

"Here?" Cash asks.

Hailey kooks dubious.

"Not a bad idea. How many bedrooms do you have here? Not weird-named rooms like great rooms, solariums, crafting rooms, wineries, or whatever, but actual bedrooms?" I ask.

"Jack, we don't have a winery. Actually, that might not be entirely true, but if we do, it's not here. Here we have a wine cellar," Hailey says.

"Quit stalling and answer the question," I say and wink at her.

"Fine." She nods her head up and down and moves it slightly left and right, her eyes following as if she's viewing some kind of mental map. "Not including the guest house and the apartments in the horse arena—eight."

"Jesus Christ. I bet there are rooms your parents haven't been in since last year," Cash says.

"They're out of town anyway. Okay, fine, she can stay here, but only until they get back," Hailey says.

"So, we put the plan in action?" I ask.

"It's not a plan, Jack. Unless you think a plan to get rid of a piece of dynamite you're locked in a closet with is lighting the wick, then yeah, I guess it's a plan," Kelly says. Cash shrugs—he won't be in until Hailey and Kelly are.

"First, didn't you say something about two plans?" Hailey asks.

"I did. For the second part, we need Casey out of there. And at least hear me out on this, okay?" I get blank stares. I wait.

"Okay, fine, tell us," Kelly says. Cash and Hailey nod.

"So Maggie—" and I don't even get the sentence out of my mouth before I'm cut off.

"Nope, just no," Kelly says.

"Hard pass," Cash says in disdain.

"You're serious?" Hailey asks.

"Can I just fucking finish, please?" At this point, I'm a little pissed. I get that my plans might be half-baked, but at least I'm coming up with something. It's super easy to just say no to everything. They can tell I'm mad, and their body language softens.

"Go ahead, Jack. Sorry, we'll listen," Hailey says.

"Okay, so Maggie, aka BlackForestPI. You know how many people follow her?" Cash starts to guess, but I cut him off—he can't help himself with numbers—"Almost three thousand. I went through her followers: two writers from the Black Forest Weekly, one from a big paper in the city, two reporters from TV stations in the city, and a reporter from USNN." I pause and let that sink in.

"The national news channel USNN?" Kelly asks.

"Yep, the very one. Casey is a pretty girl who went missing from a small town. Remember how big of a deal her disappearance was the first couple days when people still thought it was a kidnapping? Then the BFPD comes out and says she ran away, and it all stopped. I'll give you two guesses which cops were behind that investigation. Anyway, this thing was about to blow wide open. USNN had three stories on it in the first three days. And then it just died," I say.

"Exactly, they don't care anymore," Cash says.

"They don't care anymore because the cops made it clear she was a runaway. But if we get her out, and she records a video saying what happened, and Maggie aka BlackForestPI posts it, and all of her followers see it, well, that's a whole different story, right?"

"That's not the worst idea I've ever heard," Hailey says. Coming from her, that's high praise.

"What if she doesn't want to do the video? Or if she does and Maggie doesn't post it?" Kelly asks.

"Or what if we put it up and no one cares? No one believes her?" Cash asks.

I can't help but shake my head in irritation. "What if we leave her there and they move her, and we never hear about her again? Or worse, what if they fucking kill her? What if we don't do anything, and they show up and kill all of us? What if the sky falls?"

"Okay, we get it. We get it. I think everyone is just freaked out," Hailey says, trying to ease the tension.

"Of course everyone is freaked out," I add calmly, "but I feel like you guys are acting like it's okay to do nothing. I think doing nothing gets people dead. Us included."

"What about the FBI or the state police?" Hailey asks.

"I'll answer that one," Cash says. "I bet they either don't believe us, or they call the BFPD and talk to the cops there. And the cops say something like, 'Yeah, these same kids called us. We're looking into it, but they are known liars, and one of their dads is a drug dealer.'"

"And then for sure they move her, or worse. And then what do we have? Our word against two cops? Casey's not around anymore. They clean the cabin. We have no leverage, and two cops that want the four of us gone," I say, hoping they come to their senses.

"What about the DEA agent? Is no one looking for him?" Kelly asks.

"I have an alert on my phone, and I search on multiple keywords every day. Not a peep. No doubt that's gonna be a big deal at some point, but not yet. I guess we could call the DEA, show them the guy's somewhat blurry picture I found, and say we saw him dead. But again, kind of the same deal. There's no body, and they'll probably reach out to Damon and Buck," I say.

The three of them look exhausted. The small bit of levity from hopping in the pool is gone. They just look worn. Hailey's lip trembles, and I know she's a moment away from crying. I put my arm around her. She breaks down and sobs into my shoulder. Kelly grabs the roach off the bar and lights it. She manages to get a decent hit before burning her fingers and dropping it in the pool. She quickly scoops it out.

"Sorry," she says to Hailey.

Cash looks ashen, his pale skin bordering on translucent.

Hailey grabs a towel from the end of the bar and wipes her face.

"I think Jack's right. We need to get Casey out of there. Without her, it's our word against theirs. If we can make sure... umm, what are their names?" Hailey looks to me.

"Damon, he's the bald one, and Buck, the short one with the big beard," I say.

"So yeah, if we can make sure Damon and Buck are at the bank, they physically can't get there faster than twenty minutes. And I think even that's stretching it. If we can get Casey out of there and go wide with the video, then it opens up all kinds of things. We can sit here and send emails and make calls. Reach out to the DEA if we want. The FBI, the state police. More news outlets. And Casey will be here to tell her story," Hailey says, looking around for support.

Cash and Kelly aren't smiling, but they no longer look scared to death.

"That's a pretty good plan, Hailey," Kelly says.

"Yeah, I agree," Cash says.

"But wait, that was literally my plan, just said differently," I say, exasperated but also happy everyone is on board.

"Not just different, better," Hailey says and gives me a playful elbow.

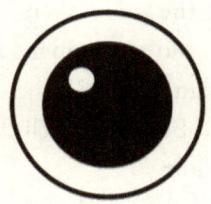

CASH AND I GOT TO HIS HOUSE ABOUT an hour ago. My mom sent me another true crime tip—*call the cops*. It spanned several messages, but it boiled down to: if you think something is amiss, call the police. I didn't ask what to do if the people you need help from are the police. Instead, I replied with several smiley faces. "What if we just moved?" Cash asks. I think he's only partially kidding, "Like to a beach? Where we just swim and fish? Our only problem being that once in a while it's cloudy? I'd even take the Arctic. Like, super flat so you could see in all directions for miles," he says.

I love Cash. I really do. But man, on occasion, I wish he was less reluctant. I give him my best frown and say, "Dude, I hear you. I'd love nothing more than to make this all go away. Last summer we kind of..." and Cash gives me a *are you sure you want to go there* look. "Okay fine, I kind of put us deeper and deeper into shit. But this, this was just bad fucking luck. Wrong place, wrong time. Now we need to get out of it, but that takes doing something."

"Running away is doing something." He thinks for a moment, sighs, and says, "Okay, you're right, but it doesn't mean I have to like it."

"We definitely don't have to like it. My mom sent me one of her hot tips. Want to know what it said?" I ask, hoping to stop his mind from spinning.

"Bleach is no match for Luminol?" he asks, and I get a chuckle out of him.

"She said always go to the cops."

Cash can't help but laugh and says, "Oh man. That's rich."

"Okay, so back to the plan."

"I think we drop the bike before we get there this time. That way we don't have to backtrack. We park it a few hundred yards away, turn it around and everything. All we have to do is jump on it. We need to dig through my dad's tools. Get bolt cutters, maybe a sledgehammer." Cash says, switching from death spiral to solution mode. He's up off the bed, out the back door, and headed for the garage. We search through his dad's tools and can't find bolt cutters. I feel like that should be a standard tool for drug dealers. But again, his dad is *C-level* at best. We find a crowbar, a hacksaw, and two flashlights. We should be able to get done what we need to get done with those. I put everything in the backpack and sit on the garage floor. I try to convince myself this is safe, that we've covered all the bases, but I'm not buying it.

I can tell Cash is in the same place when he says, "Let's run through the whole plan again. You know, just to be sure."

"We park the bike like you said. After that, we hide a good distance from the cabin. Kelly and Hailey should be at the office parking lot next door to the bank by then. Hailey has her mom's bird-watching binoculars. She's gonna call in a break-in at the bank from your dad's burner. We hang tight until we hear from them that Damon and Buck have arrived. Even from a distance, they should be able to spot Damon's bald head and Buck's huge beard. Once they confirm, they give us the go-ahead. We go to the cabin. Break in somehow, get her out somehow, and run. Hailey and Kelly pick us up at your house, and we go to Hailey's. We prep Casey for part two of the plan, where we record her statement and get it to Maggie. She posts it online, and now there's a spotlight on Damon and Buck. State cops, feds maybe, bigger papers from the city. Maybe even TV," I say in what feels like a single breath.

"Lot of somehows and maybes in there," Cash says. "You ever brok down a door?"

"You know I haven't, but that cabin is old as shit. I'm more worried about the handcuffs or whatever is attached to her arm. What if it takes like thirty minutes to saw through them?"

"That's what I'm saying."

"We can figure it out. We're smart fuckers."

"Smart fuckers wouldn't be doing this."

"I guess that's true."

My phone vibrates. It's a message from Hailey—they're on their way to the bank. I message back that we're leaving and that I'll text when we get close to the cabin.

"That's our cue. Now or never," I say.

"Is that a choice?" he asks, but gets up and grabs the bag.

We hop on his bike and take off. It's scary at night. The trees look cold and heartless. We stop a couple of hundred yards before the cabin. We find a suitable bush and stash the bike behind it. I can't believe I didn't think of this before, but if we get Casey out of there, there's no way all three of us are fitting on that bike. I decide against bringing it up to Cash because I fear it will push him over the edge. We walk toward the cabin, and as we approach, it's clear there are no cars in the driveway. No lights on the ground floor of the cabin either, but there's a faint glow coming through the upstairs window Cash broke. I text Hailey saying I don't see the car and wait for a reply. After a few moments, she texts that she's made the call. I tell Cash.

He nods and says, "Did I ever tell you about the only memory I had of my mom?"

He has not. In fact, one of the first things I recall after meeting Cash was him telling me he didn't remember his mom at all. I've heard him tell other people the same. I don't want to correct him, so I just say, "No."

"Well, technically I don't have a memory of her, but for the longest time I thought I did. I was at the zoo, and she was tying my shoe in front of the giraffes. I had one of those pink animal popsicles with the gum ball eyes, you know those?"

"Love those."

"That was it, that's all I remember, but it had, like, a warmth to it. I brought it up to my dad when I was ten or so, and he said he remembered the day and that it wasn't my mom. I was with our neighbor. He did this weird laugh and said my mom was in the hospital from one of her many ODs and that's why she wasn't there. I wish he would have just let me have that memory, you know?" Cash wipes at a tear from his face.

"That's fucked," I say, not sure why he's bringing this up now.

"He wasn't saying it to be a dick. Worse, he didn't even realize how brutal learning I didn't have a single memory of my mom would be. Fucking people."

"I'm sorry, man," I say and set my hand on his shoulder.

"Thanks. It just sucks," he says.

"My dad talked about generational trauma. Parents fuck up their kids, those kids fuck up their kids, and so on and so on."

"Casey seems like a good person, you know? I didn't know her mom, but seems like she worked her ass off at Bigmart trying to support her. Her dad seems like a fuckup, but she loves him, right?" He looks to me for confirmation.

"Yeah, I think so."

"Let's get her the fuck out of there then."

We don't talk for a while; we just stare at the sky. It looks like a black sheet with pinpricks of light. In a different circumstance, it might project a sense of calm, but right now it feels like a physical representation of our smallness. Like the universe could give a fuck how tonight turns out.

My phone buzzes. It's Hailey calling on video.

I hold the phone between Cash and me, hit accept, and say, "Go for Team Leader One."

Hailey's inside the car, Kelly is sitting next to her, and they both say, "Huh?"

"Never mind. Are they there?" Cash asks.

Hailey looks up from the phone and then back down and says, "Two cars just pulled up. One is a police cruiser, and the other is not. They're in front of the bank."

"Do you see Damon and Buck?" I ask more urgently than I intend, my nerves getting the better of me.

"Not yet," Kelly says.

We stare at my phone. I can see the right side of Hailey's face and maybe the left third of Kelly's.

"Okay, they're getting out. There's a tall guy, has a similar build to Damon, but he has a hood on. The guy getting out of the passenger side is definitely shorter," Hailey says.

"Yep, there's that stupid beard. That's for sure Buck, and his left arm is in a sling. Guess he got hurt after all," Kelly says happily.

"Is the other guy Damon? Tall? Bald?" Cash asks.

"I can't tell; he has a hood pulled over his head. They're walking toward the bank. Looking around. What do we do?" Hailey asks.

"We need confirmation that it's actually that bald fuck before we do anything," I say.

"Okay, we'll just watch... wait," Hailey says, "he's pulling back his hoodie. Fuck, he put it back on. I only saw for a second, but he was definitely bald, though, right, Kelly?"

"If you're asking Kelly for confirmation, that doesn't sound very definite to me," Cash says.

"I mean, it was quick, but yeah, the dude with the hood is bald. It's him," Kelly says.

"Are you sure? Once we go to the house, we lose service," Cash says.

"It's them. They're walking to the front of the bank now," Hailey says.

"Okay, setting our timer for twenty minutes and heading down," I set the timer on my phone and say, "We'll check in soon."

"Be safe, you two," Hailey says.

"Cash, don't screw around in there. Get out fast," Kelly says, her voice wavering.

"You don't have to tell me; I'm spending as little time as possible in there. It's this fucker you need to worry about," Cash says, meaning me.

"Jack, don't fuck around," Kelly says.

"Roger that. We gotta go." I end the call and drop my phone in my pocket.

I make eye contact with Cash; he nods. I take a deep breath, and we're off. We don't try to be sneaky; we just run straight for the house. Cash has the backpack and stops a couple of times to adjust it. I think I feel a buzz from my phone, but I'm not positive, so I keep going. The cabin looks old in the day, but at night it looks downright terrifying. No lights on the porch or in the yard, just the faint glow coming from the upstairs window. We get to the front of the house and realize the door is more substantial than we thought.

"Fuck," Cash says.

The metal loop the padlock is on is thick, and it's attached to the wood with several huge lag bolts. Cash pulls off the backpack, removes the crowbar, and hands it to me as if I'm the expert. I wedge it between the padlock and the door. I pull as hard as I can. The thing doesn't move. Cash helps, but it's clear we aren't getting in this way. I think about the hacksaw for a second, but I feel like it will take forever to saw through the lock.

"Window?" I ask.

"God damnit," Cash says and walks toward the side of the house.

Somehow the ground-level window looks even older than the rest of the cabin. I try to open it, but it doesn't budge. I do a baseball swing imitation with the crowbar in my hand for Cash to see. He shakes his head, pauses, then nods. The window is in four panes. I swing hard, and the pane I hit breaks easily. It's loud, and we freeze. Nothing happens, so I knock out the other three. The panes are held in the window with thin strips of wood in the shape of a plus sign. I take the crowbar to it and quickly break it apart.

I turn on my flashlight and point it inside. It's a big room with a couple of folding chairs. One end of the room has a small kitchen. In front of us is a wall and a hallway with stairs leading up. There's an overflowing trashcan in the middle of the room. The floor next to it is littered with beer cans, vodka shooters, spent water bottles, and used fast-food bags. On top of the pile is an empty bag from a costume store that gives me an uneasy feeling.

Cash nudges me from behind. I climb through the window, and he follows. He turns on his flashlight, and we do another sweep of the room. Just a big area that thankfully doesn't have anyone in it. The door at the bottom of the stairs is ajar. We creep toward it, trying not to make a sound. My legs feel weak, and it's hard to catch my breath as we ascend the stairs. When we get to the top, I slowly open the door. I stop because I hear muffled yelling, like someone shouting into a pillow. Maybe they gagged her? I scan the room with the flashlight as I step in. Cash is right behind me. The muffled noises are coming from behind the door directly in front of us. Light spills from the gap at the bottom of the door. I muster up the courage and yank open the door. It leads into a small bedroom. There are two twin beds with a side table in between them and a lamp sitting on top. Near the head of the twin bed on the right sits Casey. She has duct tape across her mouth, and she's handcuffed from behind. On the other bed sits Damon. He wears a predatory look on his pockmarked face. His bald head is shiny in the lamplight. A huge gun rests in his right hand. His left hand is in his pants, playing with himself. What the fuck is wrong with this guy?

"Hey, dumb fucks," he says.

My legs are jelly, and I'm super close to pissing my pants.

Damon looks from Cash to me and then back to Cash and shakes his head. "It just keeps getting worse for you guys."

I can't tell what Casey is yelling from under her gag, but since she's facing Damon, I'm sure it's something along the lines of, *Go fuck yourself.*

"Bank robbery, come quick. Calling all cars. My God. We got one of our buddies to wear one of those things that make you look bald." His smile is a black hole.

"If you fucking touch them," I say.

"I think you've got bigger problems to worry about at the moment, Jack," his sick grin broadens, his teeth on full display. Even in the dim light, it's clear how yellow they are. His gums have receded, making his teeth look unnaturally long.

My desire to live overtakes my fear, and I start searching for a way out. My hands shake, but I keep my grip tight on the crowbar. My jaw is clenched so tight my face trembles.

"Actually, maybe I should let you guys live. What do you

think? You're spunky. Actually, nah." His eyes look dead. Pleading with him would be like pleading with gravity.

I look at my feet to make sure they're still attached because they've gone numb. I notice an outlet near my left foot with an extension cord plugged into it. I follow the cord out of the corner of my eye and see it's plugged into the lamp. If I kick the plug hard enough for it to pop out of the socket, this room goes dark. Cash moves next to me. I'm hoping he noticed me eyeing the extension cord and the outlet, because there's no way for me to tell him to drop to the ground when the light goes out. I take a deep breath. Although I'm not looking directly at him, I can tell Damon's spider sense has come alive. He begins to say something, but before he can get it out, I kick my left foot at the outlet. I connect with the plug, and the room goes dark. I drop to my knees and swing the crowbar as hard as I can. I hear a loud explosion and a blinding light just before the crowbar makes contact with something firm. I hear the sound of wood cracking from what I imagine is a bullet flying through the door where I was just standing. Immediately following the crack, Damon screams. He sounds like a girl. I pull on the crowbar to take another swing, but it's stuck. I pull harder. I feel resistance, but it comes free. Damon screams again. I fumble in the dark for Casey and connect with what I think is her leg. I pull her partway off the bed. Cash turns on his flashlight and races out the door behind me. Casey gets the message and stands. We sprint for the door. Halfway across the room, my foot kicks something hard into the hall. It skids to a stop against the wall. It's Damon's gun. He must have dropped it when I hit him with the crowbar. I grab it and follow Cash down the stairs. We fly across the bottom floor and back to the busted window we entered through. Cash does a crazy dive roll out of it—it's pretty fucking awesome. I stop at the window and help Casey out from the inside. Cash helps her down from the other side. I climb through after her. I remove the duct tape from her mouth. She whimpers in pain.

"Is he coming?" she asks through panicked sobs.

"With our luck, he's halfway down the stairs. We gotta move," I say.

That's all the convincing it takes, and the three of us sprint from the cabin. When we're about fifty yards away, the most pissed-sounding howl I have ever heard comes from the house. When he stops howling, Damon yells, "I'm gonna pop your fucking eyeballs out. You're gonna die with blood in your mouths!"

He yells this with such venom that I don't know if I ever want to fall asleep again, because I know my nightmares will be filled with his threats come to life.

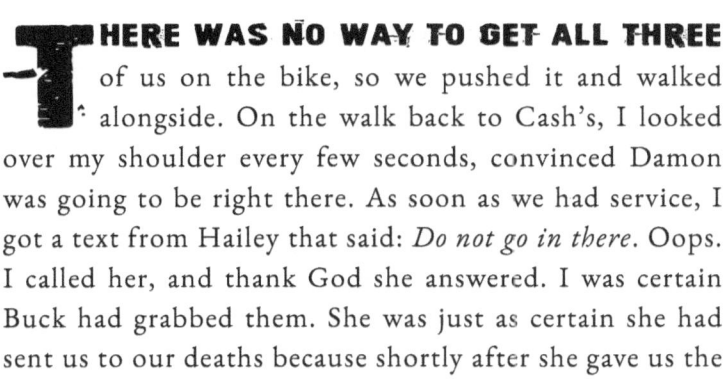

THERE WAS NO WAY TO GET ALL THREE of us on the bike, so we pushed it and walked alongside. On the walk back to Cash's, I looked over my shoulder every few seconds, convinced Damon was going to be right there. As soon as we had service, I got a text from Hailey that said: *Do not go in there.* Oops. I called her, and thank God she answered. I was certain Buck had grabbed them. She was just as certain she had sent us to our deaths because shortly after she gave us the all-clear, she saw "Damon" take off his hood and saw hair poking out of his bald head. She realized it was a disguise and the whole thing was a setup. When she didn't hear back after her text, she and Kelly got in the car and raced to the cabin. During the drive, Kelly tried over and over to get in touch with us, but her calls went straight to voicemail. She said the fifteen minutes it took for me to respond were the longest of her life. They were only a mile away from the cabin when we connected. At that point, they turned around and headed to Cash's.

My mom sent a message when we were out of range as well. It said Black Forest has an unusually high per capita homicide rate. She ended it with a smiley face. If she only knew. During the walk back, Casey filled us in on what she knew, which wasn't a lot. Her dad is somehow wrapped up with Damon, Buck, and the DEA agent. She thinks they took her because her dad has something they want, but what that is, she doesn't know.

When there was a lull in the conversation, I said, "So, Casey, we went by your house, and, um..."

"I know. Damon shared every detail of that with me. All the more reason my dad needs to get out of this. I can't lose him too," she said and started to cry. She leaned over and placed her head on my shoulder as we walked. At first, it seemed normal—or as normal as trying to be supportive of a girl you just saved from kidnappers while she discusses her dead mom can be—but then she didn't let go. Eventually, I moved away.

When there was a lull in the conversation, Casey picked the story back up and said that Buck was a pedophile and a rapist, and the DEA guy was a prick, but for the most part, both of them were—or had been, in the DEA guy's case—sane. She said Damon was a fucking sadistic pig. She had heard an argument the other day in the cabin. She was locked upstairs; the three of them were downstairs. She couldn't tell what exactly was going on, but she heard the DEA agent yell in fear, "What the fuck," and then she heard scrambling. She never saw the DEA agent, nor heard his voice, again. I asked her when that was. It was the same time we were at the shooting range. She said she heard a couple of gunshots and figured they had finished him off in the woods. Not that we needed more evidence, but it was clear those guys killed the DEA agent.

I told her about us target shooting up there and about Kelly thinking she shot the DEA guy. Casey assured us he was probably well on his way to death when he left the cabin.

When we reach the meetup spot near Cash's, we sneak behind a large tree and look around. The only car we see is Hailey's. She and Kelly stand in front of it, Kelly with a joint in her mouth.

Casey sees them and says, "Fuckin' A, yes," and takes off in a run.

Hailey and Kelly hear her coming and turn. Big smiles spread across their faces when they see we are all in one piece. Casey runs to Kelly, and Kelly seems taken aback, but then puts her arms out in anticipation of a hug. Casey skips the hug and grabs the joint out of Kelly's hand. She takes three giant hits off it. The joint is hotboxed, and less than half an inch remains when she returns it. Kelly attempts to grab it with her fingernail, burns herself instead, and drops the joint on the ground. She stubs it out.

"Thanks, I needed that," Casey says.

Kelly says, "I couldn't tell," and they both laugh.

I hug Hailey, she hugs me back harder, and doesn't let go for a long time. Her hot tears run down my neck.

"Let's get the fuck out of here," Cash says.

"Amen to that, brother," Casey says, and we pile into Hailey's car.

We pull out of the lot and wind through the roads behind Cash's. When we arrive at Hailey's, she grabs a snacks and drinks, and we sit around her living room and gorge.

"Do you have any way to get a hold of your dad?" I ask Casey.

"My phone is long gone, but I can send a message from a computer," she says.

"Follow me," Hailey says and leads Casey out of the living room.

When Hailey returns, she says, "I gave her an old phone. It doesn't have service, but all her apps and stuff will work if she's on the Internet. She's in the other room figuring it out."

"Do we reach out to Maggie now? Or do we film the video first?" Kelly asks.

"Let's shoot the video and the reach out," I respond.

Kelly says, "Maybe now that Damon and Buck no longer have Casey, they'll just blow town."

"You said blow," Cash snickers.

Kelly laughs and says, "Have you ever blown a town?"

"Hilarious," Cash responds.

I take out my phone and search for any new info on the dirty cops, the DEA agent, or Casey's dad. Nothing. I sit on the soft couch and feel the gun I stuck in my waistband rub against my back. I take it out, set it on the table, lean back, and shut my eyes.

I'm startled awake when I hear Casey walk into the room. I rub my eyes. Casey sits uncomfortably close to me. Hailey, who is on the other side, scoots closer and puts her arm around me. I enclose her hand in mine and do my best to lean toward her.

"My dad and I use this encrypted app to communicate. When I was younger, I thought it was fun pretend-spy stuff, but then I realized it was necessary. Nothing in there from him, but I sent him a message saying I was safe. I'll keep trying to reach him."

"How about I start setting up in the other room for the video?" Kelly asks.

"Sounds good, I'll help," Cash offers.

"I'm just gonna sit here for a minute if you guys don't mind, I'm tired as hell all of a sudden," Casey says. We all agree it's fine.

After a few minutes, Kelly calls Hailey and me into the next room to help. We move some lamps around and set up a table to put the camera on. We move some art off the walls to make sure there is nothing in the shot that is identifiable. Kelly heads to the other room to grab Casey and returns within seconds.

"She's fucking out. Like dead to the world out," Kelly says.

"I'm sure she's exhausted, she's been through hell," Hailey says.

"I guess we let her sleep and shoot the video in the morning?" Cash asks.

"I really want to get that thing to Maggie, but yeah, it'll have wait until tomorrow," I say.

"I'll grab her some blankets," Kelly says.

"All the alarms set?" Cash asks.

"Yep, and the motion detectors are on the most sensitive setting." Hailey says. She grabs my hand and pulls me toward her room.

"See you guys in the morning. Don't get killed," I joke.

"Not even funny," Cash says, but he laughs a little.

Once in bed, Hailey says, "I'm fucking terrified, Jack. I mean, I don't know, I just can't with this anymore."

"I know," I say lamely.

"I've dealt with anxiety since middle school. It's been like an annoying little brother. It was surface level though, like it didn't go below the skin, you know? Now, it's like it evolved. It's in my bones. Like miniature spiders creeping around in my bone marrow," and with that, she breaks down in uncontrollable sobs. I hold her and rub her back.

The sobs turn to sniffles, then stop. Then we're asleep.

HAILEY'S SOUND ASLEEP WHEN I WAKE.
I quietly get dressed and head to the kitchen. Cash is already in there struggling with her high-tech coffee machine.

"I got this," I say and take over. "Everyone else still asleep?"

"I think so," Cash says. He takes a seat at the table and rests his head in his hands. The kid looks more stressed today than he did yesterday.

"You okay?" I ask and hand him his coffee.

"I thought I'd feel better after we got her out of there. I mean, I do, but I also don't."

"The second I woke, that psycho's threats of popping out our eyeballs started bouncing around my head," I say and sit next to him.

"How bad do you think you hurt him?"

"I bet I broke something. I heard a crack. When I tried to pull the crowbar out, it was stuck. That's when he screamed the second time."

"Well, that's something. Might have just made him more mad, though. A couple of kids doing that to him. We already put that other dude in a sling."

"Slows them down on one end and pisses them off more on the other. Maybe it's a wash," I say and sip my coffee.

"Did you talk to Casey about the video yet?" Cash asks.

"I haven't. We should as soon as she gets up." I drain my coffee and get up to make another.

I hear Casey wandering around the house, so I bring her to the kitchen and make her coffee. Cash brings up filming the video, and she says she's ready whenever. Hailey and Kelly wake up and join us in the kitchen. Hailey grabs each of our phones, one at a time, and installs her alarm app on them. She gives us a quick tutorial on how to turn the alarms on and off. Once that's done, we decide it's high time to record the video. We wait around as Kelly sets up her phone to do the recording. The phone Hailey gave Casey vibrates. Casey picks it up and gasps.

"What?" I ask, fearing the worst.

"It's my dad. He's on his way back to Black Forest." I can't tell if she's excited or terrified—maybe both. "He's messaging me right now."

"Where is he," Cash asks.

"No idea, but he's close. Not sure where he's coming from either."

I move closer but can't make out what she's reading.

Luckily, she translates, "Says he left because he found some kind of coded logger? Wait, he's retyping. Legger? Hold on, he's retyping again. Legging. Oh Jesus. Hold on, I'm going to call him." She gets off the couch and walks outside. We watch as she paces on the deck talking to her dad.

It feels like she's been out there forever when she returns and says, "This is long and super complicated, but we've got a plan. Ready?"

"Very. Especially since it's not one of Jack's non-plan plans," Cash says, teasing me.

She wasn't kidding when she said it was long and complicated. With all of the questions we ask along the way, it takes her close to twenty minutes to explain everything. She starts with how her dad, aka Reed, got mixed up with Damon, aka Bald Cop, and Buck, aka Beard Cop, to begin with. We knew, based on his past arrests, that her dad likes to steal cars, and Damon and Buck busted him a couple of times for it. He was on his third strike when the two cops gave him an out—they wouldn't turn him in—if he became their personal, on-demand car thief. Whenever they came across an expensive car, he'd have to drop whatever he was doing and steal it. The cops would hang back during the job, and if it got called in, they'd make sure they were first on the scene and that Reed got away clean. He took the offer. Once stolen,

Damon and Buck would take the cars to a chop shop and split the cut with Reed (split's a strong word, but they'd give him a small percentage).

This partnership of sorts, between Damon, Buck, and Reed, went on for a good while without a hitch. Then a DEA agent—yes, the same DEA agent Kelly killed until she didn't—came to Black Forest to do a training at the Black Forest Police Department. Damon, Buck, and DEA guy hit it off, as dirty cops are wont to do. DEA guy goes back to Texas, and they don't hear from him for a spell. Then DEA guy loses his job (why he still wears the badge is anyone's guess) and was in search of a payday. He found one and reached out to Damon and Buck because he remembered their car-stealing scheme. DEA guy knew the address of one of the higher-up members of the Juarez cartel who was based in El Paso and drove a $400,000 Rolls-Royce. DEA guy got a tip that this dude was about to get raided and figured it would be a good idea to relieve the gentleman of his car first. He gave the address to Damon and Buck. They forced Casey's dad to drive with them to Texas and steal the car. Reed said it was one of the easiest jobs he'd ever done. Or so he thought. When the owner of the Rolls realized his car had been stolen, he killed himself because he left a vitally important ledger inside the car and did not want to face the wrath of the cartel. The cartel proceeds to move heaven and earth to find this notebook. Someone tells them to talk to DEA guy, which leads them to Damon and Buck. Damon and Buck didn't know about the ledger because Reed didn't tell them. Reed found the notebook in the car and slipped it in his jacket before either of them saw it. He didn't even know what was in it; he just thought it might be valuable. The cartel wants this ledger back— like yesterday. Damon and Buck ask Reed about it, Reed plays dumb, and then splits town. Damon and Buck can't find him, so they kidnap Casey in an attempt to motivate Reed to return to Black Forest and give them the ledger. Impatient as Damon is, he decides, in the meantime, to call on Casey's mom to see if she knew anything about said ledger, and, well, that did not end well. They finally get in contact with Reed yesterday afternoon; they tell him they have Casey, and Reed starts his trek home. He's on his way back to Black Forest when he gets the message from Casey that she's free. He reaches out to Casey, and, well, now here we are.

"That's a crazy fucking story," I say.

"Umm, yeah, it is. I think I only retained half of it," Hailey adds.

"I didn't hear a plan in there, though," Cash says.

"Oh right, yeah," Casey says. "So the plan is, Hailey and Kelly, you stay here. And, ummm, Jack, Cash, and I go meet my dad."

"And then?" Cash asks.

"That's it. That's the plan," she says.

"Jesus Christ. You and Jack don't understand what a plan is. That is not a plan. That is a step. If there are a bunch of other steps—preferably steps that keep us out of danger and get rid of the bad guys in the end—then that is a plan," Cash says.

"And why are we meeting with your dad? Why don't we just film the video, give it to Maggie, you guys go somewhere, and we lie low until it's clear Damon and Buck are busted or whatever," Kelly says.

Casey takes a deep breath, steels herself, and says, "I'm not doing the video."

"The fuck?" Cash asks.

"I meant I'm not doing the video... yet. We discussed it—"

"Who discussed what?" Hailey asks, pissed.

"My dad and I. I'll do it, but not until he's out of this shit, not until you guys hear his plan."

"Casey, are you kidding? We just saved your fucking life. Do you not understand that? And because of that, these psychos are after us. And you aren't willing to help?" Hailey yells. I don't think I have ever seen her this mad.

"Fuck you, you rich fuck. Look at this fucking mansion," Casey says, waving her arms about, matching Hailey's fury. "You got your perfect mommy and daddy? You think you're the only one in this? My mom is fucking dead. My dad—yeah, he's a fuckup, but he steals cars. That's it. And now he's running for his life because of these guys. And yes, I'm really fucking thankful for what you all did. I am. Because I don't think I could have made it through one more day in there, but my dad is all I have, and I need him to get out of this." And with that, Casey bursts into tears and runs out the door onto the deck.

Hailey does have living and married parents. And financially, her life is easy. But she also lost her brother several years ago, and her family has never fully recovered.

"That was fucking heavy," Kelly says. "I'm sorry, Hailey."

"She's right, though. I mean, we're right too, but I guess I just saw her holding up so well, I didn't really think about what she has been through and, well, what her future looks like."

We watch Casey through the windows, smoking and pacing.

"Want me to talk to her?" I ask. Not that I want to, but I know her better than the rest of them, and I feel like in some sense this is my doing.

"No, I'll go," Hailey says and stands.

"You sure?" Kelly asks.

"I got this. It'll be fine."

I give Hailey's arm a squeeze as she leaves the couch. She opens the door and walks outside. She stands at a distance from Casey. At first, Casey has her back to her, and it looks like Hailey is doing most of the talking. After a couple of minutes, Casey turns toward her and responds. Casey wipes tears from her face. Then Hailey does the same. Then they both laugh loud enough that we can hear it through the windows. After a minute, they hug and walk back in.

"I think we have a plan," Hailey says, her eyes red from crying.

"Sorry I freaked out like that. I'm just a bit overwhelmed," Casey says.

"Not at all," I say. Kelly walks toward Casey with open arms and gives her a hug.

"Casey's gonna do the video after you guys meet with her dad and hear him out," Hailey says, looking at me, Cash, and Kelly in a way that says, *please just fucking agree.*

"Just meet with him? We don't have to agree to anything, or do anything. Just hear him out? Then Casey films the video and we send it to Maggie?" Cash asks.

"Yep, just meet with him. Cool?"

Cash and I agree. Kelly seems skeptical—I know she wants to film the video and get the cavalry involved as soon as possible—but she says okay.

"You guys are gonna love my dad. He's a sweetheart," Casey says.

"Is he, though?" Kelly asks.

"He is. Like a big fucking teddy bear. And he's got a plan, I'm almost sure of it. I can promise you, he really probably does," Casey says.

"So when do we meet him?" I ask.

"Tonight," Casey says.

"Okay... and where?" Cash asks.

"The Black Forest Inn," Casey says, and the four of us groan.

READY? CASEY ASKS.

"As I'm gonna be," I respond.

We spent the entire day hiding out at Hailey's. I don't think I went more than five minutes without checking the alarm app. It's time to go meet Casey's dad, and Hailey said we could borrow one of her parents' cars. This will be the first time I've driven past the Black Forest Inn since all the shit happened there last summer. In a town this small, that is no easy feat.

"Full fucking circle coming back here," Cash says.

"At least there's no Zufelt," I say.

"I'd choose Zufelt over Damon and Buck any day," Cash says.

"Who's Zufelt?" Casey asks from the back seat, her head buried in her phone.

"That's a story for another day," I say and park in the lot opposite the Inn. I can't help but wonder if it's the same spot my dad parked in the day he disappeared. Of all the places to meet. I grab the gun from beneath the seat.

"You wanna carry this?" I ask Cash, knowing the answer.

"Fuck no."

I look back at Casey; she shakes her head emphatically. I slide the gun in the back of my waistband.

As we approach the entrance to the Inn, I pull on Cash's shirt. He stops. When Casey is a few feet ahead of us, I whisper to him, "Let's just agree with whatever her dad says. I have no intention of getting mixed up with this guy, but if he thinks we're on board, then all the sooner we can get back to Hailey's and have Casey film the video. Agree?"

"Hundred percent," Cash says.

Casey calls back to us, "You guys coming or what?"

Cash and I catch up with Casey as she reaches the front door. This place has a ton of history, little of it good. It's modeled after an old ski lodge, like something you might find in Austria. White wooden walls rest on a stone foundation. A dark roof extends over a large patio. There are five or six guest rooms inside and a handful of standalone cabins dispersed across the property. We pry open the oversized doors and walk in.

It's been years since you were allowed to smoke inside public buildings around here, but the place still reeks of cigarettes. In front of us, a long bar extends to the back of the building. The dining room to our left is filled almost to capacity. I'm searching the room for Reed when a hand seizes my shoulder. I let out an involuntary yelp. I turn to see Casey's dad—he has one hand on my shoulder and one on Cash's. He looks the same as his booking photos—like a skinny biker with shifty eyes and a patchy beard. His grip on my shoulder is somewhere between aggressive and reassuring. Closer to aggressive. He lets go when he sees Casey. Anger spreads across his face; I'm guessing he wasn't expecting her. He grabs her in a huge hug anyway and doesn't let go for a long time.

"I told you to stay away," he says and gives me and Cash a reproachful look.

"I stopped listening to you a long time ago, Reed," Casey says.

"Ain't that the truth," he says and tussles her hair. "I got us a table over there." He points and guides us to a booth in the corner. Casey and Reed take seats facing the front door. Cash and I sit opposite.

"There's an article on the wall over there says someone found a bunch of Nazi gold hidden here. Imagine that," Reed scoffs.

"Bullshit," Casey says, disguising the word as a cough.

"Don't believe everything you read, I guess," Cash says and gives me a knowing look.

"I'm Jack, and this is Cash," I lean over and shake Reed's hand.

"Nice to make your boys' acquaintance," he says. "Y'all can call me Wheels." He raises his middle finger, like he's flipping us off. Running along the length of his finger is a tattoo that says "Wheels." Real cute. I give the expected chuckle, but no fucking way am I calling this guy Wheels. At least I know the meaning behind the car tattoo with the "Wheels" license plate on Casey's forearm now.

"You guys ain't trying to get in my daughter's pants, are you?" he asks, trying to sound hard.

"Jesus fucking Christ, Reed," Casey almost shouts. "Don't answer that, you two."

I want to tell him he may want to reconsider who's trying to fuck whom, but instead I say, "Umm, of course not. We both have girlfriends."

"Shit, that's never stopped anyone. Sometimes it's even better that way, but she's only twenty. Wait until she's an adult," and he laughs.

"Reed, seriously, knock that shit off," Casey shakes her head in practiced exasperation. "Besides, I'm sixteen."

"Oh, right, yeah," he says and stares at his hands in defeat. Like a child that's learned, maybe for the thousandth time, that he's a dumbshit. Not that Casey said it in a mean way, but this interaction between them feels old. Casey realizes she's hurt his feelings and puts her hand on his arm. He looks up. She gives him a warm look and squeezes his arm. Just like that, he's back with a shit-eating grin on his face.

"I'm not gonna mince words, boys. I'm in about as deep of shit as you can get. Up to my receding hairline. Until recently, I've been able to keep Casey and her mom—God rest her soul—out of it," they share a look, "I'm a car guy. I like to steal 'em and drive 'em fast. Like them so much I made a career out of it. Tried to keep my head down. I'd only done four years locked up by the time I was thirty-five. I mean, pretty damn good. That's twenty-seven years free and clear."

Cash nudges my knee under the table. Like what the fuck? That's a success? Only four years locked down out of thirty-five? Jesus. This guy might want to raise the bar a bit. How about zero years? Also, he's not great at math.

"But they get their hooks in you and then want more," he pauses as the waitress approaches.

"You all ready to order?" she asks.

I'm about to suggest she give us a minute when Reed looks to Casey, which causes the waitress to look to Casey, and Casey says, "Four cheeseburgers and fries, please." Guess she's used to driving when her dad's around.

"And four beers," adds Reed.

The waitress looks at me. Then she looks at Cash. On a good day, we look seventeen. There's this kid Bobby in our grade, probably went through puberty when he was seven, had a full-on beard by the time he was in middle school. That's not us.

Before she can laugh, I say, "One beer and three Kola Kountrys."

She forces a tired smile, the kind that says *she's just hoping to survive the rest of her shift*, and walks off

"Wait, you guys ain't old enough to drink either?" he asks.

"We're all sixteen," I say.

"Yeah, okay, that's right. Just feels like Casey is older than me at times. Sixteen, wow. Yeah, goddamn it. Those were the days."

Cash and I mumble some kind of agreement about how awesome youth is.

He nods and says, "You guys meet Charlie Murray before he met his demise?"

Cash and I look at one another in confusion.

"The ex-DEA agent," he says.

"Oh, yeah, we just call him DEA guy," Cash says.

"And we only met his dead body," I say.

"Well, the prick deserved whatever he got. Anyway, they all had their hooks in me. Jumped out of my lane, I did. I didn't even grab that ledger thing with a plan; I just figured there was an escape hatch for me in there somewhere."

"What's in this ledger?" Cash asks.

"Just a bunch of random numbers, letters, and symbols, as far as I can tell. Can't make any sense of it. Don't really get its importance in all this, really," Reed says.

The waitress approaches, puts a beer down in front of Reed and Kola Kountrys in front of the rest of us.

Reed laughs as we drink and says, "So where was I?"

"The ledger," Cash says.

"Yeah, the ledger. I take the notebook from the car. The moment I get back to Black Forest, I hide it in the forest, 'cause I figure it's got to be worth something. Then I split town, figuring I'd come back when I knew everything was cool. Well, I guess the cartel tracked down Damon and Buck and they realized I must have taken the notebook. I'd gone off the grid by then, and they couldn't find me. Well, they're cops, so they eventually get ahold of me, and sent me a picture of my Casey chained up. Worst day of my life. I hightailed it back here, and thankfully, before I was able to meet with Damon and Buck, Casey sent me that message saying you all got her out. I thank you both for that." Reed pauses to take a sip of his beer.

"So now you get the ledger and give it back to them?" I ask. "They give it to the cartel and all is well? Is that the plan?"

"In theory, yes," he says, with no indication that he is going to elaborate.

"In theory and not reality, because..." Cash asks.

"Because I can't remember where it's hid."

He's not even embarrassed or ashamed about this. It's just a fact that he's sharing, as if he played no role in it.

"You fucking kidding me?" I ask. "Like no idea at all?"

"I have a general idea. It's in a tree in the forest. But I got what they call geographic dyslexia," Reed says.

"That's not an actual thing," Cash interjects.

"True, it's not an actual thing. But it is actually a thing," he says as if it clears everything up.

"What are you actually saying?" I ask, checking the time on my phone.

"I'm glad to go looking with you boys—"

Cash cuts him off and says, "Wait a minute. Looking with us?"

"Yeah, that's plan one. The three of us," he points to me, then to Cash, and then to himself, "we go looking for it. Casey told me you two was born and raised here."

"Do you have any idea how many forests there are in Black Forest? How many trees?" Cash asks.

"How many," Reed asks in a way that makes it seem like he expects us to give him an actual number.

"A lot, man, a lot," Cash looks like he's ready to give up.

"Okay, Reed, plan one might need some work. What's plan two?" Casey asks.

"This is a good one. This plan is for sure gonna work," Reed says and rubs his hands together. He continues, "I call Damon and Buck and tell them I have the ledger. They meet me in the woods, and when they show up, you two are there, and Bam!" He slaps his hand on the table hard enough to make half the restaurant jump. Then he says, "You two take care of them."

"Take care of them?" I ask.

"Yeah, you know. Like end them," Reed says.

"That's your plan? We kill them?" Cash says, the second part in a whisper.

"You guys were born here. You're probably big-time hunters," he says confidently.

"Dude, we've never hunted a goddamn thing. You want to pass off your world of shit onto two kids?" I say, joining Cash in anger. I can't help myself.

"Okay, to be fair, when I came up with plan two—" he starts.

"It's not a fucking plan," Cash says. I knee him under the table to let it go.

"Okay, okay. When I came up with... idea two, to be fair, I thought you boys were twenty."

Casey can feel our frustration. She says, "Hold on a minute. Let's just slow down. Reed, is there a third plan? If so, it's gotta be better than the first two, right? Please tell me it is."

"Well, yes and no," he says, and I can't help but sigh. I know this guy is older than us, but honestly, it doesn't even feel disrespectful talking to him or dealing with him this way. It's like talking to a kid—a middle school kid.

He continues, "See, someone else helped me hide the notebook."

"Great, problem solved. We just ask that person where it is," Casey says in relief.

I can't believe this guy needed someone to help him hide a

fucking notebook. A two-year-old could hide a notebook. Can he do anything on his own?

"Well, that's where the no part comes in. I don't know where he is."

Of course he doesn't.

Casey sees that Reed has lost us and says, "If you tell us who this person is, maybe we can help you find him."

"His name is Wilkinson. Erik Wilkinson."

Cash and I look at one another in astonishment.

"Did you just say Erik fucking Wilkinson?" I ask.

"Minus the fucking part, yeah, Erik Wilkinson. He helped me hide the ledger."

This is going from bad to worse. Wilkinson is a match tumbling toward a lake of gasoline sitting atop a planet made of dynamite. He's a grenade with the pin pulled inside a grenade factory. Pick your expression—the kid is bad fucking news.

"Just how in the world is Wilkinson involved in this?" Cash asks in exasperation.

"Oh, you know him? He's a great kid. We've done some work together."

"Of course you have," I say.

Even to Reed, it's clear that his mentioning Wilkinson's name is having a triggering effect on Cash and me.

He says, "Okay, listen, forget Wilkinson. I can find it. You guys can help me. I'm like one hundred percent sure there's a decent chance I can find it."

I take a deep breath. The mention of Wilkinson's name is giving me emotional hives. The last time I saw him, he unnecessarily buried a chef's knife in the back of a barely conscious, and entirely subdued, skinhead.

Enough of this. We've got to get the fuck out of here and film that video. Who cares about the ledger? Who cares about Reed's plans? If you can call them that. Who cares about Wilkinson? We agreed to come to the Inn and hear him out. We did that. Now it's time to get back to Hailey's.

"How about this: We meet tomorrow morning. Reed, do you remember anything about where you hid the ledger? Anything at all?" Casey asks.

"Let me see. We parked at the donut shop, the one with the fat oriental dude on it. We went up a trail from there," he says proudly.

"Of fucking course. Cop central," Cash says.

Casey jumps in before Cash and I can go off. "We'll meet at the bank. It's only a block from there. Nine a.m., cool, Reed?"

Personally, I'm thinking there is a zero percent chance we meet him at the bank tomorrow. We go home and make this video and send it as wide as the internet allows. Then Damon and Buck will be more concerned with staying out of jail or staying alive than they will with us.

"Yes, that's cool. You need to stay with your friends, though, Casey. Don't want you getting caught up with me."

Casey says, "That's fine. Nine a.m., though, right? Do I need to call you to wake you up?"

"Yeah, just in case," Reed says without an ounce of shame. She grabs his phone.

I think we're done and I get up to leave, but Reed motions us to wait.

"Are you guys sure you don't want to go with my second plan?" Reed asks. Cash and I look at each other, confused.

"You know, you *two* take those *two* out. I don't even have to be there," he says.

"What the fuck is wrong with you?" I ask. "You're like fifty, we're sixteen, and this is your mess."

"I'm thirty-six," he says and gives that sheepish, woe-is-me look again. Casey puts her arm around him and looks at us. It's clear where she stands.

"Reed, Jack and Cash are going to help, okay? But it's not fair to think they're gonna kill two police officers," Casey explains as if she's talking to a toddler.

"Sorry, guys. That part wasn't cool. You helped my Casey and I'm grateful for that," Reed says and perks up. "I hope it's as easy as sending out the video Casey is gonna make. I really do. I'm sorry I suggested you should kill Damon and Buck. I guess, just pure and simple, they scare me. Which one of you did that to Damon's foot?"

"That was me," I say.

"He was yelling at me about it when he got me on the phone. It fucked up a couple toes bad. Like they are no longer totally attached to his foot bad," Reed says.

"I get it, he's pissed about his toes. Even more reason to let as many people as possible know, as soon as possible, what they've done," I say, ending the meeting and standing up.

As I feared, this was a big waste of time. We met with him, we heard his plan, and his plan has left me wanting. Fuck the ledger hidden in the woods. Fuck Damon. Fuck Buck. And fuck Reed too. Baby driver.

"We're gonna go, Reed," Casey says. "You need to lie low tonight. Don't do anything stupid. We'll meet you tomorrow at nine."

"Okay, I'll see you all in the morning. You best take care of my daughter," he says with an amount of self-righteousness that makes me want to punch him in the mouth. The only thing that stops me from listing the multitude of things he has done to not take care of his daughter is Casey's hand in my ribs, pushing me away.

"Don't forget my wake-up call," Reed reminds Casey.

No way am I traipsing around the woods with this guy looking for a fucking notebook. I feel like we could do that for two years and not find anything.

We walk outside. It's warm and dark. The road in front of the Inn is silent. The trees tower above us in all directions. Cash stands at the edge of the patio; a shadow cuts him in half. Parked on the side of the road is a neon green muscle car. The license plate says "COCH-MYK." I laugh and point it out to Cash.

"You see Cock Mike inside?" I ask.

Cash shakes his head. Reed gives Casey a hug and says, "Good luck with the video," and walks to Cock Mike's car. At first, I'm thinking he must have parked past it, even though I can't see any cars, but then he slips a long thin piece of metal out of his pants and eases it between the window and the door frame. After a moment the door pops open and he hops in. He leans below the steering wheel, and the engine rumbles to life. He revs it unnecessarily loud several times. Casey jumps and looks terrified.

"You okay?" I ask her.

"Fine, fine, just jumpy," she says, but she does not look fine. The sound of that car scared the shit out of her.

Cash asks, "Umm, Casey, did your dad just steal Cock Mike's car?"

Without looking up from her phone, she says, "Fuck Cock Mike."

The silence of the mountains is replaced by the screeching of tires as Reed peels out in our teacher's car. Just before he rounds the first corner, I can almost swear I see a head pop up in the backseat. I convince myself it's my imagination.

"I TOLD YOU GUYS MY DAD WAS A sweetheart," Casey says from the backseat as we drive to Hailey's.

"Yes, you did say that," I agree.

"You think he's being lazy, or insensitive about bringing you in to solve his problem. But I tell you what, he's actually doing you both a favor," Casey says, and both Cash and I laugh at the same time.

"I'm gonna have to disagree," I say.

"Reed is a professional fuck-up. You don't want him running the show. He can drive, and I shit you not, that is about the only thing he can do. He can't parent, that's for sure. I love him, but he's hopeless. I hope the video works, but if not, please do not rely on Reed for any serious help in the matter."

I don't need Casey to enlighten us about her dad's dumbshitness; I witnessed it firsthand. But we don't need him, nor do we need the ledger. A video tell-all from an attractive, young, recently kidnapped teenager, that involves dirty cops has to be about as viral as it gets.

We walk into the living room at Hailey's and can see that Hailey and Kelly have put a dent into a bottle of Jack. Casey hustles to the table, grabs the bottle, and takes a swig. She passes it around, and Cash and I do the same. I sit next to Hailey and lean into her. Touching her makes me realize how exhausted I am. We texted them most of the details on the ride here, so they're up to speed.

"I got my phone all set up for the video. Just tell me when you're ready," Kelly says to Casey.

"A few more shots of that," she points to the bottle, "and I'll be good to go."

I feel like it's a good time to send Maggie a note letting her know what's coming. I'm vague, but ask in the message if she would post a video pertinent to Casey's kidnapping. She responds almost immediately that she can pass it on to BlackForestPI. God, I thought we were past that. At least I know she's around.

"Okay, I'm ready," Casey finally says. She fusses with her hair using her phone camera as a mirror.

Kelly switches her phone to video and double-checks the shot. She turns on the lamps next to Casey and repositions them slightly. She waits for Casey to enter the frame and says, "I'm gonna hit record. You just start talking. It's not live, so stop, start over, do whatever. We can fix it afterward."

I stand next to Kelly and watch. Hailey asks if Kelly turned off the location settings, and Kelly assured her she had.

Casey takes a deep breath and says, "Ready."

Kelly hits record and gives Casey an offscreen thumbs-up.

Casey looks scared, but when she starts talking, her voice is steady. "Hello, everyone. My name is Casey West, and I was kidnapped. I was kidnapped by..." and then my phone vibrates on the table. Then it vibrates again. Casey starts over, "Um, okay, so I was kidnapped..."

Then my phone vibrates again two times in quick succession. Everyone looks at me. As Kelly hits the stop button on the video, I grab my phone.

"Sorry," I say, looking at my phone. I have four new messages, all from the same unknown number. Each message contains a single photo. The first one is dark, and I have to zoom in to see what it is. When I do, my stomach drops. It's my mom's room. It shows her bed and nightstand. Visible in the corner of the photo is a hand holding a gun. The gun is pointing at a photo of my mom and me that sits on her nightstand. The message is clear. By the time I realize what I am looking at, Casey, Hailey, Cash, and Kelly must have seen the look on my face, and I position my phone so they can see. The next photo is of Cash's brother getting into his car outside of Cash's house. The third picture shows a close-up of a hand holding a dog's collar. The collar is still on the dog, and you can see the dog's face. It's a German Shepherd. The tag dangling from the collar says Barney, and it lists a phone number. It's Kelly's dog. The final one is so dark it's hard to make out, but as I zoom in, I can tell it's a finger. A finger not attached to a hand. And the finger has a tattoo running along it that says "Wheels." The same exact finger we saw attached to Casey's dad an hour ago. Casey screams and walks out of the room. The dots start dancing on my phone, indicating a new message is being composed. When the message finally comes through, it says, *Probably best to not send that video.*

"They cut off Reed's finger. Oh my fucking God. I just called him and got no answer," Casey says as she returns to the room.

Hailey walks over to Casey and attempts to comfort her.

"We send the video and everyone dies?" Kelly asks.

"I think that's the message," I say, willing myself not to throw up.

"I'm so sorry, Casey," Hailey says, holding her. Surprisingly, Casey lets her.

After a minute, Casey wipes her eyes and nose with her sleeve and says, "We can't send that video, not while they have my dad."

I agree. I'm not sending out a video knowing they've been inside my mom's room.

"They only sent a photo of Barney, but man, that's enough for me," Kelly says and lights a joint.

"I'm guessing there's no picture for me since my parents and sister are in New York."

"I mean, Wes is a dick, but of course I don't want him killed," Cash says.

"First things first, I need to call my mom. Cash, you need to call Wes, and Kelly, you need to call someone at your house about Barney," I say. Everyone nods, and we start making calls. Cash gets Wes's voicemail and can't leave a message because the mailbox is full. He texts him and gets a quick response. Wes said he will stay at a friend's house. Kelly gets ahold of her mom and makes up something about a person kidnapping dogs for ransom. Her mom locked Barney in the house while they were on the phone. I get ahold of my mom, and she's at her boyfriend's. I make up a lie about me and my friends wanting to have a several-nights-long board game marathon and was hoping we could use our apartment for the next couple of nights. Why she isn't suspicious, I don't know. Or maybe she is, but is just happy to have an excuse to stay at her boyfriend's longer. After we finish with our calls, Casey clears her throat to get everyone's attention.

"There's really only one solution to our problem," Casey says, meeting each of our eyes in succession.

"FBI?" Hailey asks hopefully.

"No," she takes a swig from the bottle and then points at Cash and me. "You guys need to find Wilkinson and find that ledger before Damon and Buck do."

"Like Wilkinson, Wilkinson?" Kelly asks.

When texting Hailey and Kelly earlier, we conveniently left out the part of the conversation with Reed about Wilkinson.

"What in God's green earth does he have to do with this?" Hailey asks.

I fill them in about how Wilkinson helped Reed find a place to stash the ledger in the woods.

"No on Wilkinson. Just plain no," I say, and Cash nods in agreement.

"Okay, fine, you have a better plan. And before you start,

remember those photos. And also remember they currently have my dad. And they"—her voice catches—"they chopped off his fucking finger. There's just no way my dad's gonna be able to find something hidden in the woods. He can't find something in his pocket." I don't have a better plan. I don't have a plan at all. I can't stop seeing the photo of my mom's room, the weird green light in the dark. The gun in the corner pointing at her picture.

"We don't even know where Wilkinson is. We haven't seen nor heard from him in almost a year," Cash says.

"What about your brother?" Kelly asks.

"Maybe he has. I mean, I can ask," Cash says.

Cash grabs his phone and calls Wes again. Miraculously, he picks up.

"Hey man, um, weird question," Cash says into the phone, "but you by chance know where Wilkinson is?" He pauses, listening, then his face drops.

"Positive?" he asks into the phone. "Okay, cool, no. All good, I'll tell you later. Make sure you don't go home." And he hangs up.

"He's in Echo Mountain," Cash says.

"Again?" I ask. Cash nods.

"What's Echo Mountain?" Casey asks.

"Juvie," Hailey says.

Casey hasn't been in Black Forest for long, but most every kid around here is familiar with Echo Mountain. It's the juvenile detention center partway down the mountain. Wilkinson's been in and out of there since he was twelve. A frequent flyer is what they call them. The kids in there refer to it as *Gladiator School*— basically, you fight or die. I doubt kids are dying in there all the time, but the point is, the place is not safe.

"God fucking dammit," I say. Wilkinson was pulling fire alarms in elementary school when the other kids were concerned with getting a good swing at recess. He completely wrecked a house that was under construction by hot-wiring a tractor and driving through it.

"You guys know him, I mean pretty well, right?" Casey asks. "Like you could go visit him?"

"Oh, we know him all right," Cash says.

"What if it's as easy as him telling you where the ledger is? I mean, you could go see him tomorrow," Casey says.

"I don't know Wilkinson all that well, but I do know nothing is easy with him," Hailey says.

"She's right, that kid's probably done more dumb shit today than you have in your entire life," Kelly adds.

"They have my dad. They cut off his fucking finger," Casey barely manages to get out before she plops on the ottoman and the tears start flowing. I'm not good at the consoling thing, so I'm thankful Hailey and Kelly go to her. After thirty seconds or so, when the sobs not only don't end but actually intensify, Hailey motions for us to leave. I tap Cash on the shoulder and nod toward the door leading to the deck. He gets it, and we walk outside.

"Sucks, man," Cash says, staring into the darkness.

"Yeah, it does." I spent many a night trying to figure out my dad's disappearance. I'd tell myself it had something to do with him being on some kind of adventure, saving the world in some way that was so important he couldn't tell me about it. I was thirteen, mind you. I also spent nights thinking about him being dead or being tortured. Casey is living that right now. If there is a way we can help reunite her with her father. I don't see how we can't try.

"I know what you're thinking, but dude, these guys are fucking crazy," Cash says, reading my mind.

"They have her dad. Like literally right now they do. Would it be the worst idea to at least try and talk to Wilkinson?" I ask, kind of knowing the answer.

"Do you hear yourself? Yes, actually, it would be the worst idea. Like the definition of the worst idea," he says, exasperated.

"Okay, let me try that again. Is it a worse idea than doing nothing? Or a worse idea than sending out a video of Casey after seeing those pictures?"

"They're all terrible ideas," he says.

"We need to pick one. They were in my mom's room," I say.

"Now that they have Reed, now that they have a way to find the ledger, do they still care about us?"

"I'm gonna say yes."

"I think this is Reed's problem. He got himself into this mess. He's had his whole life to get his shit together and chose not to."

"I can't disagree with the last part. Look, I really don't wanna do this on my own. And I'm not gonna try and force you or Hailey or Kelly to do anything. I'm just not convinced we have a choice," I say.

"We always have a choice," Cash replies.

We do, but I think in this case the choice might be we fight for our lives or wait to be killed. We can't sit back and watch as strike after strike comes across the plate and not swing.

"Should we go back in and see what's up?" I ask.

Cash nods. The girls are sitting in the same place. Kelly pulls out her phone and hands it to Cash.

"Who's this?" Cash asks.

"Dave Higgins," she responds.

"Why's he asking where you are?"

"He's one of Cock Mike's wrestlers, right?" I ask.

Kelly nods. "We worked on a group project like three years ago. The last message from him before this was literally from middle school."

"It's because Cock Mike is looking for us," Casey says. We look at her, waiting for her to elaborate. She doesn't.

"Umm, why would Cock Mike be looking for us?" I ask.

"Because he's a fucking pedo, that's why," Casey says.

I don't know what to say to that, nor do I know what Cock Mike being a pedo has to do with him looking for us.

"I told you Buck's a pedophile and rapist. And I told you how I had to fight him off when they had me in that cabin. But what I didn't tell you was, one night"—she pauses, taking a moment to steady herself—"the night before you guys rescued me, he gave me juice with my crappy fast-food dinner. All I wanted was a Kola Kountry, but I drank the juice, and not long after, I started feeling... drunk, like really out of it. The last thing I remember was hearing a car pull up to the cabin. Growing up with Reed, you get to know the sound of cars. This one was a muscle car, and the timing was off. When Reed drove away in Cock Mike's car, I knew—it was the same one."

"So you think Cock Mike is what, like part of these guys?" I ask.

"I have no doubt he was at the cabin that night. I was late to class one day, this was the beginning of the semester. He had me stay after and clean the whiteboards. He came up behind me, put his hand on top of my hand that was erasing the board. He moved right up close to me and pressed his gross hard cock against me. I froze. He made some comment like, 'That's nice, right,' as he moved my hand to erase the words."

"I'm so sorry, Casey, that is beyond fucked up," I say.

"Fuck these guys," Kelly says.

"You think Cock Mike is having his wrestlers track us down now so he can tell Damon and Buck where we are?" Hailey asks.

"Makes sense," Cash says.

Kelly jumps as her phone vibrates. She reads the message.

"Now he's saying, 'Never mind, forget he even reached out,'" Kelly says.

"I think that means they know we're here," Casey says.

Hailey gets up and peers through the window. Her phone buzzes on the table. It's an alert from the alarm app. I take it to her.

"The alert's from the back gate," she says and turns the phone so we can see. It's a live video showing a car stopped in front of the gate. The headlights shut off, and Buck and Damon step out.

WE WATCH DAMON AND BUCK TRY TO get the gate open. It's chained and padlocked and doesn't budge. Damon notices the camera covering the gate. He waves. He walks over and taps the screen. A muffled pop follows each touch.

"Is this thing on?" he says and laughs.

Damon searches his jacket pockets, then his back pants pocket, and then his front ones. He pulls something out—no, he pulls two things out. One is shiny and reflects the moonlight.

He brings the other thing to his nose and smells it, like a cigar. Then he places it up next to the camera. It takes a moment for the autofocus to work, but when it does, it looks like—

"That's a fucking finger," Cash says, gagging.

He's holding Reed's finger so we can see the tattoo that says "Wheels." Casey turns away. Damon places the finger back in his pocket and puts the other thing in front of the camera. The focus moves in and out but eventually gets it right. It's a spoon, but pointier, and it has serrated edges on both sides.

"What the fuck? He has Casey's dad's finger and a grapefruit spoon?" Hailey stammers.

Damon clears his throat and says, "Your dad's predictable, Casey. All we had to do was tempt him with a shiny car. Too bad I was waiting in back. Only took losing one finger for him to tell us you two boys have the notebook."

I look at Cash and then to Casey and then back to Cash. *We* have the notebook?

"Can we talk through this thing?" I ask. Hailey hits a button and nods.

"We absolutely do not have the notebook. Never even seen it," I say, sounding slightly less scared than I feel.

"Sure you don't," he sounds almost reasonable. "Come on out and we'll talk about it." Then he spits on the lens of the camera and the feed goes blurry.

"What the...we have the notebook? We don't have the fucking notebook," Cash stammers.

"Casey, what the fuck did your dad tell them?" I ask, genuinely confused.

"I say we figure that part out later. Right now we have to get out of here," Hailey says as she runs around grabbing keys and bags.

"Casey, what the—" Cash starts, but she cuts him off.

"I'm sure he told them whatever the fuck he needed to tell them to get them to stop cutting off his fingers. Can we fucking leave it for a second? Get the fuck out of here and make sure he's okay?"

"Sounds like a plan to me," Kelly answers.

I make eye contact with Cash and shrug. I've never had a finger chopped off, but if I did, I'd probably say just about anything to keep the rest of them.

"Yeah, fair," I say. I make sure I still have Damon's gun in my waistband, and we run for the front door.

"Cash, you, Kelly, and Casey take Hailey's car. Hailey, you drive your parents' car and I'll ride shotgun. We'll pull out first. Follow close. No headlights, cool?" I say.

No one moves.

"Ready?" I say louder, and then we hear Hailey's phone buzz.

"That's the motion warning at the back deck. They're about to get in the house," Hailey says and turns her phone for us to see.

The video buffers. When it loads, we see Damon and Buck approach the glass door on the back deck. That gets us sprinting for the cars.

"Meet at Deadese Park," Kelly yells as she jumps into the car.

Hailey and I pull out, and Cash lines up right behind us. I have the window down and my gun ready. Hailey rolls slowly down the driveway and onto the road. As we drive, I see the cops' parked car through the trees near the back gate.

"Pull over," I say. Hailey looks at me like I'm insane. "Seriously, pull over. I want to slash their tires. Give us more time." Hailey shakes her head but stops the car, and Cash stops behind us. I run to Cash and he rolls down his window.

"I want to pop their tires. You have your pocketknife on you?"

Cash hands me his knife. I jog up the dirt drive and swing around the back of the car. I crouch down next to the left rear tire and stab the knife in. I pull it out and hear the tire hiss as the air forces its way out. When I do the same to the front tire on the same side, I hear the rear passenger door open. I crouch behind the car. The car raises up on the shocks as the person in the back seat gets out. We watched Damon and Buck hop the gate. We saw them on video near the door on the deck. Did one of them double back? I crawl around to the front of the car.

I'm guessing the person has seen the flat tires, because he says, "What the fuck?" It takes me a minute because it's so out of context, but I know exactly whose voice that is. I've heard it drone on in monotone, listing mundane facts about American history from 1776 to present. It's Cock Mike. Casey was right. I debate pulling out the gun, but I don't think it would be wise to shoot my teacher. I inch my way around to the other side of the car. I think he's on the opposite side, but I hear a footstep behind me and feel a hand grip my shoulder. It's like a fucking vice. I flinch and spin around as fast as I can, completely forgetting about the knife in my hand, and I bury it in the underside of his left forearm just below the elbow. There was almost no resistance. It just sunk in. Like stabbing jello. Without thinking, I reposition my grip on the knife and yank it out. I take a step back but keep the knife pointed at him. Fuck, fuck, fuck, I just stabbed my teacher. He looks at his arm, and I think he's for real trying to figure out what happened. He still has his phone in his hand—he must have been using it as a flashlight. The confusion on his face is quickly replaced by anger.

"You...you fucking stabbed me," he says.

"Shit. Sorry, coach. I just... I didn't mean to, you just, like, snuck up on me there and I turned," I back up as he takes a half step toward me.

"I always hated that I had to feel sorry for you," he says. "The poor kid whose dad disappeared. You always looked like such a pussy. Do you even bench, bro?"

Each time he takes a step toward me, I take a step back.

"Look, man," I start to say, and fuck, what do I say? "Look, Cock Mike, I mean—" but he cuts me off, and even in the dark, I can see the fury on his face.

"Don't fucking call me Cock Mike. C-O-C-H is way closer to coach than cock. Goddamnit," and before he finishes the sentence, he lunges at me. I jump back, and this time I can say it is one hundred percent his fault. He reaches for my hand, I don't know, like he's grabbing for the knife maybe, and he impales his hand on the end of the blade. Just right through the meat of his palm. The sound and feeling of the knife sinking into his skin makes me nauseous. Without thinking, I pull the knife out and take another step back. I just stabbed my teacher. Again.

"What the fuck?" he says, looking at his hand.

"That one was all you. Just fuck off, man. Get back in the car," I say, shakily pointing the bloody knife at him.

"Your girl... I can't wait, never had me a good girl," he says and dives for me, both of his hands reaching for my neck. I scramble, slip on the gravel, and fall on my ass. I don't want to release my grip on the knife, so I drive my fist into the ground and feel dozens of small rocks and pebbles cut into my knuckles. Cock Mike is fast, but I'm faster still. I know if he gets a hold of me it's over. I scramble halfway up just as he comes even with me. He crouches down, I assume to smash my head like a grape, when I hear a loud thwack. His phone lands next to my hand. I watch as he tips over sideways and falls off the side of the driveway. He lands on his side in the ditch. I look up and see Cash with a softball-sized rock in his hand, and I know he just saved my life.

"Dude, is that fucking Cock Mike?" he asks.

"Yes. Crazy, right? Oh my god, thank you," I say and pop to my feet. Cash grabs my arm to steady me. I reach down and pocket Cock Mike's phone.

From the ditch, we hear him say, "Stupid...students...expelled. F's. F's for both of you."

"Let's get the fuck out of here," Cash says, and we race to the cars. I close the bloody knife and hand it to Cash.

"You might want to wipe that off. It's got Cock Mike blood all over it," I say.

"You stabbed Cock Mike?"

"Twice."

We drive in silence most of the way except for the occasional outburst when I say I can't believe I stabbed Cock Mike or when Hailey says she can't believe I stabbed Cock Mike.

We're almost to Deadese Park when Hailey squeezes my hand and reaches over and kisses me on the mouth. It's nice, but a bit too long, knowing there is no way she's watching the road.

I pull away and say, "Watch the road, lady." She smiles back and does just that.

We're sitting on benches in Eagle's Park. It's a common place for kids to hang at night in the summer and drink. Right now, though, it's empty.

"Dude, you better hope you don't have him for history next year," Kelly says, laughing.

"I can't believe you stabbed Cock Mike," Cash says. Hailey and I exchange a knowing glance.

I can't get the feeling out of my head of the knife scraping over bone.

"Why was he even there?" Kelly asks.

"Because he's a fucking pedo and Damon and Buck probably have their claws in him just like they do Reed," Casey says.

"I really hope your dad's okay," Hailey says.

"Reed is too dumb to die," Casey says. It's not that she doesn't care about her dad, because she clearly does, she just really does think he's going to be all right.

"We've gotta figure something out soon, though, because they're gonna be pissed as fuck now," Kelly adds.

"One more thing, why did he have a grapefruit spoon?" Hailey asks.

In all the confusion, I had forgotten about that. Then it hits me—a grapefruit spoon cutting through a closed eyelid in search of the eyeball hidden beneath. My eyeball. Or Cash's.

I look at Cash, and from the ashen look on his face, I think he's come to the same conclusion.

"I don't know," I say, "but we need a real fucking plan."

"We've got to get that ledger or notebook or whatever it is, it's the only thing that's gonna get Reed back," Casey says.

"How though? We don't know where it is. This entire place is just one big fucking forest if you haven't noticed. It could be anywhere. And your dad knows where it is a hell of a lot more than we do," Cash says.

"Have you not been listening? You know why my dad got

into stealing cars? Because he could never find his keys. So he learned how to hot-wire his *own* car."

Cash and I look at each other in confusion.

"I said it before, but I guess I have to say it again, there is no fucking way he's finding that notebook in the forest. Whether he hid it or not. He couldn't find that thing in his left hand," Casey says.

"I can't believe I'm the one suggesting this, but I feel like our only option is Wilkinson," Hailey says. Casey nods enthusiastically.

"I'm assuming Damon and Buck will keep my dad alive because they think you guys have the notebook. If they find out you don't, and then Reed can't find it, none of us are of any use to them," Casey says.

"Okay, fine. We'll see if we can get to Wilkinson," I say, looking at Cash. After a moment, he nods. "It's the only thing we can do, but I think we need to split up." Hailey looks alarmed.

"I think the three of you go back to your house, Hailey. If Cash and I aren't there, maybe they won't come looking. And if they do, hide. There's a hundred places they won't find you in that house. Just keep the alarms set," I say.

"You don't have to tell me that," Hailey says, and surprisingly doesn't put up a fight.

"I don't feel great about leaving you guys," Kelly says.

"We'll be fine. Jack, we can sleep in the attic above my garage. It'll suck, but it's pretty clean up there," Cash says, and I shrug in agreement. I've seen that attic, and I'm not sure I'd call it clean, but it does seem safe enough.

Hailey gives me a big hug. Kelly and Cash give each other hugs. Casey pretends to hug herself, and we manage a laugh.

WHEN WE ARRIVE AT CASH'S, WE DO a quick sweep of the perimeter of his house. His brother's car is out front but that's it. We peek in the front window and see Wes in his usual spot on the couch with his favorite three-foot bong he calls "Tiny" in front of him. He's not supposed to be here. Cash shakes his head. We walk through the front door and

I lock it behind us while Cash checks the back door. I hear him mumble "not even fucking closed" from the hall. He stomps back to the living room.

"The fuck?" Wes asks blowing out his bong hit.

"Dude, I fucking told you it's not safe to be here," Cash yells.

"Whoa, man. It's fine. I can totally see the driveway."

"What if they came in through the back door? The not-even-closed back door?" Cash asks.

"Oh, right. I didn't think about that."

Have I mentioned that Wes is not a genius?

After Wes loses a staring contest with Cash, he says, "Fine, fine. I'll get going. But fuck, seems like every summer you guys make this house unsafe."

"Trust us, we know. Sorry about that," Cash says.

"It's cool, little bro. Bong hit?"

"No thanks," Cash says. Wes looks to me, and I shake my head.

"Wes, you know how long Wilkinson is in for?" I ask.

"Not that long. He tried to steal some plants from a grow house. A few months, I think," he says and loads another bowl.

"We're gonna grab some shit and take off ourselves. You need to get going," Cash says. I'm guessing he either doesn't trust Wes with the information that we're just going to the attic above the garage or doesn't want to put him in harm's way by giving it to him.

"I am, bro, jeez. I'm like, so close to not being here, that I'm barely here."

Cash sighs and we head to his room. We grab some

blankets and pillows and Cash grabs a half-empty twelve-pack of beer from under his bed. We walk out the back door and make our way to the attic. The sun is just starting to rise.

The attic is not as bad as I remember. In fact, it's pretty close to clean. Sleeping on plywood is gonna suck, but I'm so fucking tired I might not even notice.

"Think we can get in to see Wilkinson tomorrow?" I ask once I've finished making my bed.

"Yeah, for sure. Pam's older brother got sent there when we were in elementary school, she used to visit him."

I look up the facility online. They don't have set visiting hours, but as long as someone isn't locked down or in some kind of class, you can see them between 8 a.m. and 4 p.m. I think it's unlikely that Wilkinson isn't locked down, but stranger things have happened.

"I'll ask Hailey if we can take the car up there. And then I guess we just show up at 8, huh? Like, only a few hours from now?" I ask.

"Sounds like another bad step in a non-plan."

"Super excited about it. I'm sure some really safe stuff is gonna come from it."

This thing goes from bad, to worse, to worse still. When do we hit worst? Probably with Wilkinson. I lay back on my wood mattress, put the pillow under my head, pull the blanket over me, and fall asleep.

We wake with barely enough time to make it to Echo Mountain by 8 a.m. We hustle out the door to Hailey's car. It takes us about forty-five minutes to get there. As we make the final turn, the place comes into view. Kind of looks like our school, but a lot bigger, which is scary. It's also surrounded by a giant fence. A number of kids wander around inside. A group of them plays basketball. No adults in site, but it seems orderly. We pull into the lot and park.

"Just roll in there?" I ask.

"After seeing how tall that razor-wire-covered fence is, I'm thinking no way they're gonna let two random kids meet with an inmate."

"I feel the same, but we gotta try," I say.

"Fine, fuck," Cash says.

The fence ends on either end of a one-story stone building that serves as the entrance. Cash follows as I walk to the double front doors and open them. Inside, about twenty heavy plastic chairs are bolted to the ground in rows. Backed against the wall on the left are a number of ancient vending machines. One spits out cups of coffee and hot chocolate, and it only takes coins. The opposite wall has posters featuring different rules. One poster has a super long list of what is considered contraband. Other than the woman sitting on a stool behind the glass-partitioned counter, the room is empty. Hopefully that's because it's early and not because no one comes to visit. The woman's head is shaved on the sides and back and the remaining hair on top is spiked in a thousand directions. It's mostly gray, with some fading purple. She has so many earrings in each ear, you can barely see flesh. She's wearing a short-sleeve button-up collared shirt that has the Echo Mountain logo on the left breast. Her arms are covered in faded tattoos, as is her neck. Also her hands. I'm not great with the age of old people, but she's gotta be in her sixties. The contrast between her age and her piercings and tattoos makes me dizzy. She's like a teenage grandma. Her suspicious eyes follow us as we approach.

"Umm, we're here to see Erik Wilkinson," I say, doing my best to sound confident. Like I visit people in juvie all the time.

"Boys, I happen to know the entire Wilkinson family tree, and you two are definitely not on it," her voice thin and gravelly.

"No, we're not. We're friends," Cash says.

"Oh, in that case, head right in," she says sarcastically.

"I guess we don't really know how this works. We thought there were visiting hours," I say.

"For family, yes. Friends are what got kids like Erik in here," she says. I bet Erik got himself in here all on his own.

"We aren't those kinds of friends," Cash says.

"Of course you're not."

"No way we can see him?" I ask. "It's really important."

She looks at Cash and tilts her head to the left, like a dog hearing a high-pitched sound.

"You're a McDermid, aren't you?" she asks Cash.

"I am, yeah. Cash."

Then she smiles. Not a half-assed one either.

"I could feel it in my insides. How's Wes?" she asks.

"Umm, pretty good. You know my brother?"

"I know Wes," she says. And it doesn't seem possible, but her smile gets bigger. I bet Wes's parents didn't even smile like that when he was born.

"Let me show you something," she says to Cash. She slowly scoots her stool back from the counter; it screeches the whole way. She struggles off it and shuffles to the table behind her. She rummages through her bag, grabs something, and trudges back. She winces, pauses, and rubs her hip before attempting to mount the stool. The whole process takes a long time. She manages, with a number of grunts, to get herself back on the stool, but then realizes that she is some distance from the counter. She reaches for the edge of the counter to drag herself closer, but it's out of reach. Her outstretched, vein-ridden hand is still eighteen inches shy of being able to grab on to anything. She looks around; I think she's contemplating getting off the stool, pushing it closer, and then getting back on, but doesn't seem thrilled about that idea. She's breathing hard. I don't know what to do, so I reach my hand through the smallish opening in the glass and offer it to her. She hesitates but then grabs on. Her hand is cold and papery, but her grip is surprisingly strong. She weighs so little that when I pull, I almost yank her off the stool. Cash sees the problem and leans through the opening on his belly. He grabs the edge of the stool, and between the two of us we are able to slide her to the counter.

"Thank you," she says and places the item she pulled from her purse face down on the counter. From the back, it looks like a Polaroid. She turns it around and hands it to Cash through the opening. Sure enough, it's a Polaroid. And one she should not be sharing. It's a shot of Cash's room. In the frame is his bed, and on top of the bed is the woman in front of us. But in the photo, she's naked. Her legs are positioned in a way that you can't see anything below her waist. Her arm covers her nipples—the nipples that are close to her belly button due to the sagging of her breasts. She has the same huge smile on her face. The most disturbing part of the photo, and there are many disturbing parts, is the giant wet spot below her crotch.

Cash stammers, but finally manages to get out, "Why?"

The woman looks at him with genuine dismay and says, "Why? Why? He's kind. He's smart. He's beautiful."

Now I'm confused because she can't be talking about Wes.

"Wes is all those things?" I ask.

"Umm, yeah. Do you not know him?" she asks.

"Oh, I know him," I say.

"But why my bed?" Cash asks again, a hint of despair in his voice.

"Well, his was too wet," she says without a trace of embarrassment.

At this point, it seems all too much for Cash. He tries to say something—what, I have no idea—but can't get the words out.

"So no way we can see him, huh? Wilkinson?" It's hard not to get distracted by thinking about her and Wes, and the picture, but we came here for a reason, and if it's not gonna happen, then we need to get a move on.

"Well, things have changed, haven't they?" she says.

"Have they?" I ask.

"Wes changes everything," she says.

I say, "Well, of course he does. He's Wes, after all."

"Yes, he is."

She gets lost in some reverie I'm glad I'm not privy to. Cash still hasn't said anything. Wes, plus this grandmother, is apparently not a math problem he can solve. The woman looks at Cash and then looks to me. Then she makes the same arduous journey off her stool to her purse, searches through it again, finds something, ambles back, this time pushes the stool closer to the counter, and manages to seat herself back on it. She manages to catch her breath as she fondles what she emoved from her purse—a folded piece of paper covered in drawings of hearts. She brings it to her nose, smells, and closes her eyes.

She opens them and says, "I'll let you see Erik Wilkinson if you promise to give this to Wes."

I look at Cash, but he's still gone. I'm not sure what his deal is. I mean, it's weird, for sure, but I guess Wes likes his girls a little bit older. Or a lot older. But whatever.

"Deal," I say to her. "That's it? That's all we have to do?"

"That's all you have to do. I've done the rest with my words and incantations," she says and smiles. She touches a tattoo on the inside of her forearm. It's a symbol of intersecting ovals and circles. Maybe she's a witch? She slides the folded piece of paper to me through the hole in the glass. I grab it, and because she is watching me so intently, gingerly slip it into my pocket. It is not new; my guess is she's been holding on to this for quite some time.

"I'll have them send down Erik. There are lockers along the wall to your left. Put everything in there. Keys, phones, belts, syringes. Everything but your clothes and note. Note does not leave you until it is in Wes's possession, understand?" she asks.

"Understand," I say. She didn't use *the* when talking about her note, like she was talking about a person.

She picks up the phone as I nudge Cash toward the lockers. I open one and place the contents of my pockets inside. Cash should be doing the same, but he's not.

"Dude. Snap out of it. Put your shit in the locker and let's go see Wilkinson before she changes her infatuated mind," I say.

"Why would he do that?" he asks.

"Fuck, man. Wes is Wes. Nothing to figure out there."

Apparently, that's enough because he starts unloading his stuff in the same locker I used. Once he's finished and has patted down his pockets to make sure nothing remains, I close the door and set a four-digit PIN per the instructions. We walk back over to the woman behind the counter.

"I'll pop the door on your right. Walk through it and enter the room on your left. The one with the orange door. Have a seat at the table, and a corrections officer will bring out Erik shortly. Do not—I repeat, do not—sit on note," she says.

I make a show of taking the note out of my back pocket, saying sorry to it, and putting it in my front pocket. She nods.

We walk to the door on our right and hear a metallic click as it opens. We enter a short hallway that cuts right after about ten feet. Halfway down on our left is an orange door with a large rectangular window next to it. We open the door and have a seat at the small round table and wait for Wilkinson.

CASH AND I SIT IN UNCOMFORTABLE SEATS behind a cold metal table. The chairs are hard, plastic, and small, as if they were made for children. I hope there aren't kids in here small enough to fit in them correctly. In the center of the table is a metal U-shaped hook that I think is for handcuffs. I see movement out of the corner of my eye and spot Wilkinson and a guard headed our way. Wilkinson's hair is buzzed. He looks like he's aged five years in the year since we've seen him. He's only seventeen, but easily looks in his mid-twenties. The tattoo above his left eye that was newish the last time I saw him has faded. It's written in script and says, *kill me.* He's added another one on the other side of his face that says, *now.* Not that I am surprised, but it seems as if things have not been going well for him. The guard opens the door and lets Wilkinson through. No handcuffs.

The guard stands next to the door as Wilkinson enters. He says, "The door locks from the inside. It will not open no matter how many times you try the knob. I will be outside. When fifteen minutes have transpired, I will enter the room and take the inmate back. If, before that time, you would like to terminate the meeting, knock on the door. I will proceed to open the door and escort the inmate back. The door will not open from the inside. Is all of this clear?" He says his spiel while staring at the wall between Cash and me. It takes me a moment to process because there was no inflection of any kind. Clearly, he's said this a million times and has lost all sense of the flow in delivery necessary to convey actual meaning.

"We got it. Don't try the knob. Knock when done," Cash says.

The guard turns and closes the door. If Wilkinson is shocked to see us, he doesn't show it. He has on blue sweatpants and a long-sleeve white thermal shirt. His shoes are blue canvas slip-ons. No laces.

He grins and says, "Cash Money. Jackson Five. Sup?"

"Hey, Wilkinson, long time," Cash says.

"Hey, man," I say.

His hands rest on the table, the thumbs and pointer fingers

of each hand meeting in a diamond shape, in plain view of the powers that be.

"Let me guess, Reed West," he says.

I don't look at Cash, but my guess is his jaw dropped like mine.

"How the fuck?" I ask.

He looks at his hands. He has twice as many shitty homemade tattoos on them as he did last time I saw them. My favorite is the kitchen knife across the top of his left hand. On the handle, it says, *I tried.* I'm thinking that has everything to do with the kid he stabbed last summer. And I would agree, if by try he means "tried to kill him."

"I know shit," he says.

"Yeah, it does have to do with Reed," Cash says.

"Figured. Life chews you up. Swallows you. Becomes you."

Here we go. Wilkinson makes sense about twenty percent of the time. I hope this isn't a complete waste.

"We got like fifteen minutes here. We're in a world of shit. We're looking for a ledger that you apparently helped Reed hide," I say.

"A document," he says and looks out the window.

"Yeah, I guess so. Like a notebook of some sort? You know where it is?" I ask.

"Could very well be that I do, Jacky boy. But my arm's a bit short to reach it."

"Maybe you can tell us where it is?" Cash asks.

Wilkinson shakes his head. I hear a door open down the hall and fear our time is up. No way it's been fifteen minutes, I'm not even sure it's been two. Wilkinson leans in close.

"You want the ledger? I want out of here. A win-win, as they say. The easiest way to escape is through the laundry. Wes can help; he knows the driver. Pick-up is today at four."

Then the door opens and the guard steps in. Wilkinson stands and puts his hands in the same diamond shape, but this time behind his back. He walks past the guard and stops in the middle of the hall, his toes touching a white line on the floor, apparently indicating where he is supposed to wait.

"Once you hear the door close at the end of this hall, proceed to the door you came through, and they will pop it for you," the guard says, equally as excited about this dialogue as he was the previous.

"Thanks," Cash says.

Wilkinson walks down the hall and as he rounds the corner, he sings, "Fly Like an Eagle."

When they're clear of us, Cash says, "Well, that's a terrible fucking idea."

"This whole thing is fucking terrible," I whisper as the door pops and we walk back into the lobby. The woman is still sitting on her stool. From this distance, she actually does look like a witch. We go to the lockers, grab our stuff, and walk back to the counter. I pull out the note to show her I took good care of it.

"Thank you," I say. "We'll get this to Wes immediately."

"I know you will," she says and rubs her hands together. The sound is like sandpaper, and it gives me the chills.

"What's your name?" I ask.

"Candace. Candace Clay," she says and winks.

"So what would a date with Wes be worth to you?" I ask.

She shivers. Her face trembles and she moans.

"The world," she says.

"Okay. Thanks again," I say, and we walk out the front door.

Once we reach the car, I buckle up and start the engine.

"Umm, so dude. Wilkinson wants us to break him out of juvie," I say, still processing our meeting.

"That's not fucking happening," Cash says and stares out the window as the trees fly by.

I fucking love Cash, but goddamn if I'm not getting sick of trying to convince him of the level of shit we are in. Now that Reed has told Damon and Buck that we have the ledger, they're gonna come looking for it. I'm not positive they'll try and kill us if we have it, but I have no doubt they will if we don't.

"I kind of feel like a broken record here, but what do you think happens if we do nothing? They track us down and we don't have the ledger?"

Cash doesn't respond.

I give it a moment, and then, "Or let's say we release the video of Casey that Kelly shot. Or, I don't know, go to the FBI or something. I don't have to remind you of the photos they sent last night."

"No, you don't, although I'm not quite as attached to Wes after seeing that picture." He takes a couple of deep breaths and turns to me with a helpless look on his face.

"Do we really have no other choice?" he asks.

"I mean, we always have a choice," I say, giving him a sly look to make it clear I'm teasing by turning his words back on him, "but I'm not sure any of those other choices keep the people we love safe."

"Ourselves included," Cash says.

"Ourselves included," I repeat.

"Okay, so we not only have to convince Wes to go on a date

with a grandma, but we have to convince him to help us break Wilkinson out of juvie? And do it today?"

"Yep," I say, realizing how preposterous this whole thing is, "and he needs to convince Candace to help us."

"Fuck me," Cash says and returns to staring out the window.

During the drive back to Cash's, I was able to convince him we didn't need to immediately replace his bed. Currently, Cash sits on his bottom bunk, his hand rubbing the blanket (not where the wet spot was), as we wait for his brother to return home. I get that you don't want to see a picture of an old-ass woman naked on your bed, but I'm having a hard time understanding the depth of effect it's having on him.

"I thought your brother said he'd be home by now?" I say.

He just looks at me like, *have you met my brother?* Yeah, being on time is not at the top of his brother's priority list.

Just then we hear the rumble of Wes' Camaro pull into the drive. Cash takes another look at his bunk bed, shakes his head, and walks toward the front door. I follow him outside, and we meet Wes on the path from the driveway.

"What's the fucking emergency, man? You tell me I have to leave, then you tell me I have to come back," Wes says.

Cash stares at him and shakes his head. I figured Cash was gonna start yelling, but from the look of dismay on Wes' face, this must be worse.

"What, man? What the fuck?"

Cash continues to shake his head. Then he snickers and huffs. With each overwrought reaction from Cash, his brother gets visibly more upset. Cash is like some evil puppet master.

"Just tell me. What the fuck did I do wrong?" I kind of feel sorry for him.

"On my bed? On my fucking bed? Candace Clay?" Cash says. And I don't think he's just laying it on to fuck with Wes. He's really upset.

It takes Wes a minute to put two and two together, but when he does, he says, "Oh, fuck. How? I'm sorry." And he looks it. Both of them are eyes down on the driveway. Neither seems to be in a hurry to continue the conversation.

I break the silence with, "We went to see Wilkinson at Echo Mountain. Candace works there. Wouldn't let us in unless we gave you this," I say and pull *note* out of my pocket and hand it to him.

"She gave you this?" he asks excitedly.

I nod. He brings the note to his nose and smells it. Just when I think he's not going to open it, he does. As his eyes move down the page, a look of joy spreads across his face. When he finishes, he says, "Awwww."

What a weird fucking morning.

"I'm sorry, Cash. I know it probably won't help, but I loved her. I love her. And, well, she was so uncomfortable about our age difference. I was too. And this was the first time. Well, it was the first time in the day. In the light and stuff. And she was so happy. Like she could see I didn't care. And she was like, 'Grab your phone.' So I did. And then she's in the hall, and before I know it, she's on your bottom bunk. And I'm thinking, *oh fuck*, but I don't wanna say anything, you know? Like make her feel bad or whatever. Like she didn't even cry after we did it. I just took the picture."

"It's okay, man," Cash says.

"Really?" Wes asks hopefully.

"Really, but you fucking owe me big."

"Anything," Wes says and gives Cash a hug. "I'm really sorry."

I don't think Wes has any idea how literally we are going to take his *anything* statement.

"Well, Wes, about that, we do have a couple of things in mind," I say.

"Yeah, what do you guys need?" he asks.

"First, I think you're gonna need to go on a date with Candace," Cash says.

"Okay, twist my arm," he says and laughs at his own joke.

"And secondly," I say, pausing for a moment to think of how best to present it, then I decide on brutal honesty, "we need you to help us bust Wilkinson out of juvie."

I expect him to start laughing, but he doesn't. I guess he can tell I'm serious. But he does turn white.

"Ah, fuck. For real? You guys, Jesus."

"Wes, I'm not gonna lie. I wouldn't ask if there was another solution. And no, I don't think you owe me this because of that photo. I'm asking because I don't know what else to do," Cash says and sticks his hands in his pockets. He's not used to asking his brother for help.

"So what kind of shit are you guys in?" Wes asks.

"The less you know, the better. But remember last summer with Zufelt?" I ask.

"Yeah, still see that fucker in my nightmares," he says.

"Well, multiply that by a hundred and that's the shit we're in," I say.

"You fucking guys. Cash, you're a fucking math genius. And I don't know about you, Jack, but you seem like you got it together more than most. But holy hell, you guys make me look like a choirboy."

"It finds us," Cash says.

"Like a fucking magnet," I add.

"Why Wilkinson, though? Jesus," Wes asks.

"He has something we need in order to get out of our jam. And we need him out of there in order to get it," I say.

"Sucks for you. But of course I'll help. And fuck, man, maybe go to camp next summer or something," Wes says and manages to look paternal.

"Not a bad idea," I say.

"Okay, what do I have to do?" Wes asks.

It takes about an hour to figure out a plan. And like all of our plans, it's terrible. Wes is currently in the other room on the phone with Candace. Cash and I are in his room waiting. Cash sits on the bottom bunk, and I sit on the couch.

"I know I've never told you, just felt kind of childish, I guess. But my mom used to lay on this bunk and sing to me as I fell asleep on the top bunk. I don't remember it, but Wes told me. Said she'd do it almost every night. It's why I never sleep down here. Pretty weak memento, a shitty twin bed, but it's what I have."

"Oh, man. I'm sorry. The picture makes sense now," I say.

"It's time I moved on anyway. I don't like sleeping up there. It's way too small and not even remotely comfortable. I know Wes is a dick ninety-nine percent of the time, but seeing that picture, I was just like, are you kidding me?"

"Ninety-eight percent of the time, I think, but he sounded genuine, at least to me," I say.

WES WALKS INTO CASH'S ROOM BEAMING and says, "I just got off the phone with Candace. We're back together."

"Congrats, I guess. And the part about helping us?" I say.

"Oh, right, yeah, she's in," he says.

Although this is what we were hoping for, my stomach flips and I feel dizzy hearing it just the same. It's one thing to talk about breaking a kid out of kid jail, it's quite another to do it. I take a few deep breaths, but my throat feels too narrow for the air.

Wes notices something's off with me and says, "Dude, you don't look so good."

Cash leans over the top bunk, and whatever he sees must be alarming enough that he jumps off the bed, runs to the kitchen, and brings me a Kola Kountry. He opens it for me and everything.

I take a couple of sips. I'm not sure soda is a cure for anything, but I do feel better.

"I'm fine," I say and will my face to look fine. "I just got freaked out for a second thinking about getting Wilkinson out of there and then, what, just hoping he doesn't do his usual and make this whole thing worse?"

"Dude, you know how you give me shit about how we have to do this or we have to do that? How we can't just sit around and hope everything just works out? Well, I'm willing to bet that feeling of fear you just had, that I guess is rare for you, is the feeling that has been running through me since this whole thing started," Cash says, giving me shit, but in a nice way.

"Ha, you're probably right. I'll do better," I go in for a big hug, and he pushes me away.

"Okay, I'm okay. I swear. So what did she say?" I ask.

"She said Echo Mountain isn't very secure at all. She said Wilkinson was right, the laundry pick-up and delivery is by far the weakest point. They don't search the truck coming or going. And the in-house laundry is run by an inmate."

Hmm, maybe this won't be so terrible after all.

"You guys remember Heath?" Wes asks.

Scratch that, it will be even more terrible. Cash and I sigh at hearing Heath's name. Having Heath mentioned within a square mile of a plan automatically negates said plan.

"I remember Heath, and no," Cash says in perfect finality.

"Absolutely, just no," I add, although Cash's response was plenty clear.

"I know, I know. Just hear me out..." Wes pleads.

Wes is a grade-A dumbshit and a part-time sadist, but he's a fucking rocket scientist and saint compared to Heath. It amazes me that Heath can remember to breathe. Heath is seventeen, I know this because he ages out of juvy next year. From there, he'll move on to adult prison to spend the next however many years he has left on his sentence. He's spent six of his seventeen years locked up—if you think about that for a minute, it's an exceptional feat. He got sent away the first time in third grade (he should have been a grade above Cash and me, but he was a grade below). One day in class, he got up out of his chair to sharpen his pencil. Apparently, he sharpened the shit out of it, and he wanted to find out just how sharp it was, so as he walked back to his desk, he pierced the back of Kyle Lacklow's upper arm. Kyle was a bit on the chubby side and tended to wear shirts a few sizes too small (hand-me-downs, most likely), and I guess that ruddy arm sticking out was like a magnet too strong, taunting Heath's needle-sharp pencil tip. No matter how sharp a pencil is, you have to push that thing pretty damn hard to get it through three inches of flesh. Before Kyle even had a chance to start crying bloody murder, which he eventually did do, Heath pulled the pencil all the way back out. The tip must not have broken off because when the teacher came barreling down the aisle, yelling and sending spit halfway across the room (his name was Mr. Fitz, but we all called him Mr. Spitz), Heath stuck the pencil straight into the teacher's hand. The scariest part is that Heath wasn't even mad. Just curious. So off he went to Echo Mountain for his first stay. His sentence got extended multiple times for infractions inside. He got out when we were in eighth grade. He wasn't free a full week when he stole his dad's car to go get himself a Slushee Dream. On his way to Kum Quick, he mowed down a guy and his dog. The dog was fine; the guy died after a week in the ICU. I doubt it's true, but I heard he had to swerve to hit them. So neither Cash nor I are all that interested in a plan that involves Heath.

Wes continues, "Seriously, just hear me out. I know he's crazy and dumb as trash, but he is the foreman, or whatever it's called there, of the laundry. Kid's only seventeen and already has like five years' work experience. He can basically do whatever he wants. An outside company will pick up the rags and aprons this afternoon. That's the only stuff they don't wash there. Heath packs them all up in big bags, and then the driver from A-1 Wash-N-Fold takes them away. Guess who the driver is?"

"Wes, if it's some Inwood dumbshit, let's just stop right here and figure out a different plan," I say, feeling hopeless.

Wes' eyes get glassy and his mouth goes tight. If I didn't know better, I'd think he was trying to hold back tears. Oh no, he is.

"Shit, sorry, man. I know you're trying to help. Tell us the plan. I'm just tired and freaked the fuck out. I've never broken anyone out of jail before."

And just like that, his normal vacant look returns.

"Me. I'm driving," he says, looking from me to Cash and then back to me.

"The fuck?"

"Kyle Lacklow's the normal driver and he owes me. He's gonna pull over before he hits Echo Mountain Road. I'm gonna take over, pick up the load—Wilkinson will be hiding in one of the bags—then I drive back down and give Kyle back the truck."

"Kyle Lacklow? The kid that Heath stabbed with the pencil in third grade?" Cash asks as if the world has gone completely mad.

"The one and only. They're like tight now, shit was a long time ago," Wes says. "Candace is the one that buzzes people through the gate and pops open the back door to the laundry."

"Don't Wilkinson and Heath have beef? Something about a girl? Dana Clark?" Cash asks.

"Dani Clark. That's ancient, man. They squashed that a long time ago," Wes says, and I can't tell if he's looking down because he's being shady or if he's just being Wes.

"Well, shit, Wes. I mean, this sounds like a plan. Like a legitimate plan." It's not true; it sounds like a horrible plan, but the alternative is not having a plan, and that is unacceptable to my brain.

"Awww, thanks, Jack," Wes says, elated.

"I mean, Heath's a psycho, Wilkinson's a psycho, and they may hate each other. And Kyle, well, Kyle's..." I stop because I don't really know much about Kyle.

"Kyle's a psycho too. And a junkie. Like, dude will shoot anything into his arm," Wes says, trying to be helpful.

"Okay, great. So Kyle's a psycho junkie and also possibly still hates Heath," Cash says.

"No. No, I'm telling you. That's all buried under the bridge," Wes says, and yes, he is definitely trying to convince himself.

"Candace is solid, though, right?" I ask.

"Solid as a brick. Heath and Candace broke up, so all good on that end."

"Candace and Heath dated? What? When? Hasn't he been in juvy for, like, ever?" I ask, confused. And is Candace a legit pedophile?

"Well, they, like, broke up. Like completely, a while ago," Wes says, staring at the wall above my head.

"Wes, look at me," he does, but reluctantly. "When did they break up?"

"Fine. They broke up today. Right after we started going out."

"Oh my fucking God," Cash says and buries his face in his pillow.

"I'm gonna make this work. For both of you. I swear and promise. And it's Candace's plan, not mine. And she went to college."

"When? In the fucking 1940s?" Cash yells through the pillow.

"I don't know when, but she went for almost a whole year. Emily's Vocational College," Wes says proudly.

"She went to fucking beauty school? How is that helpful?" Cash asks.

"College is college, bro. And you guys came to me, don't forget." Wes smiles and puts his hand up for a high five. It takes every ounce of willpower to raise my hand to meet his. He proceeds to share with us the rest of the plan, part of which calls for me and Cash to be diversions.

"Wes, it's almost three. What time are you meeting Kyle? And what time do we need to leave ourselves?" I ask.

"Oh, I meet Kyle at three-thirty. So I need to leave right now. And you guys, well, you need to have left five minutes ago," he says, as if it's possible for us to leave five minutes ago.

IF THIS WERE A MOVIE ABOUT A JAILBREAK, and you wanted to assemble a crew of people to absolutely ensure that it fails so spectacularly that at least one person dies, everyone gets caught, and probably some shit gets blown up, you would put together a crew including Wes, Wilkinson, Heath, Kyle, and Candace. Like, literally an all-star team of absolute fuck-ups. If there was a draft for a team of idiots that included every single person in Black Forest, they'd be the first five picks. Fuck my life.

Wes dropped me off a half mile from the eastern edge of Echo Mountain. He drove dumb fast to get here and now I'm sprinting the rest of the way to only be ten minutes late. Luckily, there are big pockets of trees that give me cover. I stop on a little rise behind a few boulders. I can see almost all of the Echo Mountain facility. It's disheartening that it takes a place of this size to lock up kids in such a sparsely populated area. Other than the green of the trees and the various colored cars and trucks in the parking lot, the place is devoid of color. Would it kill them to paint a wall yellow? Or blue? Is lead gray really the only acceptable option? They want a color that accurately reflects these kids' futures? The whole place looks like it just gave up. Even the weeds are doing a half-assed job of growing.

It's four-thirteen and I haven't heard from anyone. This plan is already off to a shitty start. I decide to get in position, so I army crawl my way to the edge of the fence. I hide behind the vinyl banner spread across this portion of the fence and pull the canister out of my sweatshirt. It's a squat round container about half the size of a can of soup. The label says *Inferno*. Wes said it's lighter fluid in gel form. He has cases of the stuff. I think it's used to make meth, but I'm not positive. I pop the top and grab a handful and smear it across the back of the banner, which isn't all that easy since I have to contend with the chain-link fence in between. The banner itself is about ten feet long and five feet high. The message is facing the inside of the facility, but I can read it from the back: it says, "Make Good Choices." A little late for that.

The fence itself is about ten feet high and lined with razor wire. Candace assured Wes that the burning sign will be visible from the main building. She also assured Wes there are no cameras out here. I scoop out the final bits of gel and rub it on the sign. Still no word from anyone. We are already fifteen minutes behind schedule, so I decide to move ahead. I squat down, grab my lighter, and touch it to the gel. It only takes seconds for the sign to be engulfed in flames. The heat is so intense, I have to scramble away. Just as I make it back under the cover of trees, my phone buzzes with a new message: *running late, hold*. Fucking Wes. Too late. I write back: *already rolling*. I take another look at the burning banner. Black smoke, that I'm sure is toxic, fills the air. Candace said there are two guards that oversee the laundry pick-up. The banner Cash is supposed to light on fire is not visible from here, so I don't know if it's on fire or not. When Candace sees the smoke, she is supposed to radio the guards. Then, in a perfect world, one guard goes to one fire and one to the other, thus leaving the laundry pick-up unsupervised.

I make my way through the trees to the top of the rise and down the other side. After a quarter mile of pushing through brush and foxtails, I reach the rendezvous point. I hide behind a tree and wait for Cash.

Just when I'm about to freak out because Cash hasn't shown, I hear movement. I squat lower in my hiding place and peek out. Thankfully, it's Cash. I do a lame bird call to get his attention. He chuckles at my attempt and walks over.

"Think it's working?" I ask.

"My shit was sending out a ton of smoke," Cash says, still winded from his run over here.

"Well, we did our part. I'm thinking our odds improved to about two in a million. Let's hope your brother makes it out of there and comes and gets us." My fists are clenched so tight, there are deep indentations in the palms of my hands from my nails.

"I think it's gonna work, man. Right as I headed down the hill, I turned back and saw Wilkinson walking to the van," Cash says and mimics a rimshot on the side of a tree.

"You mean you saw Heath," I say, convincing myself he misspoke.

"No. It was Wilkinson. I saw him clear as day walking to the van, pushing a big cart of laundry bags."

"Wilkinson is supposed to be in a bag inside one of those carts. Heath is supposed to be pushing the cart." Somehow I manage to say this without screaming.

"Oh fuck, you're right. Fuck. Fuck," Cash says anxiously.

"Did he look okay? Was he running or freaking out or anything?"

"Nah, he looked fine. Just strolling along in his orange jumpsuit. I'm thinking maybe he was painting right before or something," Cash says.

"Painting? Why would you say that?" I ask, but I'm thinking *God no, Wilkinson, what did you do?*

"Because he had splashes of red paint on his jumpsuit."

"Right. Right. Like maybe blood red?" I say.

"Ha, no way, dude. Like red paint red. Like, yeah, a bloodish color, but I think too much to be blood."

And just then, our phones buzz. I open the message, squinting because I'm afraid of what it says. It reads: *Dream team. Be there in five.* My body goes cold.

Last night, Wes came up with the idea that if something goes really wrong, he would text *Dream Team* as code. When I asked how wrong, he was like, "I don't know, like if someone dies or something."

And now, although I don't really know, I one-hundred-percent know that Wilkinson fucking killed someone. And most likely that someone is Heath. Because fuck-ups like Wilkinson and Heath don't bury beefs. They just bury the people they have beef with.

ONLY A HANDFUL OF WORDS PASS between me and Cash as we wait for Wes and Wilkinson. What I thought was an unbearable weight of fear and sense of impending doom this morning is nothing compared to how I feel now. It's like I tried to solve the issue of a hornets' nest too near the front door by putting it under my shirt and smashing it against my chest. Not only do we have two dirty cops after us,

I have no doubt that once Wes and Wilkinson get here, we are going to be accessories to murder. I practice deep breathing, and just when my heart rate starts to drop, my phone rings. It's from a restricted number. I show it to Cash.

"Do I answer it?" I ask.

"They're gonna say they want the ledger. The ledger we don't have," he says.

Just when I think I'm gonna let it go to voicemail, I answer.

"A little birdie told me you have something I want," Damon says.

"We might," I say, completely winging it at this point.

"I want you to know, Jack, that I am not a patient man. It is taking every ounce of restraint for me not to destroy everything that means anything to you. My toe has turned black in parts. It's so swollen that the skin is bursting. I can feel the heat coming off it, and I can't get it fucking clean!" he screams so loud that I have to move the phone away from my ear.

"You know why your toe is all fucked up, don't you?" I ask.

"Because you smashed it with a goddamn crowbar," he spits.

"That, but mainly because you abduct girls. And you kill DEA agents. You brought this on yourself," I say. I'm not sure where the resolve is coming from. I guess I've finally reached my breaking point.

"Give. Me. The. Fucking. Ledger," he says in a whisper.

"Tomorrow afternoon is the soonest we can get it to you," I say, looking at Cash. He just shrugs.

"That doesn't work for me, Jack. Which means it doesn't work for your mom."

"You do a single fucking thing to my mom and you will never

see this ledger again. The cartel might. And maybe the press, but not you."

"Where is it, Jack?"

"Don't worry about that. We'll give it to you tomorrow. You turn over Wheels and we give you the ledger," I say.

"Okay, Jack, I'll give you until tomorrow. But if that ledger is not in my hand by then, I'm going to pop your eyeball out and I'm gonna fuck your bloody—"

I end the call. It takes a second because my hand is shaking so bad. Cash doesn't have to ask what he said, because at the end, he was screaming and Cash could hear it clear as day.

"No way that psycho is going to trade the ledger for Wheels. No way is he going to let us walk," Cash says and looks like he wants me to convince him otherwise.

"I think you're right," I say and reposition myself because crouching behind this rock is starting to kill my back. "I think he's gonna go after everyone that has anything to do with this."

"Think they'll at least leave us alone until tomorrow?" Cash asks and takes a quick peek around the tree to see if Wes and Wilkinson are coming. Not yet.

"I think they might leave my mom and Wes and everyone else alone, but I bet they'll be searching high and low for us. We just have to make sure they don't find us before we get the ledger."

A squirrel, one of the big black ones, comes tearing across the ground, sees us, stops, and then takes off the other way. Smart move, man; we'll just end up getting you killed. We hear a vehicle approaching. It's the delivery van. It stops and Wes and Wilkinson pile out. Wes' face is so white, it looks like he's wearing stage makeup. Wilkinson looks like he always looks. Not a care in the world, just puffing away on a cigarette. We come out from our hiding place and approach them.

"Cash City Rocker. Thanks for the jailbreak," Wilkinson says and gives Cash a big hug.

"Hey, man, glad you're out," Cash says unenthusiastically.

Although Wilkinson's clothes are dirty as sin, they are not bloody. But I know better than to get my hopes up. Wilkinson can see my fear mixed with fury and only gives me a slight head nod.

"So what the fuck?" I ask.

All Wes can do is shake his head. Wilkinson grins, like the cat that ate the canary.

"Seriously, what the fuck?" I ask again.

"I had to, Jacko," Wilkinson says, his eyes emotionless. Anger or hatred would be less disturbing. It's like looking into the eyes of a dead person.

"Had to...what?" Cash asks, as if he's supplying the "who's there?" part of a knock-knock joke.

"Self-defense, bro. He just couldn't get over it. I fucked his little sister. That's true. Sue me. And yes, I fucked his girlfriend. It was on the same day and it was in his house. Yes, in his bed. Fine, yeah, it was also his fucking birthday. I get it. Kind of fucked up. But how's it my fault his girlfriend lets him finger her after I came in her?" He looks around for support. "How is that *my* fault?"

I just really can't. I mean, how? It's like I went to school for this shit. How, without putting in serious effort, is it possible to get into situations as fucked up as these?

"Dude, can you just tell us what happened? Please," I beg.

"Well, of course I can, your Jackness. Candace filled me in on the plan, right? So I'm showing up at the laundry this afternoon.

There's been a keep-separate order between me and Heath Bar since I've been in there, but I'm like, okay, he must be cool with me now. Why else would he be part of the deal, you know? So I walk in and I'm like 'Pencil-cuck, what's up?' And…"

"Pencil-cuck?" Cash asks.

"Yeah, dude. Like he stabbed that kid with a pencil and he's a cuckold."

Wes, Cash, and I shake our heads at the same time.

"Well, fuck man. What am I supposed to call him? And then he gets super mad. And I'm like, 'What, fucking cum fingers, what?' Anyway, I guess things weren't so cool between us after all, because he comes at me, bro. He's like, 'I'mma fuck you up, put you in one of those bags, then give the guards a little ring ding ding when Wes tries to drive you on out of here. Two birds and shit.'"

I have no idea why I thought a bunch of super dumb people that fucked each other's girlfriends and boyfriends and fucking hated each other would work together, even if it's in their own best interest. Well, now that I think about it, I guess none of this was in the best interest of Heath. Lesson learned.

"So…" I say. It comes out sounding bored, but really it's just like, fuck.

"So he comes at me with a pencil. You fucking serious, bro? Like dude, get over the fucking pencils already. We're old now. I'm backing up, though, 'cause that fucker can sharpen a pencil. I back into a table next to the washers, and my hand hits an open container of some liquid shit. I grab it and throw it at his face. And I guess it was bleach, 'cause he's like, 'My eyes! It burns!' And I'm all feeling like the Taliban and shit. He drops the pencil and rushes to the sink to start flushing his eyes or whatever. I pick up the pencil and I see the back of his fat arm, you know, just under his shirt."

"No," I say.

"Yes. And I'm like, 'This is for Kyle,' and I fucking pierced the back of his arm, bro. Boom. Fucking jabbed that shit. Fucking laughing so hard. 'For Kyle, bro. For Kyle.'"

Then he stops, partly because he's laughing too hard to continue, and partly because he wants to light another cigarette.

"And then?" I ask.

He gets his cigarette lit and says, "That was it, man. The bleach was self-defense. The pencil in his arm, well, I just couldn't pass that up. All of you would have done the same," he looks around for confirmation. He gets three shaking heads.

"Anyway, I'm like, fuck. Heath Bar here has a hole in his arm and some super fucked-up eyes. I'm in the fucking laundry where I'm not supposed to be. And I know my boy Wes is about to roll up any moment. I try talking to him. I'm like, 'Bro, sorry I fucked your girlfriend.' He paused for a second, you know? And I'm like, *hey, maybe there is something to this talking shit.* So then I'm like, 'Dude, really sorry I fucked your sister.' And well, that was the mistake right there. Guess he didn't know about that. Pencil boy comes at me again. I'm like, *learn your lesson, bro.* I'm thinking he can't see a fucking thing at this point, so I'm not that worried—it's like a toddler is after me, right? But I guess he was up to some trickery because he came at me fast, and it was clear he could see just fine. He was washing his eyes, sure, but what he really wanted were those giant fucking scissors in the sink. Like, dudes, I didn't know they made scissors that big. He misses me by a millimeter, that cuck fuck does. I could have died. So I grab this big-ass industrial clothes iron off the table by the cord. And I swing that shit like a lasso. He keeps walking and the iron comes around and smacks him square in the side of the head. And check this out, like it was fucking choreographed, he falls back, and this beautiful arc of blood, like a red rainbow, shoots up out of his head. And as he falls back, he lands in the fucking laundry cart, on top of a bunch of bags of laundry, and every fucking drop of blood from that majestic arc lands right in the basket too. Tell me that shit wasn't meant to be?"

"He died from you hitting him in the head with the iron?" Cash asks.

"Even tried CPR, well the chest-pump part. That's how I got all bloody. I mean, the kid didn't deserve to live, but, well, he didn't deserve to die either," he says, unaware of the contradiction.

"Umm, why's he got that pencil sticking out of him though?" Wes asks.

"Well, that's kind of another part of the story," Wilkinson says and pops into a squat position like he's excited to tell us.

"Fuck, man," Cash says and walks off shaking his head.

"I'm not a doctor, right? Checking a pulse, like you need some kind of degree to do that shit. So well, I was like, if I stick a pencil in him, if he's alive, he's gonna wake up."

"No, you didn't," I say this, and at the same time, I know that he did.

Wilkinson nods and says, "He didn't wake up. Fucking self-defense though, bro! I mean, not the pencil parts, and I may have thrown in one more 'for Kyle' at the end there, but I kind of whispered it. Anyway, bro was trying to kill me. How the fuck do they allow those scissors in Echo Mountain anyway? We get those rounded ones in group. Like the ones little kids use."

This is so fucked. I can barely contain the fear and frustration rushing through my body. I didn't ask for these fucking cops to try and kill us. I didn't ask for Reed to sell us out and say we had the ledger, whatever the fuck the ledger is. I didn't ask for psycho Wilkinson to kill psycho Heath. And it's like the more I try to dig out of this, the deeper the hole gets. Now we have a dead kid? I don't care that he's mostly a piece of shit, I don't want him dead. I sure as shit don't want to have played a part in his death. Heath's a severely fucked-up kid, but I guarantee his parents did their part in making him that way. And Wilkinson killed him, which means we killed him. This kid we go to school with named Andrew Parker has an older brother who was the getaway driver for what he thought was a burglary. The kid was seventeen years old. It was a dry cleaner's, I think. He was like three blocks away, waiting in the car. Turns out the dry cleaner's wasn't empty and one of the guys ended up shooting and killing the owner. Gordon's brother had no idea he even had a gun. Too bad. He got life. The kid's still in there. Breaking someone out of juvy and having someone killed in the process has to be a million times worse than being the getaway driver. We turn ourselves in and what? We get killed because Damon and Buck don't want us talking. And they kill Casey's dad because he can't find the ledger? And maybe they kill my mom, and Wes, and Hailey's family, and Kelly's fucking dog? As fucked as it is, the only way out seems to be going deeper in.

"No one's gonna know," Wilkinson says and starts doing jumping jacks for some unknown reason.

"Literally everyone is going to know," Cash says in disbelief. "No one's *not* gonna know."

"No one's gonna know he's dead. They'll think he escaped along with me; we just have to disappear the body," Wilkinson says, and it's kind of hard to understand him now because he's out of breath from his calisthenics.

"Disappear the body? Oh my God." I can't believe we're in this situation. Wilkinson can't not stab people, I guess. Another lesson learned.

"I know where to do it. No one will ever find him. I've been disposing of cats and dogs up there for years." Now he's doing one-handed push-ups with his other hand behind his back. This kid is too fucked up for words. I don't even know what to say, so I take a seat on the ground. Cash is not handling this any better; he's pacing around in circles and, for some reason, counting on his fingers. Wes looks at the back of the van and then walks closer to us—he actually seems to be fine.

"I'll drive you," Wes says to Wilkinson.

"Now we're talking. You guys need the ledger. We got to deal with Heath first," Wilkinson says. I just marvel at the fact that he can talk about getting rid of a dead body the same way he'd talk about eating a sandwich.

"Wes, no..." Cash manages, but it's not terribly convincing.

"Yes. When I talked to Candace on the way to Echo Mountain this morning, she was having second thoughts. She was afraid Heath wasn't going to play nice. I told her it would be fine. I wanted it to work so bad. It's my fault and I want to help make it right," Wes says. His eyes well up. Fuck, how many times can I make Wes almost cry in a day?

"It's not your fault, Wes. You were just trying to help. We appreciate it, man, you didn't ask for this," I say.

"Thanks for being there for us," Cash says and walks over and hugs his brother. And not like a side hug, but an actual hug. A sob escapes Wes, and when they separate, they both wipe at their eyes.

"We'll drop you two at your car," Wes says, looking at Cash and me, "and then Wilkinson and I will drive to wherever this fucked-up pet cemetery is and deal with Heath."

Wes and Cash share a look of gratitude toward each other.

"Fuck, okay. I don't know what else to do," I say and stare daggers at Wilkinson.

"Don't look at me, bro. How is a single part of this my fault?" Wilkinson asks, genuinely.

"And then you get us the ledger, right?" I say to Wilkinson with more menace in my voice than I intend.

"Shit yeah. It's about an hour hike from the burial grounds. I'll head out after we're done with Heath. I'll swing by your house tonight, Cash, and then I'mma bounce. Probably gonna have a few piggies after me."

THE LAUNDRY VAN SMELLS LIKE BLOOD, SO
I do my best to breathe out of my mouth. We're less than
a mile from where we parked Hailey's car. The van has
two seats up front, and the rest of it is wide open to make as much
room as possible for the laundry carts. The cart that has Heath
in it is splashed with a fair amount of blood. Heath is lying on
his back on top of several bags of laundry. A sheet is spread over

him, and the pencil sticking out of his chest creates a tent effect. Wes drives over a bump, I stumble and grab one of the carts, and find myself staring directly at Heath's body. This time, though, the pencil is gone. I guess Wilkinson didn't stab him as hard as he thought. I turn away from Heath and look out the windshield. We are on a narrow service road that, until now, I didn't know existed. It looks like it hasn't been serviced itself since the day it was built. The left side of the road is bordered by a three-foot-high cut in the forest. The right side drops into a steep ravine that ends about thirty feet below. Thank God it's not raining. I want to look back and check on the missing pencil, but I also don't.

Eventually, I can't take it anymore and I turn around. The sheet on top of Heath has moved, and I can see part of his arm, thankfully not the part Wilkinson stabbed. It shouldn't be surprising that he's moved with the way the van has been bouncing around, but it gives me the creeps. Before I can turn away, we hit another bump and Heath's arm shoots straight into the air. My heart skips a beat. I can't wait to get out of here. The moment I convince myself his arm movement was solely because of the bump, Heath sits bolt upright. The sheet is still covering him, so he looks like a ghost. Maybe he is. He turns his head left and right under the covering. I can't make a sound. I reach to tap Cash on the shoulder, but before I can, Heath starts screaming.

"You fucked my sister!" he shrieks. In response to Heath's scream, Cash, Wes, and I scream as well. Only Wilkinson remains unfazed. Wes, who's not paying attention to the road, jerks the wheel to the right, heading us straight for the ravine. I dive for the wheel to try and straighten us out.

Heath screams again, "Where's my pencil!?"

Thankfully, Wes realizes we are headed off the road and

yanks the wheel back left. But he overcorrects, and now we are fishtailing. Cash is holding on to a laundry cart for dear life. I fall to my knees, skid across the floor, and look out the front window just in time to see us go over the edge. The van flips as we tumble down the embankment.

The next thing I know, the van is still and I'm lying on the roof, which is now the floor since the van is upside down.

Wilkinson was the only person wearing his seatbelt, believe it or not, and he seems totally fine. He's hanging upside down, still buckled in, minding his own business. Wes groans while he massages his wrist. He has a few scratches on his face and arms but seems to be okay. Cash peeks his head out from under a laundry cart. He's dazed, and I'm not sure he knows where he is. Lucky him. I fared pretty well myself. I landed on top of a bag of laundry, and that must have cushioned my fall. My head hurts, though, and when I touch the back of it, I feel a knot the size of an egg. I pull my hand away—thankfully, there's no blood. I'm not sure why it takes me so long to think about Heath, but when I do, I see the cart he was in is on its side and pinned against the wall of the van.

"I guess I should have checked his pulse," Wilkinson says, still hanging upside down.

"What the fuck?" Wes mumbles. "Everyone okay?"

We agree that, for the most part, we are. Miraculously. There's still no movement from the cart Heath was in. The back door is ajar, and I vaguely remember it flying open as we flipped.

"Where's Heath?" Cash asks.

I put a finger to my mouth—*Shhh*—and point to the laundry cart on its side. Wilkinson decides it's time to stop hanging upside down and releases his seatbelt. As he falls, he spins over and lands perfectly on all fours. Like a cat.

"Heath in there?" he asks, pointing at the cart and rubbing his shoulder. I nod.

Wilkinson crawls to the cart. He grabs the edge, pulls with all his might, and yells, "Boo!" The cart skids across the roof, which is still the floor, but no Heath. I search the van in desperation, throwing dirty laundry everywhere. I've just finished looking in every possible place Heath could be, when we hear from outside the van, "You fucked my sister!"

We look through the back doors and see a white object streak across our field of vision.

"The fuck?" Wes asks. I scramble over the laundry, push the cart out of my way, and climb out the back. Cash is right beside me. Wes and Wilkinson join us. Heath is running down the ravine, covered in a blood-stained white sheet, his hands outstretched in front of him. He makes it a good fifteen yards before he trips over a fallen tree. He shakes his head underneath the sheet, then gets up and starts running again. The sheet covers every bit of his body, like it's his skin. The ravine bends left after about twenty-five yards. We watch Heath run, stumble, run, stumble, and yell until he disappears around the curve.

"See, nothing to worry about, Jacky. Old Heath Bar is fine," Wilkinson says while staring at something on the ground a few feet away. He walks over and grabs it. It takes me a minute to figure out what it is—the yellow color gives it away. It's the pencil that Wilkinson buried in Heath. Wilkinson hoists it above his head like a trophy. The tip still razor sharp, and there are streaks of blood on the sides. He places it behind his ear.

"Finders, keepers," he says.

"Motherfucker," I say, and now that the fear of Heath turning ghost on us is ebbing, the relief that he is not dead, and that I am not a murderer by association, floods through my body. "Dude just popped up and ran off. And Wes, fuck. That van flipped like five times." We are all giddy.

"Not only did we survive that.... Literally it took some kind of car crash to make Heath undead," Wes says. I don't correct him by pointing out that Heath becoming undead is actually what caused the crash.

"Wes, that van is all fucked up," Cash says. I follow his gaze to the van. It is indeed all fucked up—smashed windows, dents all over. That thing is done.

"Yeah, I think Kyle's gonna have some explaining to do," Wes says. I can't help but laugh.

Wilkinson pulls a plastic bag out of his pocket. It's filled with what looks like chunky yellow flour. He digs his fingers in, grabs a handful, and shoves it in his mouth. He feels my stare and turns.

"Cornbread, bro. Took it from Heath," and he continues to help himself to a couple more handfuls. "So it's been pretty sweet, guys, but I'm gonna head on out. Got a hike ahead of me," and Wilkinson starts walking away.

"You're gonna go straight from here to get the ledger?" Cash asks.

"Yep. No more Heath to bury, so might as well get on with it." He stops and looks at me. "Jack, I think you'll be glad to know that I learned a valuable lesson today." He looks earnest as he says it.

"Oh yeah, what was that?" I ask.

"You fuck a guy's sister, it's best not to tell him about it."

"Well, that's something," I say, marveling at the human being that is Wilkinson. "Bring the ledger by Cash's tonight. We'll be in the attic above the garage," I say.

"Toodle-oo," he yells back as he walks down the ravine in the opposite direction of Heath.

On the walk back to Hailey's car, we came up with a plan that I think might keep Cash and me out of juvie and Wes out of jail. Before we left, I got a text from my mom saying she wants to have dinner tonight. She also shared a true crime tidbit about how some killer tossed the latex gloves he was wearing in a trash can a couple of blocks away from the crime. The cops found them and were able to pull his prints off the *inside* of the glove. It made me think of the overwhelming number of surfaces we touched inside the van—not just the door handles, but the roof and the walls, as we flipped over and over. I suggested we do our best to wipe it clean. It took us a good forty-five minutes, and I'm sure we missed a ton of spots. We also filled a laundry bag with the bloody rags from the cart Heath was in. Wes is going to dispose of it in a dumpster somewhere. After we made it to Hailey's car, we dropped Wes off at his car. He said he'd wait there for Kyle.

Candace actually came up with most of the plan. She's a devious one. She told us they haven't done checks yet, so they don't even know Heath and Wilkinson are missing. Candace said they are terribly understaffed and underfunded there. Wes is going to drive Kyle back to Echo Mountain, and Candace is going to sneak Kyle into the laundry room, tie him up, and lock him in a utility closet. When they do the next inmate count for the day and notice Wilkinson and Heath missing, they'll lock the place down and do a search. They'll find Kyle, and he'll tell them a story about how he was overpowered by Heath. We decided we could leave Wilkinson out of it, make it a little more confusing for them to figure out. Candace swears it'll work. She also said everyone that works there is going to be elated that those two are gone. She doesn't think they are going to dig too hard for the truth. I hope that's the case. I'm cautiously optimistic, but even if it goes south, at this point, getting busted for breaking someone out of juvie sounds like a treat compared to being charged with murder.

WE'VE BEEN LYING LOW IN CASH'S attic for about an hour. The thrill of not being an accessory to murder has been replaced by the fear of our overall situation. It was nice while it lasted. The fact that it's about a million degrees up here, doesn't help anything. We found an old box fan in the garage and it's on high, but it does little more than push around hot air. I've been messaging with Hailey and I filled her in on the whole shit show. Most of her responses have consisted solely of exploding head emojis. I'm still supposed to meet my mom for dinner, so I hope Wilkinson shows up before I have to leave. Hailey has been messaging with her family from her sister's lacrosse tournament. I can't imagine how much all of that travel costs. Hailey would probably die if she had to spend that much time with her parents, but at the same time, I know it bums her out how involved they are in her sister's sport. Both of her parents played lacrosse growing up. Her mom has turned supporting her sister's sport into a full-time job. She carpools all the kids to practice, runs the booster club to raise money, and holds some kind of volunteer position with the club. Whatever it is her dad does for work, he can do it from anywhere, so pretty much all summer, they travel with her sister to different tournaments across the country. Hailey used to have to go with them. Hailey is easy and doesn't get in trouble—well, didn't used to get in trouble—and her parents just expect she's gonna be okay, which leads to her being ignored. I message her that I'm gonna try and take a nap. It takes me all of five seconds to fall asleep. I wake drenched in sweat, disoriented, and far from refreshed.

"Dude, you awake?" I ask the mound on the floor that is Cash.

"No," he says and sits up. He's got more color to him, but he doesn't look great.

"You look like you have leukemia, bro," I say.

"Fuck you, man," he says and lays back down.

"I look like I lift?" I ask, thinking back to Cock Mike's comment. I pull up my sleeve and flex my bicep.

"Absolutely not."

"God damnit. Fucking Cock Mike."

"Yeah, he's said that same shit to me. His muscles didn't help much the other night though, did they?" Cash asks with an exaggerated smile.

"No they did not. Who's the pussy now?" I say and laugh.

"What time you think Wilkinson's gonna be here?" I ask and drop to the floor to knock out some pushups.

"Fuck if I know, I just hope he remembers to show. Or remembers where he was headed and what he was supposed to do when he got there," Cash says.

I look at my phone and it says 6:30. I'm supposed to meet my mom at seven.

"I'm gonna roll. Hopefully I'll be back before Wilkinson gets here."

"Yes sir. I told Kelly by the way," Cash says.

"I figured. I told Hailey. How stoked is she you aren't a murderer?" I ask.

"Almost as stoked as she was when she found out she wasn't a cop killer," he says as he rolls up his sleeping bag.

"How insane is it that what happened today is only like the fourth craziest thing that's happened in the last week," I say shaking my head.

"I'm wondering if it'll even make the top ten before this thing's over."

I meet my mom at a Chinese restaurant that is a twenty-minute walk from Cash's just before 7 p.m. I suggested it since I'm still trying to keep her away from the apartment. The fact that she doesn't work overnights anymore has done wonders for her. She looks ten years younger. She's dressed in a comfortable-looking exercise outfit and I can see her arms are starting to look toned. Does everyone have stronger arms than me? Fuck Cock Mike. We talk about nothing of consequence while we eat. I never consider bringing my mom in on what's happening. She's just not a resource in that way. She must notice that mentally I am somewhere else and says, "You thinking about the board game?"

For a moment I have no idea what she's talking about. And then I remember I told her we were having a board game marathon at the house. Oops.

"No, but yeah," I stammer, "I mean, it's been fun."

"I'm glad."

My mom reaches over and sets her hand on my shoulder. Mom is not a toucher, never has been. Maybe when I was a baby. Anyway, it feels nice. I put my hand on hers and hold it there until eating one-handed gets too hard and I pull away.

After dinner I walked back to Cash's and have been here for exactly thirty-eight minutes. I'm finding it impossible not to check the time on my phone every thirty seconds. Where in the fuck is Wilkinson? Wes called Cash from Candace's before I arrived. He told him that the people at Echo Mountain bought the story Candace concocted. They found Kyle tied up and asked him about Wilkinson. He said he only saw Heath.

I message Hailey that we're still waiting for Wilkinson

to return with the ledger. She's as anxious as I am. Cash and I throw a tennis ball back and forth. The rule is we can only throw and catch with our non-dominant hands. We make it to forty-three before I drop it and we start over. We're approaching our record of consecutive catches when we hear a knock at the trapdoor leading to the attic. No doubt Wilkinson has had the cops pounding on his door on a number of occasions, so he gives it a nice quiet tap. It's appreciated.

Wilkinson must have stopped off in the house before heading up here, because he has Wes' giant bong already loaded. He always looks unwell, but right now he looks barely alive. He takes a seat on the floor and lights up. He cashes the bowl in one hit. He holds it in for an impossibly long time and blows out an awesome amount of smoke.

When the last bit of smoke exits his lungs he says, "I remember when I was fifteen, I was like *I'm gonna fuck two chicks in the same day.* Teachers and counselors and shit were always like, you gotta set goals. So I set one. Kid you not it wasn't a week later when I fucked Amy Collins after school inside that giant tractor wheel on the playground of the elementary school across the street from our school. You know, the one that always smelled like piss? And then that night, I went to Kristen Irwin's and fucked her in her mom's closet."

Even with the insanity of everything going on, and the fact that this conversation has nothing to do with anything, Cash and I find the second part of Wilkinson's statement so hard to believe that, at the same time, we both say, "Bullshit."

"No way you fucked Kristen Irwin," I say, probably sounding jealous. I mean, Amy, sure, I can believe that. But Kristen? She is like a goddess among mortals. And then I realize, who fucking cares.

"I did fucking too. And her clit was the size of my thumb."

"No way," Cash says vehemently, "but also what the fuck does that have to do with anything?"

"Jeez. Nothing, man, just thought, you know, we're friends. Friends share stuff. I learned that in group," he says and casts his eyes to the ground. Before this moment, I didn't think Wilkinson had feelings. I'm still not fully convinced that he does, but maybe.

"Sorry, man, you're right. Thanks for sharing. We're just a little keyed up here. You know, sitting in this hot-ass attic, terrified that you weren't going to be able to find the ledger," I say in an attempt at amends.

"I understand," he replies, then leans back on his elbows and closes his eyes.

"You okay, man?" Cash asks.

"I don't feel so great, Cash. I think there was something wrong with that cornbread. Also, I drank a bunch of stream water. And, well, my stomach wasn't feeling so great out there looking for the ledger..." Then he lies on his side and curls into a fetal position.

I look at Cash, concerned. Wilkinson didn't say he doesn't have the ledger, but he also didn't say that he does.

"You found it, right?" I ask, trying to keep my panic at bay.

"So I'm so sick up there on the mountain, I'm kind of

delirious. I finally find the place, the hiding place, and..."
Wilkinson covers his eyes with his hands and stops talking.

"And, what?" Cash asks.

"Well, I hid a bunch of acid up there too. And I was like, I know this is just paper, but maybe it'll soak up some of that stream water in my stomach. So I snacked on some. And then I fell asleep," he says, and I wait for him to finish, but I think he is finished.

"And you woke up and found the ledger?" I ask. At this point, I'm not doing a great job of keeping the frustration out of my voice. It's always something with this guy, never a straight line from here to there.

"When I woke, I was tripping balls. Still am, of course. And well, right before I got locked up I was at my mom's—" he says, but I can't take it anymore.

"Dude, before you tell us some long-ass story, we need to know whether or not you have the ledger," I almost yell at him.

"Bro, it's not about the ledger," he says, exasperated.

"Hey, Wilkinson, I get it. For one second though, let's pretend it is about the ledger. Do you have it?" Cash asks in a remarkably calm voice.

It works and Wilkinson says, "Bro, I got the ledger. Okay?" He sits up and looks around. His pupils are gigantic.

"So I'm at my mom's. I'm digging through boxes looking for my old comic book collection so I can sell it. I come across this old DVD. It's called *Pregnant and Filled 7*. It's got this woman on the front. She's legit pregnant. She's got a dick in her mouth and looks like two more in her other holes. Like literally filled. Hence the title. I see her face, man, and it looks just like my mom. I mean not exactly, but yeah, basically," he pauses and stares into space.

I look at Cash, like I often do when dealing with Wilkinson. He rolls his eyes. I decide to let Wilkinson get to the ledger when he's ready. At least we know he has it.

"And then I look really close at her stomach. And I see a handprint. But you know, like coming from the inside. The impression of a baby's hand pushing out from the stomach. It was unreal. And then fucking right under it is my stamp collection. I forgot about the DVD and put the box back. Then, you know, I'm tripping balls on the mountain and it all became clear, you know?" He looks at us.

"Um, no, not clear, not clear at all," I say.

"On my way down the mountain I call my mom. I ask her about the DVD and she breaks down. She just starts crying and she tells me the whole story. She's not my fucking mom, bro, she's my aunt. My fucking aunt, bro. My mom is the woman on the cover of the movie. And guess what?"

"That little handprint is yours," Cash says. How he made that connection I have no idea.

"That little handprint is mine," he says and closes his eyes.

"Whoa, that's heavy," I say.

"The heaviest, Jack. She lives in Cali, brah—my real mom does. So I'm heading west, that's why I had to get out of juvie."

As long as Wilkinson gives us the ledger, as far as I'm concerned the farther he is away from here, the better. Weird story, but I could give two fucks at this point—give us the book and take your tripping ass on out of here.

"I always knew I was meant for LA," Wilkinson says. He reaches in the back of his waistband and pulls out a notebook. It's weathered, but is still in decent shape. It's brown and is made of normal-sized paper. Printed in bold type across the front, I shit you not, it says *The Ledger*. He passes it to Cash. Cash flips through it.

"Definitely in some kind of code," he says.

"It's been swell, boys. I'm gonna get on the road before I start peaking."

"I hope you find your actual mom out there," I say.

"That means a lot, Jack," Wilkinson says.

"Yeah, good luck," Cash says.

"Luck is for pussies, if anyone should know that, it's you two," he says, in a not unkind way, and then he turns and climbs down the trapdoor.

"How did that guy get made?" I ask Cash.

"I don't know, but he sure as fuck came through for us," Cash says, turning the pages of the notebook.

He's right. Maybe fucked-up situations call for fucked-up people. I know that was the case last summer. All of that said, I'm glad to be done with Wilkinson. We have the ledger and we aren't accessories to murder. Doesn't even seem like we'll end up being wanted for breaking him out of juvie. All in all, a pretty good day.

THE FIRST THING WE DID WHEN WE GOT TO Hailey's was double check that all of the doors were locked and the alarms were set. We devised escape routes in case Damon and Buck showed up. Cash is busy trying to decipher whatever code the ledger is written in. Casey has been hovering over his shoulder the whole time. He's so deep in it, he hasn't even noticed.

"Crack it yet?" I ask Cash jokingly. He has the ledger in front of him, his phone to one side and a notebook he's been using to take notes on the other. He'll look at the ledger, then search something on his phone, and then write down a bunch of random shit in the other notebook. And then he'll do it all again.

"It's a bunch of nonsense," Casey answers for him.

"I don't know what it is yet, but I know a bunch of things it's not," Cash says.

"Gee that's great," Casey says and sits with an audible hmph.

"This'll take time, but I don't think it's all that sophisticated," Cash says.

"Why don't we just give it to them now? Trade it for Reed. Who cares what the fuck it says?" Casey asks.

"We've already agreed to make the trade tomorrow. And I think the more we know the better," I say.

"That's because they don't have your dad," Casey says.

I let the comment slide. I know that trading the ledger for Reed tonight, when we don't have a plan, isn't the smart move.

"The more we know, the better chance we have of walking away from this."

"You walking away, or Reed walking away?" she asks.

"All of us walking away," Cash says.

"All they want is the ledger. Give them the ledger and they give us Reed," she says, but I don't think she fully believes it.

"They kidnapped you. They know, that we know, that they killed the DEA agent. They admitted to you they killed your mom. Buck, well, Buck... Do you think they are just gonna let us go?" I say as kind as I can, but it's not kind enough, because Casey starts crying.

"You're gonna let him die," she says through her tears.

"We are not going to let him die," Kelly says.

"Well why the fuck wouldn't you? What's he to you?" Casey asks. Not in an accusatory way, but like she really doesn't understand. She's so used to feeling alone in this world, she can't fathom it being different.

"Well, because we're not. Because he's your dad," Hailey says.

"You're gonna get bored and need to deal with your horses or fly somewhere or some shit," Casey says to Hailey.

"Whoa, man. Easy," I say.

"No it's fine, Jack. Casey, you don't know me, I get it. But we are all in this together. None of us are going anywhere. Cause if we do that, then someone dies. And that's not gonna happen."

"We'll see," Casey says. She sounds like a child when she says it. Gone is the tough, smart-ass. What remains is a little girl that is struggling to believe she's not on her own on this.

Cash's eyes are buried in the ledger. He used to get this way when he'd work on the math puzzles his teacher would give him. One time, we were hanging out in his room, and he started working on one. I sat there for what felt like an hour and then got bored. I walked to Kum Quick, got a Slushee Dream, came back and he was still doing it. Then I watched a movie on my phone. A whole movie. He was still in it when I was done. My mom texted me that she wanted to pick me up and take me to dinner. We went out to dinner, she took me home, I showered, changed clothes, and then she dropped me off at Cash's. He was still doing the same fucking problem. He hadn't moved. The blank notebook he started with was almost full with notes. He didn't even know I left. He worked on that one problem, without moving, for almost eight hours.

I feel Casey staring at me.

"What?"

"You have to get my dad. You have to save him," she says.

"I mean, yeah, of course—"

She cuts me off, "No, you fucking have to. I cannot lose him. If that psychopath reaches out, you give him what he wants. Okay?"

"Absolutely."

She takes a deep breath, a slow blink, and says, "Jack, no fucking scheming. No plotting. No stupid mousetrap plan. I want my dad back. Give them what they want or I will."

And she turns and walks away. I feel like the enemy all of a sudden. Like it's my fault her dad got caught up in this shit. I want to yell back, *Hey, I'm just trying to keep my fucking eyeballs in my head*. But I don't. I let her go.

DUDE, WAKE THE FUCK UP, I FIGURED IT OUT."

I open my eyes to Cash towering over me. It takes me a moment to get oriented. I'm in Hailey's bed. She's still sound asleep. Cash heads towards the door, stops, and looks back to make sure I'm following.

"Fine, fine, I'm coming." I hop out of bed and get dressed.

I barely hear him say, "That's what she said," as he barrels down the stairs. I look at my phone; it's not even six a.m.

I grab my shoes and slip them on as I walk across Hailey's room. I turn back and look at her. I want to jump back in bed, hold her, and not let go. I want to tell her just how fucking scared I am. But I follow Cash instead.

I find him in the kitchen. He must have moved here at some point last night. He's sitting at the counter with five empty energy drink cans next to him.

"Dude, did you even sleep?" I ask.

"Let me show you this," he ignores my question, flips the ledger and his notebook back to the first pages.

"It's a pretty simple code all in all. People are fucking stupid. It would be so much easier to do this online somewhere and write it in normal fucking language and then encrypt. Dude's probably old though, so..."

"Dude's also dead, so..."

"That too."

"What's it say?" I ask and walk to the coffee maker and hit the button.

"It's account numbers, accounts, and amounts of something, I'm assuming cocaine or heroin, meth maybe. Look here, see this line of numbers? Five digits," and he points to a line midway down the open page on the ledger, "that's an account. I'm guessing for a person, a gang, a dealer, whatever. This line here? This one is three digits. Some of this type have two digits, some have three and some have five. I think this is the amount of drugs. Then this number here. That's the price. That's what is owed them. I can follow these numbers all through the ledger. In here, there are thirty-seven accounts. And all the money, from these thirty-seven accounts, eventually makes its way into five bank accounts," Cash looks up smiling. Not like check me out, I did a good thing, he's just genuinely happy he figured it out.

"Whoa, you got all that from these random numbers?" I ask.

"Yeah, but there's more. Like that part is interesting, but not all that helpful. You see this page?" he asks and points at a page near the end.

"Yeah." It looks like all the other pages, except there's some writing in Spanish at the bottom.

"This page has all of the account numbers. And not only that, in the same fucking code, corresponding to each one, is a seventeen-digit alphanumeric password. This one page has all the account numbers and passcodes for all the accounts. All of it on one fucking page."

"That's dumb, right?"

"So fucking dumb. Check this out," and he points to the bottom of the page where it says, "donde esta la vaca."

"Where is the... wait, I know," but Cash doesn't wait.

"Where is the cow."

"Right, where is the cow. I don't know.."

"Well if you take this through a different decoder thing I came up with and rearrange the letters it says Vericontinental."

"Is that the digital currency Vericontinental that Kelly uses?" I ask.

"The very one. She uses it to buy sneakers from Russia,

or China or wherever, and she might be one of the few people that uses it legitimately. Most people use it to buy shit on the Dark Web."

"So you think these accounts are all on Vericontinental?" I ask.

"I know they are. I woke up Kelly and she walked me through it. She logged in to each and every one of them. Between the fifteen accounts, guess how much money?"

"I don't know. Sixty grand."

Cash laughs and says, "Twenty-seven million dollars. Can you fucking believe that?"

My heart flips. We have a ledger that leads to $27 million in cartel money. There is nothing safe about that.

"Can they tell you logged in there? And why didn't they change the passwords?"

"I look new to you? Of course they can't. I used VPNs and relays and all that shit. And they didn't change the passwords, I think, because the guy who would know how to reset them, would a) need this ledger and b) would need to be alive. I think the only place any of that info exists is right here in this notebook. They must not even know the email or phone he used to sign up, otherwise they would have reset the passwords. They aren't worried about someone finding this ledger and using it as evidence in a case against them, they want this ledger back because they can't get their twenty-seven million dollars without it."

"Oh fuck. This is terrifying," I say as a chill runs through my body.

"Yeah it is. I'm not sure how big of a deal twenty-seven million dollars is to a cartel at the end of the day, but I guess big enough. Another interesting part of this is what the rest of the text says. I won't bore you with the translation, decoding, etcetera. But what looks like random sentences is actually another account number and another passcode at a different digital bank."

"And that means?"

"I think the guy thought he was being clever by leaving the final digit off the passcode. But since all the other passcodes had the same total numbers and letters, it was pretty easy to spot. And at the end of the day, there aren't that many letters, numbers, and special characters. I was able to get a list and it only took me forty-three tries to come up with the right passcode. So I get in and there is 1.5 million in there."

"I mean that's a lot, but why's this account different?" I ask confused.

"I think the guy who kept the ledger was stealing from the fucking cartel. I think he did a lot of rounding from the other accounts and stashed it in his own personal account. Nothing has gone in or out of that account recently either, which makes sense since he's dead."

"So he uses a separate bank to stash the stolen money, but writes down all the details in the same ledger," I say shaking my head.

"Yeah, a real dumbshit."

"I know I'm kind of slow, but how does that help us?" I ask.

Cash shakes his head in mock annoyance and then dives into everything.

Right as he finishes, Casey walks into the kitchen.

"Figure out how to get my dad yet?" she says angrily. Clearly a night's sleep did little to improve her mood.

"Um, no, I just woke up, but Cash figured out the code," I say.

"I fucking warned you, Jack," she says and stares me down.

"Yeah, and I heard you. But I think you're forgetting I didn't get us into this. I didn't ask for this," I say, in a harsher tone than intended, but I'm pissed enough at this point that I'm shaking.

She just stares at me. Then she grabs the coffee out of my hand and walks out of the kitchen.

I yell after her, "We aren't fucking wizards," although I think Cash kind of is. She doesn't respond.

"What the fuck was that?" Cash asks.

"She thinks we should have already traded the ledger for her dad."

"We're in a better position now that we know what's in the ledger than we were before. And what, they're just gonna do a swap and let us walk away?"

"Preaching to the choir, sir."

We sit in silence and finish our coffees. As I am putting the mugs in the dishwasher and tidying up the kitchen, Kelly and Hailey walk in. Hailey looks concerned, so I'm assuming she saw Casey on her way in.

"Anything more come of the ledger?" Kelly asks.

"A lot actually, and I can't wait to fill you guys in," Cash says and grabs the ledger.

"I have to feed the horses first. Can you guys give

me fifteen minutes? Maybe you can get some breakfast together while I go?" Hailey asks.

"Oooh, I want to feed the horses," Cash says.

"Who are you and what have you done with Cash?" Kelly asks.

"I agree," I say and give him a sideways look, "Cash volunteering to do a chore?"

"I need to get outside. I've been at this all night," Cash says, "but you're right, I don't really plan on doing anything, just watching."

"If you're coming, you're helping," Hailey says.

Cash seriously contemplates for a minute. He really is incredibly averse to doing anything that resembles a chore. I think it's gonna be a rude awakening for him when we start our summer job and he realizes that it's basically chores eight hours a day, five days a week.

"Okay, fine, let's go," he says, and Cash and Hailey walk out the door. I make Kelly a cup of coffee. She digs through the cupboards for cereal. It takes us a few minutes, but we are able to put together a decent spread. Orange juice, coffee, milk, cereal, and some powdered donuts. We lay it out on the black marble table in the middle of the kitchen. As Kelly sets down the final fork, both of our phones buzz. It's an alert from the alarm app. Someone tripped the alarm somewhere, and the fifteen-second grace period to enter the code has begun. We hear the beeping from the room down the hall where they keep the alarm. It beeps for a few seconds, then it stops.

"Think that's weird?" I ask Kelly.

"I mean if her parents or sister were home, no, but..." and she leaves the rest unsaid.

We head to the room where the alarm system lives since we are so close, and the screens are bigger than on our phones. I haven't been given an explicit tutorial on how the main system works, but I've watched Hailey enough that I have a pretty good handle on it. On the screen is an alert that says the perimeter alarm for the "back gate" has been triggered. The same place Damon and Buck were at two nights ago. It takes me a minute to find the right live feed of the camera. Damon's spit has long since dried on the lens, but the image is still blurred. I am able to see well enough to tell that everything looks normal there. No cars and the gate is still closed. I turn up the audio and everything sounds normal. Kelly grabs her phone and dials Cash's number and hits speaker. I hear it ringing on Kelly's phone, and then it starts a feedback loop because we also hear a ringing through the camera.

"What the fuck?" Kelly asks.

After several rings, it goes to voicemail. I pull out my phone and dial Hailey and hit speaker. The same thing happens. I hear the ring on my phone, and then after a moment, there is a muffled ring coming through the monitor.

"Does that mean their phones are close enough to the camera to pick up the sound?" Kelly asks.

"I don't know. Are you able to see where Cash is on your phone?" I ask. Hailey and I share our location, so I pull up the app we use. Kelly does the same. We put our phones next to each other, and it looks like they are in the same exact spot—the back gate.

"Oh fuck," I say, and we bolt for the back door.

When we make it to the back gate, we yell their names, but no one responds. I approach the gate and look at the ground, but I don't see anything amiss. I hop the gate and look at the other side.

"Jack, over here," I follow Kelly's voice and see she's found the phones. We each grab one. They're on, but Hailey's lock screen is set, and I don't know her code. Apparently, Kelly knows Cash's though, and she spends a few moments searching in it.

"Anything?" I ask, holding Hailey's phone, realizing I'm getting my fingerprints all over it. Then I realize a dirty cop probably has something to do with this, so it doesn't matter.

"Nothing. But the last app that was open was the alarm app," Kelly says, kicking the ground with the toe of her shoe.

"Maybe they made him type in the code to silence the alarm?"

"Maybe."

"At least there isn't any blood."

"Jesus, Jack," she says, her breathing speeding up as she escalates toward a panic attack.

"I'm sorry. I'm sorry, look. Kelly, look at me," she finally does, terror in her eyes. "They're gonna be fine, we're gonna find them. I swear, okay?"

She manages a weak nod.

"Let's look at the video. I'm pretty sure I know what we are going to see, but…"

Kelly can't bring herself to say anything, she just starts jogging toward the house. I spend the trip back to the house trying to come up with the right thing to say. Something light, but not insensitive. We reach the back door before anything comes to mind. I open it and, out of instinct, look for the ledger on the kitchen table. It's not there. But what is there, written in the dusting of powdered sugar, is a single word—"Sorry."

"Fuck!" I yell.

"What?" Kelly asks.

I point to the table.

"What the fuck does that mean?"

"It means Casey sold us out and took the ledger."

"How? Why?"

"I guess she didn't think we were gonna turn it over. That we weren't gonna help save her dad. I think she reached out to Damon and Buck."

"Why didn't she just take the ledger, why'd she have to bring them here?"

"Maybe the ledger wasn't enough for them. Maybe they demanded more for her dad. Casey made it pretty clear, on a number of occasions, that she'd do anything to get Reed back. Fuck, we should have moved faster," I say.

"Jack, they have Cash. And Hailey. Those fucking psychopaths have Cash and Hailey," Kelly says and starts to cry.

My brain, or more accurately, my heart, can't handle thinking about it.

We walk to the alarm room to view the footage. We scan the footage and sure enough, we see a cop car pull up to the gate. It's blurry because of Damon's dried spit, but two figures are visible through the windshield. It's Damon and Buck. Damon puts his phone to his ear, steps out of the car, walks towards the gate, and trips the alarm. Damon pulls his gun and yells for them to shut off the alarm, We can't see Cash and Hailey because they are off screen. The beeping stops. Damon tells them to drop their phones, hop the fence, and climb into the back of the car. Cash and Hailey walk on screen, they look at each other, I think deciding on whether or not they should run. Cash shakes his head. Maybe I never shared the *what do you do in case of a kidnapping* tip my mom sent me. Basically, you run, you fight, you do not go willingly, because there's never gonna be a better chance to get away from a kidnapper than before you are kidnapped. Cash and Hailey drop their phones as they were told and scramble over the gate. Once on the other side, Hailey glances back at the gate, she looks terrified. They pile in the back of the cruiser. Damon holsters his gun and gets behind the wheel. Buck closes the back door on the cruiser, hops in shotgun, and they drive off. That's it. They kidnapped them in all of thirty seconds.

"They looked fine though, right?" Kelly asks.

"Yeah, they looked fine," I lie.

"They have Cash and Hailey, and I assume Casey is about to give them the ledger. We are full-on fucked."

"Actually, we're not," I say and reach into my pocket.

OH MY GOD, YOU ARE THE FUCKING BEST!
Kelly screams and wraps her arms around me with such force that she knocks me back in the chair and falls on top of me. If she wasn't so excited, I think she'd be a bit embarrassed by the position we end up in, which looks very sexual. But it doesn't even register. She jumps up, still holding the sheet from the ledger.

"Actually Cash is the best," I say, "he's the one that ripped it out and handed it to me this morning."

Her eyes brighten. "This is the page with all the account

numbers?" she asks, marveling at the sheet with the random numbers and symbols scrawled across it.

"Yep. Cash said all the other stuff is just accounting—who bought what, how much they paid, etcetera. The only page that really matters, at the end of the day, is this one. Without this, they don't have the passwords to those accounts, which is the main thing the cartel wants." I grab the sheet back, place it on the table, and smooth it out. I take a picture of it, then fold it and put it in my pocket.

"Now we get ahold of that bald fuck and tell him his ledger is useless without this sheet? And that he needs to trade Cash and Hailey for it?" Kelly asks, but it's not really a question.

"Yes. Only thing is, we need to get his number since he always calls me from a blocked one," I say.

"It can't be that hard to get, right? We could call the station," Kelly says. I don't feel comfortable calling the station, but it gets me thinking that we actually know someone who knows him. *Cock Fucking Mike*. I don't know his number either though, and after me stabbing him twice I don't think he's gonna be helpful. Thinking about Cock Mike and phone numbers makes me feel like I'm missing something. And then it hits me. I tell Kelly to hang on and I run downstairs. I start digging through my bag and eventually find it—Cock Mike's phone. After I accidentally stabbed him, he dropped it, and I picked it up. I put it in my bag and promptly forgot about it. I run upstairs as fast as I can, yelling Kelly's name excitedly. She comes barreling toward the top of the stairs looking alarmed.

"No, it's all good," I say and show her the phone. "It's Cock Mike's. He dropped it when I stabbed him. I totally forgot about it."

I attempt to power it on, but it's dead. Kelly runs to grab a charger. When she returns, I plug the phone in and we wait. After a couple of minutes, we're able to power it up. And we get a big fat lock screen of course.

Kelly can see that I'm crestfallen and says, "It's fine, Jack, we'll figure it out."

I don't mean to, but I scoff and say, "Really?"

"Maybe Cock Mike's dumbshitness extends to what he chooses for a passcode," Kelly says.

"This thing is going to lock up on us after a certain amount of failed attempts though, right?" I ask.

Kelly grabs her phone and searches. After a minute, she says, "Okay, six failed attempts will lock us out for one minute, seven for five minutes, and eight for twenty-four hours."

"We get eight guesses then?" I look to Kelly and she nods. "What do we know about Cock Mike?" I'm doubtful this is gonna work, but at the same time, Cock Mike is as dumb as a box of rocks.

"Let's see," she says as she grabs a pen and paper. At the top she writes *Cock Mike* and then double underlines it. "He likes rape, pedophilia, dirty cops, neon cars, and wrestling."

She writes down each one. I really doubt his passcode is going to be *rape*. Especially since you can't use letters. We spend the next forty-five minutes brainstorming possible passwords and typing them in. We tried a variation on his birthdate, the anniversary of his now defunct marriage—of course, that didn't work. We tried the date he won state for wrestling when he was in high school. We have one attempt left, and then we're locked out for twenty-four hours.

"I fucking hate this guy," Kelly says.

"Same."

"One shot left, I'm thinking 1, 2, 3, 4, 5, 6 or 1, 1, 1, 1, 1, 1 or 1, 2, 1, 2, 1, 2," Kelly says.

I sigh. "Your pick, all three seem equally plausible."

Kelly takes a deep breath and then types in six numbers. From her look, I can tell it didn't work.

"It was worth a shot," I say and start pacing the room. "What did you try?"

"1, 2, 3, 4, 5, 6. I could see him thinking that's harder to guess."

We sit for minute in silence. Both of us thinking about the best way forward from here.

"What about Maggie? It's possible she has a number for them, right? I mean, she had some communication with them when Casey first went missing," Hailey says.

Duh. Before she even finishes her sentence, I'm sending a message to Maggie. I call her as well, but she doesn't pick up.

"She might be working at the Kum. Let's go down there," I say.

We head to the car and start the drive to Kum Quick. I wasn't aware of how shallow my breathing was and how panicky I felt until I managed to slow it during the drive. I can't believe those fucking psychos have Hailey and Cash. I just hope to God Damon can keep his shit together until we can make a trade. I have no idea what that's gonna look like though. Two trained cops versus me and Kelly. Ha. I still have Damon's gun. I think we're gonna need to get in Cash's dad's safe and get another gun for Kelly.

Before I finish my doom spiral, we pull into the parking lot of the Kum. We walk inside, and thank God Maggie is working. She sees us and gives an indifferent nod.

"Hey Maggie, it's Jack and Kelly," I say, in case she doesn't remember us.

"I fucking know who you are, dude. Gordon's not here, just bailed halfway through his shift to go on a road trip." She turns and wipes the counter. Okay, well, off to a good start.

"We're not here for Gordon, we're here for you," Kelly says and pauses to see if Maggie will look over. She does not, so Kelly plows on. "We kind of need the number for Damon Storey, you know that bald cop that was looking for Casey."

"Looking?" Maggie says and laughs.

Kelly, starting to lose her patience, says, "Okay, let me try again. Do you have his number?" Maggie kind of scares the shit out of me, so I'm more than happy for Kelly to handle this. Kelly and Maggie stare at one another, and after a moment, Maggie looks away.

"I have his number. He stopped answering my calls and texts a while ago though. Why do you need it?" Maggie asks.

"Can we just say we need it and leave it at that?" Kelly asks.

"I mean you can, but it's not gonna get you his number." And Maggie's defiance returns. She's a hard case for sure.

Kelly looks at me for help, so I say, "Casey is fine. We found her. In a day or so we can tell you everything, and you can write all about it, but for now, it's fucking imperative that we get in touch with Damon."

Maggie looks from me to Kelly and then back to me. Her eyes soften. Maybe she senses our desperation.

"She's okay? For real? You're not just saying that?" she asks.

"She is, I swear," Kelly says.

"And the bald cop is part of this? Like not in a good way?" Maggie asks.

Kelly says, "Yeah, he's part of it, and in the opposite of a good way."

"They make us lock our phones in back now. I'll go grab his number," Maggie says and walks past the register, turns left at the hot dog roller thing, and into the back room. The door chime goes off, and Barnes walks in. He's decked out in running gear, and he's drenched in sweat. The black eye is still visible but fading.

"What's up, you two?" he asks, looking around. Our vibe must have put him on edge, because then he asks, "Everything okay?"

"Yeah dude. All good. How are you?" I ask, trying to sound normal.

"Good man, good. Hi, Kelly," he says, and she gives a polite wave. "I was out running and saw what I thought was Hailey's car out there. Three of Cock Mike's wrestlers are peering through the windows."

"Huh?" I ask, genuinely confused. But before he can answer, it clicks. Cock Mike's phone. We couldn't get into it, but we turned it back on, so now he's able to track it. He probably sent his goons to retrieve it. I bet there's shit on there he doesn't want anyone to see.

"Yeah, they're trying the door handles."

Maggie walks out of the back room with a piece of paper and places it in my hand. It has a single phone number written on it. I put it in my pocket. Barnes eyes the interaction but doesn't comment. He looks at Kelly, and she looks at her feet. He looks at Maggie, and she finds a sudden interest in her bracelets.

"Dude. What's going on? I haven't seen you this skittish since last summer," he says with genuine concern.

"Cock Mike's phone is in Hailey's car. I think he sent them to get it," I say, hesitant to tell him more.

"And you have Cock Mike's phone, because?"

"Kind of a long story, Barnes, but he's not a good dude," Kelly says. We've all heard rumors about Cock Mike and his female students. No doubt Barnes is making that connection.

"Say no more. I'm gonna walk you guys out of here."

"Oh my God, that would be great," Kelly says.

Maggie grabs my arm before I follow Barnes and Kelly out the door and says, "Here, take this." She puts a can of pepper spray in my hand. I'm not much of a fighter, so I don't argue.

"Thank you," I say and walk out.

As we round the corner, the three guys around Hailey's car stop what they are doing and turn toward us. They were all part of the group that gave me shit about calling Cock Mike "Cock Mike" at Barnes's house the other night. One of them is the guy who stole the sunglasses from me; pretty sure his name is Brandon. He's wearing the glasses right now. Another was the kid wearing an American flag bandana on his head; he has a different red, white, and blue one on now. He's still not being ironic. The third one is wearing a Black Forest Wrestling shirt, cut so dramatically into a tank top that it now says *Lack Fores restlin*. He has a gigantic dip of tobacco in his lower lip. They're gathered around the driver's door, and one of them has a rock in his hand. It looks like they were about to break the window.

"Can I help you?" Barnes asks.

"We don't have a problem with you," the one who stole the sunglasses says. He looks nervous seeing Barnes—no doubt he's heard about him.

"You kind of do though," Barnes says and winks.

"That fucking guy," this coming from the bandana kid, pointing at me, "he stole Coach Mike's phone."

"Coach Mike? Who's Coach Mike? Oh, you mean Cock Mike?" Barnes asks and laughs.

"His name is not Cock Mike," says the kid wearing the tank top. The dip in his mouth makes it sound like he has a speech impediment.

"Yeah, yeah, I know," I say, "he's a great American."

Neon guy looks upset, like I stole his thunder, and says, "Well, he is."

"We don't have his phone," Kelly says.

"Yeah, you do," sunglasses says, "and he stabbed him," and points at me.

Barnes is taken aback and says, "Really?"

"Well, to be fair, he kind of stabbed himself," I say and shrug.

"Twice he stabbed him. And then stole his phone, all because he was mad he got a bad grade," sunglasses says.

I can't help but laugh. "Is that what he said?" Cock Mike's classes are so easy that, even with him hating me, I've always gotten A's.

"Well," Barnes says reasonably, "if Jack says he doesn't have Cock Mike's phone, then he doesn't have Cock Mike's phone. So I'm gonna need you guys to move away so they can be on their way."

The boys look at each other, unsure how to proceed. One of them types into his phone.

"It would not be right for us to allow that," sunglasses says. He takes off his glasses and puts them in his pocket. When he lifts his head back up, I see that both of his eyes are a mess. The whites are bright red and glassy. There is yellowish goop drying around the upper and lower lids. His eyelashes are stuck together, and the skin around his eyes is bright red, probably from scratching.

"Oh my God!" Kelly exclaims.

"Fuck you. I got something in my eyes," he says defensively.

"Um, yeah, you did. You got fucking conjunctivitis in your eyes is what you did," she says and laughs.

Sunglasses guy looks lost and says, "You calling me a faggot?"

"What?" Kelly says, confused, before realizing he has no idea what conjunctivitis means. "Pink eye, dipshit. You have pink eye. Actually, you have pink eyes. In both of your eyes. Like a fucking toddler you are. Put those sunglasses back on, for God's sake," she says, shaking her head in disgust.

"I'm not gonna rumble in sunglasses," he says, and the others nod in agreement, like that would indeed be a terrible idea.

"No one is rumbling. What is this, 1950? Just move away and let us get going," I say. Barnes takes a couple steps closer to them. They instinctively step back.

Bandana guy glances at his phone, a look of satisfaction crossing his face. He shows it to the other two. My guess is that they have backup on the way. If so, we need to get the fuck out of here, now.

"Give us the phone, or you're all gonna be tapping out," Tanktop says.

"If you're gonna be able to tap out, that is," Bandana says, and they laugh.

"Fine, fine, you guys got us," Barnes says. "We'll open the door and you can look in the car."

"That's more like it," sunglasses says.

Barnes turns to me and winks. I make a show of grabbing

the keys out of my pocket and unlocking the doors. Barnes walks toward the driver's door.

"Let me get this for you," he says, and they give him a little space. Instead of opening the door, Barnes cocks back his right arm and hits Bandana kid with all he has. It knocks him clean off his feet, and he lands square on his back, bouncing twice before coming to a stop. It takes the other two a moment to figure out what's going on, and that's all Barnes needs. He swings with his left and connects with Tanktop's jaw. There's an audible crack, then a yelp as he drops to his knees, cradling his face. Barnes then lands a right hook to the side of Sunglasses' temple, and he falls to the ground.

Sunglasses is the first back to his feet. He backs up and gets into a wrestler's stance. He looks behind at the road, hoping to see his friends arriving. He looks at Barnes and starts moving from side to side, popping on his toes. I'm sure there is a reason for it, but it does not instill fear. He almost looks like he's dancing.

Tires screech in the distance. Sunglasses grins. His eyes are so crusty that they barely move.

"Just wait until I get you on the ground," he says, looking at Barnes.

A huge truck hauls ass toward us. I can't tell how many people are in the cab, but there are several in the bed. They are whooping and hollering, like something out of a redneck horror movie. I've seen that truck at school; its owner is another of Cock Mike's wrestlers.

"We gotta get the fuck out of here," I say.

"Why in such a rush?" Sunglasses asks. He's swaying back and forth and occasionally feinting toward Barnes. He shakes his head a few times. I think he's starting to feel the impact of that shot to the head. His movements are looking more and more like a dance routine. I know the situation is serious, but I'm finding it hard not to laugh.

"Keep your fucking eyes away from me," Barnes says as Sunglasses lunges toward him.

"What are you, a fucking pussy?" Sunglasses asks. Then scrunches up his left eye and starts rubbing it.

"No, he's just hygienic," Kelly says.

Bandana and Tanktop are still on the ground, both of them looking over their shoulders at the approaching truck. The truck's gonna be here in no more than thirty seconds. I think Tanktop is out of the fight, but Bandana is getting back to his feet.

"Fuck this," I yell and run toward Sunglasses. He backs up a step and then stops. I pull my hand out of my pocket and press the trigger on the pepper spray. The effect is instantaneous. Sunglasses drops to the ground, writhing in pain, screaming about his eyes. He takes a blind swipe at me with his left arm and manages to knock the keys out of my hand. They skid across the ground and under the car.

"Get in the car!" I yell to Kelly and Barnes as I dive for the keys. Kelly runs toward the passenger door, but Barnes stands his ground. I'm about to ask him what the fuck he's thinking when the truck comes to a skidding halt behind Hailey's car, and seven dudes jump out. All seven of them are dressed in baseball uniforms, I guess they are in some kind of summer league. Five of them have baseball bats. A random bit of information jumps into my head—Cock Mike also coaches baseball.

"My eyes are burning!" Sunglasses screams. One of the new arrivals, who must be at least 6'3", lifts Sunglasses off the ground and helps him into the truck. Tanktop follows him, gingerly holding his jaw and sobbing. I move closer to Kelly and hand her the pepper spray.

"Too much of a pussy to fight like a man," the tall one says to me, alluding to the pepper spray.

"Too much of a pussy to get conjunctivitis at least," I say.

Tall Guy looks at me and then back toward Sunglasses and says, "You calling him a faggot? You can't call people faggots anymore. My cousin's a faggot."

"It's pink eye, dumbshits. Your fucking friend there has pink eye. My God," Kelly says.

Then a smaller kid with long hair says, "Well, you're all about to have black eyes," and he goes to high-five the kid next to him. The other kid ignores him and shakes his head. In the midst of it all, I almost feel sorry for the smaller kid.

Barnes walks within striking distance of Tall Guy. His bat rests on his shoulder. The other kids with bats are doing all kinds of fancy tricks, flipping and twirling them. They either think it looks menacing, or it's just a nervous habit they do before they go to bat. I hope it's the latter, because it does not look menacing.

Barnes stops a couple of feet away from Tall Guy and says, "Last chance." This gets the whole group laughing. Barnes uses the moment to his advantage and lunges at Tall Guy, unleashing a barrage of fists. His right connects just above Tall Guy's right eye. Then his left hits him square in the kidney. As he crumples from the kidney punch, Barnes lands another right, with all his weight, in the same spot above the guy's eye. The skin splits open, and blood arcs across the pavement. The whole takedown only lasts a couple of seconds. I was hoping that seeing the biggest one of their crew drop that easily would cause them to give up, but it has the opposite effect, and they start coming at us.

Now that Tall Guy is out of the fight, a short, stocky guy takes the lead. He points to the two kids without baseball bats and says, "Get the phone out of the car." The rest split into two groups. Three come toward me, and four head toward Barnes. Kelly runs after the guys trying to get in the car, pepper spray in her hand. I catch a glimpse of Barnes—he's smiling.

Only two of the kids in the group surrounding me have baseball bats. One of them is a kid named Preston. We've gone to school together since elementary. We had to do a group presentation on Bolivia a couple of years back; it might have been the last time we spoke. I remember he was really good with graphics, and the report turned out looking awesome. He looks nervous but also determined—not a good combo. Clearly, our history holds little sway at the moment. He lifts the bat above his head and takes a pretty half-assed swing toward me. I easily avoid it. His next swing has more power behind it. I'm able to deflect it, but it connects with my forearm, sending a shock of pain all the way to my shoulder. His next attack is more of a jab than a swing, and I manage to wrap my arm around the bat and pull it toward me. Preston doesn't let go, and he gets pulled into me along with the bat. When he's right up next to me, I kick down hard with my right foot, and it makes contact with his shin. Not where I was aiming, but it works. He buckles, and I wrench the bat from his hands.

To my left, Kelly tries to keep the two kids out of the car by chasing them with the pepper spray. It reminds me of the pirate ride at Disneyland. Apparently, the kids aren't smart enough to split up and each go to a different side. I steal a look at Barnes. He has a bat in his hand too. There's a kid at his feet, holding his arm in pain. Another one in front of him, still standing, but bleeding profusely from his nose. I've never seen a bloody nose bleed that much—almost makes me wonder if the kid's a hemophiliac. I stare too long at Barnes, and one of the kids in my group takes a swing at me. I jump to the side, but the end of his bat comes in direct contact with my left hand. The pain is almost unbearable. I look down to see my pinkie and ring finger pointing in directions they should not be. Either the position of my fingers, or the pain, or both, makes it hard to breathe. I grab the bat in the middle with my good hand. When he comes toward me again, I punch forward, and the handle end of the bat smacks him on the bridge of his nose. There is an audible crack, and the skin on the bridge of his nose splits. He drops the bat as blood rushes from the wound and his nostrils. A lot of blood, but nothing compared to the kid Barnes hit. He grabs for his nose with both hands.

I feel like I am going to pass out from the pain in my fingers. My field of vision is shrinking. The sole remaining kid in my group grabs a bat and comes at me. I back up and stumble over the kid I kicked in the shin. He grabs my leg, and I go down. The bat twists under my hand, and I let go. The kid with the bat takes a big swing and connects with my right bicep. Cash's brother used to walk by us and hit us as hard as he could in the arm or leg with an extended knuckle. He'd laugh so hard. There were a couple of times I had to fight back tears. That pain was nothing compared to this. From my back, I watch three kids with bats charge Barnes. He manages to deflect a couple of swings, but is quickly overtaken. I glance at the car and see Kelly has made it inside, and she's locked the doors. The two kids are trying in vain to open them. They settle for pounding on the windows. A punch, or maybe a kick, to the back of my head brings me back to my situation. I turn to the other side just in time to feel a punch land below my eye. I'm barely holding on to consciousness at this point. I have just enough strength to pull myself to my knees. My left hand is useless, so my balance is precarious. I see a foot coming toward me and barely manage to avoid it. I push myself up to standing and scramble toward the car. Barnes is huddled in a ball on the ground. Luckily, they're kicking him and hitting him with their hands and feet, not their bats. The driver's door of the car opens, and Kelly yells my name. I look up in time to see something flying toward me. I instinctively reach out and catch it. It's the gun I picked up after hitting Damon with the crowbar. I spin around, and the kid chasing me sees what's in my hand and stops cold.

"Everyone just fucking stop!" I yell. The ones that haven't seen the gun keep doing what they were doing. Two of them are still pounding on the car windows. Four kids are still hitting and kicking Barnes. I point the gun in the air and fire off three quick shots. They all drop to the ground with their hands covering their heads.

"You fucks have five seconds to get out of here before I stop shooting in the air and start shooting in your faces," I say. That's all it takes. Baseball bats clatter to the ground as every last one of them sprints for the truck. Preston is the last person in line to jump in the back of the truck. I yell his name and he stops.

"Tell Cock Mike he needs to stay home tonight. If he gets a call, he needs to stay home. Otherwise, everyone is going to know about his extracurricular activities." Preston looks at the gun in my hand with terror in his eyes. I'm not sure he's going to be able to retain what I just told him.

"Preston, look at me," I say, and he does. "Tell Cock Mike

that if he helps tonight, everyone will know about what happened at the cabin. Got it?" He nods numbly.

"Repeat it back to me," I say.

"I'm gonna tell Cock—I mean Coach Mike—that if he helps tonight, everyone will know, uh..." he says and looks to me for help.

"What happened at the cabin," I finish for him.

"Yeah, everyone will know what happened at the cabin," he says and looks at the gun again.

"I'm not gonna shoot you, man. You know how to get in touch with him?" I ask.

"Yeah, he's at the gym right now. We're supposed to head over there with his phone," Preston says.

"Okay, good. Go right there and tell him, okay?"

"Yes, sir. We'll go right now," he stammers.

"And Preston?"

"Yeah?"

"You did a great job on that report on Bolivia," I say. He can't process the sudden change in topic, but manages a weak, "Thanks." I shoo him along with the gun, and he bolts for the truck. The kid driving backs up, turns, and takes off down the road.

Kelly opens the car and jumps out. We rush toward Barnes. It sounds like he's sobbing, but as we get closer and help him up, it's clear he's laughing. He looks pretty messed up—huge welts on his arms and legs, a swollen bump on his cheek, a fat lip, and what looks like a hole in his cheek where a tooth might have pierced through.

"Fuck, dude, you okay?" I ask.

He's dazed but asks, "How'd we do, Jacko?"

"We're alive, so I think pretty good," I say.

"Shit was fun, right?" Barnes says and then turns and throws up. His puke has a reddish tint to it.

"Well, the opposite of fun maybe," Kelly says. "We gotta get you to the hospital."

"I'm fine, those kids couldn't hit to save their lives," Barnes says, wiping at the blood dripping from his scalp into his eyes.

"Then we at least have to get out of here. Jack just fired a gun in a parking lot in the middle of the day," Kelly says, looking up and down the road.

We grab Barnes and help him to his feet. I open the side door and push him in. Kelly gets behind the wheel, and I hop in the passenger seat. We take off in the opposite direction of the truck. The first thing I do is grab Cock Mike's phone and power it down so he can't see where it is anymore.

"Oh my God, your hand, Jack," Kelly says once she sees my broken fingers.

I look down, and my fingers look even worse than before. They're starting to swell. They're still pointing in directions they're not supposed to. I cup my right hand around them and try to move my wrist. It's fucked. I don't think it's broken, but it's hard to move.

"We need to get both of you to a hospital," Kelly says.

"We don't have time," I say and reach into my pocket with my good hand. Thankfully, the number Maggie gave me is still there. I point at the number so Kelly can see it. I don't want to bring Barnes into this any more than he already is. I'm also not sure how much help he'd be. The kid has to be concussed. We drive the rest of the way to Barnes' house in silence.

We stop at the top of his driveway, and he gets out.

"See you guys at school tomorrow," he says, but then he laughs. "Kidding, I'm fine." He hops out of the car and walks to his house. He's a little wobbly, but seems okay. He gives us a wave. Kelly turns around and we drive off.

I hold the number in my hand, just staring at it.

"No time like the present?" Kelly asks and I nod.

I grab my phone and punch in Damon's number. It takes a few tries because my hand is shaking. I hit send and it rings. He's called me before so I think he probably has my number in his phone already. After five rings he answers.

"Resourceful little fucker aren't you?" Damon says.

"Are they okay?" I ask.

"Hear that? You know what that sound is?" I listen and can barely make out a tinny sound. Metal on metal. Like a grapefruit spoon tapping on something. I can't believe how quickly my mind got there.

"Doesn't sound like a ledger," I say.

"Well, I do have one of those. What's that say about you kid? She chose me over you," and he laughs.

"Casey chose her dad," I say and turn my bad hand in a way that sends a lightning bolt of pain up my arm.

"You okay there? I heard a call on the radio about a fight outside the Kum Quick. Shots fired. Wouldn't have had anything to do with you, would it?" he asks, knowing that it did.

"Are they okay?" I ask again.

Then I hear Hailey yell "We're fine," in the background.

"Shut the fuck up," Damon snaps.

"You fucking touch her and I swear to God…" I say.

"What, Jack, what are you gonna do? I have everything now.

Your friend, your girlfriend, the ledger." I can imagine the smug look on his face. He taps the grapefruit spoon again.

"Did you notice your ledger is missing a page?" I ask, and the moment I finish saying it, the tapping of the grapefruit spoon stops. It sounds like he covers the phone, but I can make out him yelling Buck's name and demanding he bring him the ledger. I hear rustling. I can almost see him flipping through it, searching for evidence of a page missing.

"You're full of shit," he says, but he doesn't sound his usual commanding self.

"Am I? Let me tell you what you have there. You have a list of transactions. How much person A bought and how much person B paid. What you don't have is the page with the account numbers and passcodes. What you don't have is the only page that matters," I say and can't help but smile. Kelly smiles too.

"You're full of shit," he says again.

"You just said that."

"How the fuck do you know what you have? It's just a bunch of numbers."

"We know because we cracked it. And yes, super dumb to not have this info somewhere else, but if they did, they would have moved the money and changed the codes once they realized the ledger was missing. And they haven't, because we checked," I say.

"Fuck!" Damon howls into the phone, and we hear him breaking things on the other end of the line. He's throwing a tantrum like a toddler. Buck yells "Fuck," in the background. I assume he just got hit by something Damon threw.

"There's a phone number on the page with the account info," I bluff, "the country code is five-two. That's Mexico, if I'm not mistaken. What happens if I call that number and tell them what I know? How do you think that'd go?" It's quiet for what feels like forever. Then I hear breathing. He sounds panicked.

"Okay, Jack. You little cunt. Let's meet for a trade. One missing ledger page for two kids."

The relief I feel is overwhelming. I know we are just trading a current problem for a future one, but I'll take it.

"10 p.m. at the old Palmer Farm, where they light the bonfires. You know it?" I ask.

"I know it. You need a few hours to set up a plan, do you, Jack? I'm gonna advise you against that. And against calling anyone. If anyone besides you shows up, I start killing kids. I fucking promise you that."

I hang up before he can say more. Kelly looks sickly white. I'd forgotten about my hand for a minute, but now the pain is back in full force.

"I've got to do something about my fingers. And we don't have time to go to the hospital. Think you can help me set them?" I ask, and Kelly nods. I'm afraid she's going to be sick, but she holds it together. She drives to the pharmacy near Cash's house. I give her a list of things to get, and she heads in. Fifteen minutes later, she's back in the car with a bag of stuff.

"You got a plan here, Jack?" she asks as she starts the car.

"Getting there," I say.

As Kelly drives back to Cash's, I work on the plan in my mind. It's not a good one. So far, all I've come up with is having Kelly hide somewhere nearby with the ledger sheet and a gun. We do some kind of timed swap—they let Hailey and Cash go, and we leave the sheet for them. We go our separate ways. A million things could go wrong. And probably will. Once I get my fingers straightened out, maybe the pain will ease and I'll be able to think more clearly.

Kelly passes Cash's house and continues to the turn-out just past it, parking the car. I'm worried Damon and Buck will try to get the missing ledger page before tonight, so we hide in the attic above the garage. Before going up, we make a pit stop inside. We head to Cash's dad's safe and open it using the combo I've seen Cash enter before. I search through the bags of pills and find one labeled Roxys. I grab a handful. I remove the pistol Kelly was shooting the other day, make sure it's loaded, and hand it to her as I close the safe. Kelly grabs a bag of chips and a six-pack of Kola Kountry from the kitchen. As we pass through the living room, she also grabs Wes's bong.

Once upstairs, Kelly hands me an opened Kola Kountry, and I use it to swallow three pills.

"Cash would tell you that if you smash them and snort them, they work faster," Kelly says with a weak laugh.

"Well, he can tell me later," I say and stare at my fingers.

Kelly spends the next ten minutes or so watching videos on her phone, illustrating the best way to set broken bones. I'm not sure they're all that reliable. At least she uses earphones so I don't have to hear the audio. When she finishes with the videos, she starts rifling through the bag she got at the pharmacy and pulls out a package with three different-sized finger splints, a roll of self-adhering bandage, and a wrist brace.

"Jack, you really want me to try and put those back?" she asks, looking at my tweaked fingers. "It's gonna hurt real bad."

"I don't know what else to do," I say.

"Okay, but don't hold it against me," she says.

"I won't. Let's just give the pills a few more minutes to work their magic," I say. I close my eyes and lie on my back. If I take slow, shallow breaths, the pain is not as biting. I rest my hand as close to flat on the ground as I can. I feel the warmth of the opiates doing their thing. From what feels like a far-off place, I hear Kelly messing with the bandages and splints.

"How's it feeling now?" she asks gingerly, touching my fingers.

"A little bet—" but before I get the full sentence out, there's a pain in my fingers like nothing I've ever experienced. Like someone is stabbing them with needles and setting them on fire at the same time. I scream and attempt to pull my hand away. Kelly must have anticipated this because her knee is on my arm with all her weight behind it.

Just when I don't think I can take it anymore, she says, "It's done."

It doesn't matter because I can't move anyway. It feels like the wind has been knocked out of me. Just when I think I might pass out from lack of oxygen, something gives in my chest and I'm able to take a deep breath.

"Fuck, how about a little warning next time," I say.

"The no warning was more for me than you. I think if I told you I was going to do it, I would have chickened out," Kelly says.

"How do they look?" I ask.

"Really inappropriate colors still, and they look like swollen sausages about to burst, but they're at least pointing in the right direction."

AT ABOUT THE SAME TIME JACK RECEIVED the gift of mace from Maggie inside the Kum Quick convenience store, across town, in a one-story house wrapped in police tape, Cash and Hailey sit back-to-back, handcuffed to one another. The house is not in Inwood, but it might as well be. The yard is littered with the usual Inwood-type stuff: an old lawnmower, a washing machine, a dirt bike, and a busted flat-screen TV. The difference here is that each of these items is partially disassembled. Hailey and Cash were led in through the back, so they weren't exposed to this visual delight, but had they been, Cash would have immediately thought, *Tweakers*. Gears, springs, bolts, and wires lay around each item, as if scattered by a small explosion. Next to the front door sits a pile of rocks, some no bigger than a kernel of corn and some the size of a grapefruit. Some are crystalline, some greenish, and some have uniform bands of varying brown. All of these types of rocks— amazonite, agate, geodes, and quartz crystal—are abundant in this state, but not in the same place. The fact that the rocks sit here, on the porch, unpolished, suggests that the meth wore off by the time the rocks made it home. It seems the chemically induced trait, similar to the intensely focused interests of someone on the autism spectrum (but on steroids), subsided before the rocks could be cleaned and displayed. The question here is: What came first? Did the meth use lead to rockhounding, or did the love of searching for rocks get leveled up from the meth? Fun thought, and it could make for an enlightening dissertation that would never pass IRB approval. Interesting, but in no way, shape, or form helpful to Hailey or Cash.

The two alleged tweakers who lived in this house were arrested for stealing rosebuds and Choreboys from a gas station. The cute paper roses encased in glass, merchandised next to checkout counters, seem harmless on casual inspection—like something a teenage boy might buy his girlfriend on their two-week anniversary. And that might very well happen, but the more common use is that the rose inside is tossed, and the tube is used to smoke meth. The Choreboy, a copper scouring pad sold for cleaning, is used in this instance as a filter to avoid inhaling a burning chunk of meth. Funny story—Andy Stater, one of the two inhabitants of this rental property (now in county jail for the past three days because the bail, set at five hundred dollars, was four hundred and eighty-seven dollars out of reach), was admitted to the hospital eighteen months ago because he sucked so hard on a meth pipe that he not only inhaled the smoke from the burning meth but also inhaled the chunk of Choreboy that was supposed to prevent him from inhaling the burning meth, which he also inhaled. It was about the size of his fingertip and was removed with forceps from his trachea. His voice was shot for a week, but other than that, he was fine.

A quick peek through the window by an officer, sent to the home after the arrest, revealed several cases of Sudafed. The officer felt that the sight of large quantities of a key ingredient for making meth was enough to request a search warrant and promptly wrapped the home in police tape. While the paperwork for the warrant makes its way to a judge for signature, the house sits empty. With their cabin blown, Damon and Buck decided this house would be perfect for their needs. If that same cop who peeked through the window a few days back were to return, and look through the same window, he would see Hailey and Cash sitting in mismatched chairs, pushed back-to-back and handcuffed to one another. The cop would also be able to see Damon pacing back and forth in the trash-filled room next to the kitchen. The room is probably meant to be a dining room, but right now it serves as a room-sized trash can. It does not smell good. Damon has kicked enough crap out of his way as he circles that he's made an oval path, a racetrack of sorts. Cash can only see part of the room from the corner of his eye, but it looks like a good portion of the refuse is made up of diapers. *Jesus*, he thinks, *there was a fucking baby in here?*

Cash twists his left wrist and gently grabs Hailey's forearm. She leans the back of her head against his. The frantic energy emanating from Damon since the phone call with Jack has Hailey terrified. When Damon hung up, he threw an empty glass beer bottle across the room that missed her by centimeters. She felt the hair on her head move from the wind as it blew past. She saw it coming, at least. Cash did not. And although it missed him as well, he screamed when it hit the wall and exploded.

Before Jack called Damon, Hailey was positive they were going to die in this shithole. But now, she has the tiniest bit of hope. She won't let it grow beyond that—higher hopes lead to deeper disappointments. Her arms ache from being twisted behind her back. For most of the time they've been in this house, Damon and Buck have been out front scheming. Watching them is like watching sharks swim around a tank—scary for sure, but nothing compared to when they are inside. Then she's in the tank with them.

As Damon paces, he attempts to keep his racing thoughts in order. He thrives on control, and at the moment, he feels like he has none. *This fucking kid. How? How is this fucking kid still breathing? Bite him. He killed my toe. He killed my fucking toe. God it's so dirty.* Pictures and fragments of thoughts bounce around his brain like kittens in a dryer. He imagines the pop of Cash's eyeball in his mouth as he bites down on it. The salty squishiness. It won't get him out of this mess, but to hear the boy scream as he does it—will definitely get him something. Some kind of relief. *Okay then, let's do this*, he thinks, and limps across the yard to the front door.

Oh fuck, Buck thinks as he sees Damon scoot toward the house as fast as his fucked-up foot allows. Damon's lost contact with this world. Buck's seen it before. Buck contemplates taking off himself. But Damon has the keys to the car, and even if he didn't, Buck doesn't think he can leave these two kids behind with Damon. *God damn this,* he curses under his breath and follows after.

Cash has the better view out the window. He notices movement and sees Damon heading toward the door.

"Hailey, Damon's heading in here and he looks like a rabid dog," Cash says in a shaky voice.

Hailey turns her head just in time to see Damon grab the door handle.

"I know we're stuck here, but I think it's time to fight," Hailey says, steel in her voice.

"With what? With fucking what?" Cash asks, his voice high and reedy.

"Your feet. Your teeth. Your head. Whatever you can move that might cause pain."

"Oh fuck," is all Cash can manage as the door flies open.

Damon limps around the island, searching the countertop as he does. He frantically reaches into his pockets, mumbling incoherently. Most of it sounds like gibberish, but Cash is able to make out four words—*Eyeball. Bite. Fuck. Socket.*

"Oh my God," Cash says, then repeats it several times before stopping as he begins to hyperventilate.

Damon moves to the table that separates the kitchen and the trash room. He madly searches under trash and porn mags. He sighs in relief as he finds the item he's been looking for.

Hailey sees the piece of metal in his hand and the sadistic grin on his face. It's the grapefruit spoon. She's never used one herself but has always thought they were both cool and completely unnecessary at the same time. She was able to understand only one word of Damon's mumbling word salad: *Eyeball*. And now the grapefruit spoon makes perfect sense.

"Oh my God," she says, "oh my fucking God."

Damon hobbles around the island toward Cash. Cash freezes. Hailey cranes her neck to see. She can just make out Damon's eyes. They might as well be marbles for all the life they have in them. He leans his weight against Cash. Hailey feels Cash's body go soft. *He passed out*, she thinks, *fuck*. She can't see what's happening, but she can feel it—a sawing motion as Damon attempts to cut through Cash's eyelid in search of the eyeball beneath.

Hailey screams, and feels warm liquid soaking her butt and legs. At first, she thinks it's Cash's blood. Then she realizes his bladder has let go. For whatever reason, this spurs her into action. *Fight*, she thinks. With all her might, she spins her body to the left. The piss-slicked floor helps the chairs spin counterclockwise. They don't quite make it ninety degrees, but it's enough to knock Damon off balance. He tries to right himself on his bad foot and stumbles. This gives Hailey enough time to spin the remaining ninety degrees. As the chairs come to a stop, she kicks forward as hard as she can. She connects with Damon's calf on the same leg as his fucked-up toe, and it's enough to send him over. He falls, and his forehead connects with the corner of the countertop. He doesn't pass out, but he drops to his knees, bringing his hand to his head drunkenly. He looks at the red liquid on his fingers like he doesn't know what it is. *It's blood, you dumbfuck*, Hailey thinks. *Hopefully, you lose enough of it to die*. But she knows he won't. She looks at his foot and sees red seeping through his sneaker.

Buck stands over him. "What happened?" he asks. He knows what happened, though—he watched it. He even reached for his gun to put Damon down. He actually believed he was going to do it, too. But his gun wasn't there. He forgot that Damon had confiscated it earlier.

"What happened?" Damon asks in return. Buck doesn't think Damon's being sarcastic, but he searches his face to be certain. Buck comes to the conclusion that Damon genuinely doesn't remember how he wound up on the ground with a head wound. The fall seems to have knocked the psycho out of him, at least for the moment. Buck shakes his head in disbelief.

"You fell," Buck says, "tripped, banged your bad toe, and fell."

Damon looks down at his bloody foot. He grimaces in pain.

"Well, help me up for fuck's sake," he says with venom.

Buck rushes to Damon, grabs him beneath his shoulders, and hoists him up. When it's clear Damon can stand on his own, Buck backs away. He sees the two kids—both terrified. They have streaks of clean where tears have washed away the dirt on their faces. The boy's eye is a mess. *Leave it to Damon to turn a grapefruit spoon into a torture device,* he thinks. The wound is bloody but it looks superficial. Buck believes the kid's eye will be fine—hopes so, at least. He wants to check, make sure the kid is okay, but he is not about to risk antagonizing Damon.

Damon leans against the counter. His injured foot, too tender to put weight on, rests an inch off the ground. He smiles and Buck feels it on the back of his neck. It would have sent a chill through the two kids as well if they had seen it.

"We have to kill them," Damon says matter-of-factly.

"Kill who?" Buck asks.

"Them," he says, pointing at Cash and Hailey.

"No, you don't," Hailey stammers, "you absolutely do not have to do that."

"There are thousands of things you can do besides killing us," Cash says, now wide awake. "Hundreds of thousands." But he sounds defeated, resigned.

"My toe is fucking dying," Damon hisses, pushing himself away from the counter.

Buck rushes to his side. "We just need to get the missing sheet back. Like we planned. We do that, we'll have so much money. You can buy your own hospital, your own surgeon."

"Why the fuck would I buy a hospital?"

"I'm just saying, we have a plan. We're so close." Buck takes a calming breath. "Let's get the piece of paper back from the other kid, and everything will be fine."

"It'll be *fine?* I don't have a fucking toe!"

"They can probably fix it, like, they can do all kinds of crazy stuff these days," Hailey adds, trying to be helpful.

"Shut. The. Fuck. Up," Damon says.

Buck makes eye contact with her and shakes his head as if to say, *do not rile him up.*

"Listen," Buck says, turning to Damon, "let me go find the other kid. Let me get the ledger back."

"He's not gonna give it to you," Damon says. "The kid's not stupid."

"I know he's not gonna give it to me. I'm gonna take it."

"What are you willing to do to get it?"

"Whatever it takes. He's standing between us and our only way out of this mess."

"I like this version of Buck," Damon says, like a proud father. "By all means, go get it, then."

Damon looks at his phone, sets a timer. "If you're not back in one hour," he pauses and stares at Hailey and Cash, "then I start biting chunks out of these two. And get me my fucking nail scissors before you go."

I **HEAR A LOUD KNOCK COMING FROM THE** back door of Cash's house. I peel back the curtains on the attic window and can just make out the edge of Buck's beard as he stands by the door. I check Damon's gun to make sure there's a round in the chamber.

"I'm gonna go down there," I say. Kelly tries to tell me no, but I assure her I'm just going to look. I open the trapdoor and quietly descend the stairs. Only having one hand makes it slow work. When I reach the door, I open it enough to see Buck. My intention is to watch and only act if he heads toward the garage, but when I see his arm in a sling, and it's clear he doesn't have a gun in his other hand, I pull out my gun and open the door.

I point the gun at his back and say, "Don't fucking move." He doesn't.

"I'm unarmed. I just want to talk," he says, raising his good arm in the air. "I'm gonna turn around, okay?"

"Real slow," I say. My hand shakes. I extend my left arm beneath it to stop the trembling. My broken fingers throb in time with my pulse.

"Damon sent me here to get the missing sheet and get rid of you, but I came to see if we can figure out something different," he says. Not that I trust him, but he sounds genuine.

"What kind of different?" I ask.

"He's lost it. I've been fine with taking something off the top, making some money on the side. I'm not a saint, but I'm not this. I'm not about kidnapping and killing kids."

"You're just about raping them, huh?" I say, and he flinches. "Yeah, I know about that. You're a piece of shit."

"You're right. I am. But I never killed anyone," Buck says in his defense.

"No, you just killed parts of them. And you came damn close to killing me the other day on the motorcycle."

"I am a piece of shit. It's not an excuse, but growing up wasn't easy for me."

"Sounds exactly like an excuse," I say.

"That's what I'm here to talk," he says and sighs.

"Talk about what a piece of shit you are?"

"No. Talk about tonight. You know he's not gonna let anyone walk away, right?"

"I figured. Yourself included?" I ask.

"Yeah, me included. But more than anything he wants you. His foot is seriously fucked up. It might be fucked up for good. He's always had this thing with his nails. Like he can't even have the tiniest bit of nail showing. So he cuts them, no joke, like five to ten times a day, but now he barely stops. His fingers are a bloody mess. He's basically cutting skin now," he says.

"Sucks for him. So what's the plan?"

"I kill him and you let me go," Buck says.

I can't help but laugh.

"Not even let me go, just give me a head start. Tomorrow you tell whoever, whatever you want. I don't want the ledger; I don't want anything other than a bit of time."

"I'm supposed to trust you?"

"No, of course not. I'm gonna grab my phone, okay? I want to show you something," he says, but doesn't move. He waits for my okay.

"So you know, the absolute easiest thing for me to do right now is to shoot you. I'm not a killer, but don't for a second think I won't do what I need to do to protect myself and my friends."

"I hear you. Super slow," and he does move super slow. His left arm in the sling stays in place, but he lowers the other toward his front pocket. I can see the outline of a phone there. He pulls it out, unlocks it, hits a button, and turns it around for me to see. It's a prerecorded video. It's starts with Buck holding the camera in front of his face inside the ground floor of the cabin they held Casey in. He frequently looks over his shoulder as he tells his tale, my guess, checking for Damon's return. In the video, he admits to coercing Casey's dad into stealing cars. He admits to being present when Damon killed Charlie Murray, the DEA agent. He even walks over and records some faded bloodstains on the floor. He walks up the stairs and shows where they held Casey, including the chain. He grabs a phone out of the drawer in the room and powers it up; the photo on the lock screen is Casey with her mom and dad. He admits to being present when Damon killed Casey's mom. He doesn't say anything about the cartel or being a rapist, but he confesses to a lot. When it's done, he types into his phone and I feel a buzz in my pocket.

"Have a look," he says. "I just sent it to you." I pull out my phone and sure enough, it's the video I just watched.

"What's stopping me from sending this to your boss at the police department right now?" I ask.

"Nothing. Other than the fact that the second a squad car pulls up on Damon, he's gonna start killing people. That's just a fact. The only thing keeping me from leaving right now, and not coming back, is that I'm not gonna leave two innocent kids with him to die. I'm not saying I'm not a piece of shit—I'm just saying I'm not that big of a piece of shit."

"I'm not giving you the sheet," I say.

"I know, I know. I hope he'll be calm enough when I return that he'll still agree to the meet tonight."

Maybe I'm a sucker, but part of me believes Buck wants to do the right thing. Or at least, not the most wrong thing.

"I fucking promise you, if I get away, I'll get help. I've never wanted to do what I do," he says. I can't help but scoff.

"I hear you, and I know I sound lame, and I'm not really making an excuse. Because it's inexcusable. I could have done something about my attraction to younger women—"

I can't help myself. "Dude, you fucking drugged and raped a kid!"

"You're right. That's what it is. It's hard for me to think of myself that way. But I need to. I could have done something about," and he pauses, struggles, but finally says, "the fact that I drug and rape young girls, and I haven't, but that doesn't mean I don't hate it. That I don't hate myself. I'll kill Damon, you just give me a head start after that."

No fucking way am I giving him a head start, but I say, "Okay, how's it gonna work?"

Buck walks me through his plan. Basically they'll pull up in their service vehicle to the Palmer Farm. He'll have a gun pointed at Cash and Damon will have a gun pointed at Hailey. He says they haven't discussed this, but this is how he sees it going. I'll be there, alone, and when Damon asks for the ledger in exchange for Hailey, Buck will shoot Damon in the head.

"Sounds too easy," I say.

"Ever shot someone in the head? I haven't, but I wouldn't say it sounds easy," he counters.

"Okay, sounds too simple then. Does he really trust you?" I ask.

"Fuck no. He doesn't trust anyone."

"You gonna give me some kind of signal?" I ask.

"The signal will be Damon's head exploding."

"Okay, that should be clear," I agree.

"And then I walk away. Call whoever you want, give them the video, whatever, just give me the night," he says.

"Okay, deal. See you at 10 p.m.," I say.

Buck doesn't say bye or wave; he just walks around to the front of the house. I hear his car door open, then close, and then he takes off. The minute he's gone, the door to the garage opens and Kelly walks out.

"No fucking way we're letting him walk away after this, right?" Kelly asks.

"Zero fucking way," I say.

PLEASE TELL ME WE DON'T HAVE EVERY single one of our eggs in the Buck basket?" Kelly asks nervously.

"We don't have every single one of our eggs in the Buck basket." Kelly looks at me with annoyance. "Most of them though, yeah."

I want to tell her it's going to be okay, but I don't think it is.

I also don't see another way. If we call the cops, I firmly believe Damon will kill Hailey and Cash. He's like a cornered, psychotic animal.

"Remember how good of a shot you were with that gun the other day?" I ask, giving Kelly my most encouraging look.

"You're joking, right?" Kelly says. "Jack, fuck. I shot that gun twice, and it's the only gun I've ever fired." She shakes her head.

"But you almost shot someone without even trying. That's gotta mean something," I say.

"You're an idiot," she says, but in a nice way. "Is me shooting someone really part of the plan?"

"Well, it's plan C. Plan A is Buck shooting Damon, and then you and I holding Buck at gunpoint until the cops arrive. Plan B is me shooting Damon. Plan C is you shooting Damon. Actually, I guess if plan A doesn't work, then plan B is me shooting Damon and you shooting Buck—or vice versa," I say, laughing at the stupidity of it all.

"It's only seven; we have a couple more hours before we need to leave. We definitely need to come up with something better by then," Kelly says, and I can't disagree.

"I'm gonna put my thinking cap on," she says, grabbing the bong.

I haven't shared with Kelly why I chose Palmer Farm. Mainly because, in retrospect, it seems ludicrous. It's no longer an actual farm—now it's open space owned by the county. It's accessible, but far enough from a main road that, for a while, until they consistently got busted, kids would go there to drink. Cash and I went to a party there once, we were thirteen and more interested in messing around than drinking. Just to the south of where everyone was gathered, we stumbled upon an old well. Almost fell into it, actually. I feel like most old wells have a circular stone wall built around them for safety. Maybe this one did at one time, but it definitely doesn't anymore. Now, it just has rotting boards running across it. Vegetation has grown up around the boards, so unless you get right up next to it, it looks like all the rest of the ground up there. Cash stepped on it, and his foot went right through. He didn't come that close to falling in, but close enough. He wanted to know how deep it was, so he started dropping rocks down it, and timing how long it took them to hit the water. They took about two and a half seconds. He said that meant the well was about one hundred feet deep.

Anyway, it's pretty far-fetched to think we're gonna get Damon—and possibly Buck—to fall down a well, so I've kept that part to myself. Besides the well part, it's actually a pretty good place for this. There are a some boulders near where we're going to meet that Kelly can hide behind.

I take two more pills since the pain in my fingers has returned. I think a slight decrease in mental sharpness is better than having unbearable pain shooting through my fingers. I set an alarm for 9:15 p.m. in case I doze off. And I do, a little bit, but I'm wide awake a couple of minutes before my alarm would have gone off. I look at Kelly and she's awake too.

"Any improvements to the plan?" I ask.

"That's your fucking job, man," she says.

"You take Buck and I'll take Damon. Don't stop shooting until you run out of bullets," I say.

"That's it? Really? You had like an hour and that's what you got?"

"And don't shoot Cash or Hailey," I say and try to smile, but I can't make it happen.

"That's not even funny, Jack. I'm seriously freaking the fuck out."

"I know. So am I. Ready?"

She grabs a pillow and flings it at me. "No, I'm not fucking ready," but she stands and heads toward the trapdoor.

It takes us about fifteen minutes to get to the spot. We don't see any other cars. It's not fully dark, but it's close. After I scan for people and don't see anyone, I knock once on the window and Kelly pops up from the floor in the back seat and slides out of the car.

I point to the boulders. "Right behind those. Just keep your gun out the whole time. If you crouch down on the left side over there, you can hide behind that bush. You should have a decent sight line, and they won't be able to see you."

"This is so fucked," she says and kicks at the ground. "That's like a mile away."

"I got a good feeling about this," I say.

"Really? You swear?"

I have a terrible feeling about this, but say, "I swear."

She gives me a quick hug and runs behind the boulders. I gave her the missing sheet before we left. I also put the picture of it, and the video from Buck, in the cloud. I copied the link and wrote a message to my mom and scheduled it to be sent at 1 a.m. tonight. Hopefully I'll be able to cancel it.

I walk to my spot and wait. It's a few minutes after ten. It's full dark and cloudy. I didn't account for the utter lack of light up here. Hopefully, Kelly can see well enough from where she is. I practice some grounding exercises the therapist I saw for a minute last summer taught me, but they do nothing. I give up and search the ground with my eyes for the old well, but everything looks the same. Just a bunch of wild grass and rocks. I see headlights approaching; they come and go as the car turns and dips up and down the little hills. It seems like it takes forever, but eventually, the car stops across the field from where I stand. The headlights shine in my eyes. Damon could very well be taking aim at me right now, and I would have no idea. My heart races and my knees feel weak. I unlock them so I don't pass out. Just when I think I'm about to have a full-on panic attack, the headlights go dark, and the doors open. I can't see a fucking thing except afterimages of the headlights. Orbs of different colors move across my vision. I hear gravel crunching under feet.

"You alone?" Damon yells from a distance.

I take a deep breath and steady myself. "Yes," I yell back.

My eyes slowly adjust. Two shapes move toward me. Pretty sure Damon is on my left, hunched behind Hailey. He struggles because he's so tall, and it looks like his limp has gotten worse. I hear him grunt a few times. Buck's on my right, with Cash in front of him. Hailey and Cash's arms are behind their backs, most likely handcuffed. They stop about twenty feet from me. Damon and Buck take small steps back from Hailey and Cash, each holding a gun in their hand. Damon's is pointed at Hailey, and Buck's is pointed at Cash. I try to imagine what it looks like from Kelly's point of view. My guess is that it's too dark to be able to tell the difference between the good guys and the bad guys.

"First thing you're gonna do, Jack, is toss me back my gun," Damon says.

I really don't want to give up the gun, so I wait.

He walks closer to Hailey and points the barrel of his gun at the side of her head. "Right fucking now," he says, and Hailey breathes in sharply.

"Fine, fine," I say and reach behind my back with my good hand.

"Slow, Jack. You don't want your girl's pretty face ruined with an exit wound from a .45," Damon says.

I slow down. My mind can't help but visualize Damon shooting Hailey in the back of the head. I grab the gun by the edge of the handle with my good hand. I extend the gun in what I feel is the least threatening way possible.

"Toss it over here," Damon says.

I'm afraid to wind up too much because it might look like I'm bringing it back to shoot him. I end up giving it a pretty weak toss. It goes all of five feet.

"You throw like a fucking girl," Damon says. "You have the sheet?"

"It's close," I say. This time, he presses the gun into Hailey's neck.

"I told you to come alone and bring the fucking sheet," he barks.

"I am alone, and I brought it. It's just not on me," I stammer.

I look at Buck and see his arm move ever so slightly toward Damon, but then it comes back. A half a second later, he does the same thing. He's probably trying to work up the courage to take a shot, but he looks like a spazz.

"I'm losing patience, Jack. Where is it?"

"Switch me for Hailey. I'll walk you to it. It's just over by those rocks," I say and point to where Kelly is hiding.

"Maybe I just shoot all of you right now and go grab it," he says.

"Good luck finding it." I don't know if he'll believe it, but I say it.

I look at Buck and urge him with every ounce of my nonexistent telepathic skills to shoot Damon in the fucking face. He does his worthless mini movement again, and then quickly moves back.

"On your knees, Jack," Damon yells at me. I freeze. He gives it about ten seconds and then says it again: "On your fucking knees, or a bullet goes in your girly friend's head."

I don't know what else to do. I drop to my knees. I watch as Damon moves the gun from Hailey to me. I take a deep breath. I sneak a quick glance at Buck. He inches his gun toward Damon. This time, Damon takes notice.

"Well, are you gonna fucking shoot me or not?" Damon asks staring directly at Buck. It's clearly a rhetorical question because as he speaks, he aims his gun at Buck and fires. The shot blows off the right half of Buck's face. He's dead before he hits the ground. Cash screams, Hailey screams, and I scream. We all scream. Then I see flashlights waving erratically coming out of a group of trees to my left. It looks like two people—maybe a younger guy and an older woman. If I didn't know better, I'd think it was—and then I hear.

"Wooo, hoooo. Where's the party, bitches?" the guy says in a terrible English accent. He has a flashlight, and he's pointing it pretty much everywhere except where it would be helpful. The woman with him has a flashlight in one hand and a bottle in the other. As they get closer, I can tell that it's Candace and Wes. What in the actual fuck? She looks straight hammered. One boob hangs out of her tank top, and she's having a hard time staying upright.

Damon stares at them, frozen. I guess he didn't factor in this contingency.

"This is a police matter," Damon yells in his most authoritative voice. "Turn around and head the other way."

"I'm gonna choke on some cock tonight! Bonfiiiiiiiire!" Candace yells. And thankfully not in an English accent, but in a Southern accent. She does this pretty well. Either she heard Damon and is doing a masterful job of ignoring him, or she didn't hear him at all because she keeps walking. She's swaying so far to the side with each step, I'm shocked she hasn't fallen. Her saggy boob swings like a pendulum. There's no way they've showed up here actually looking for a party. Well, I guess knowing them, it's possible, but man, the chances are slim. It doesn't look like they have guns, so I don't know what the fuck they're trying to accomplish. I really hope Kelly is taking this opportunity to line up a shot on Damon. I can't yet process the fact that Buck is lying dead on the ground with half his head missing.

Damon, losing his patience, yells, "Turn around. This is a police matter. You will be arrested if you proceed."

But proceed they do. Damon looks back at me and then at Cash to make sure neither of us has moved. Just then, it becomes clear to me what Candace and Wes are doing. They're decoys. Two new figures sneak up behind Damon and join our standoff. I can't fucking believe it. It's Casey and her dad.

"Don't fucking move," Casey yells as she points a gun at Damon. This prompts him to swing his gun away from Hailey and toward Casey.

"Do it, and you're dead, Damon," her dad yells from the other side. Damon jerks his head towards Reed and then back to Casey. He's not sure who to point his gun at, there are too many targets.

"You didn't think I'd leave without saying goodbye, did you,

Jack?" Casey says. I can't totally make out her face, but I bet she's smiling.

Damon pulls Hailey closer to him and jams the gun under her chin. The pressure causes Hailey to cough. Kelly decides it's time to show herself, so she pops out from behind the rocks, her gun aimed at Damon.

"Let her go," Kelly says.

Now Damon has three guns pointed at him. I spot the gun he had me toss on the ground and walk toward it. As I do, Damon fires off a quick shot near my feet. I jump back.

"Get the fuck back, all of you," Damon yells.

"Dude, it's fucking over," I say. "Let her go. We'll let you leave."

"Okay, okay," he says, walking with Hailey toward me. "I'm gonna let her go, then you're gonna let me go."

"Absolutely," I say and can't wait to beat him within an inch of his life before calling the cops.

Damon still has his gun under her chin. When he's within ten feet of me, he stumbles, cries out, and drops the gun.

"Fuck, my foot," he says, pushing Hailey off of him. As I reach for Hailey, I realize Damon's fall was a ruse. He lunges at me, in his hand he has what looks like a small pair of scissors. I move backward and stumble over a rock. I manage to grab the item out of my pocket that Hailey gave me earlier. I hope it's pointing in the right direction. When he's about on top of me, I dive toward his foot and squirt the pepper spray all over it. He's not expecting me to come at him, and he ends up tripping. I scramble away before he's able to right himself.

He's having a hard time getting back up, and it's not just because of his fucked-up toe. It looks like his good foot is stuck.

I'm about to give up hope on the pepper spray having any effect when he lets out a primal scream—guess it took some time to soak through his shoe.

"You're mean," he yells, like a little kid. He looks at me with pure hatred. I inch toward him. He's in a deep hole, hanging on to a rotting board. I can't fucking believe it—he fell into the well. I move a couple of steps closer to him. Too close. With some kind of superhuman strength, he lifts himself up with one arm and grabs my leg. His grip feels like it could break my ankle. He starts pulling me toward him, pulling me toward the edge. The ground is slippery, and I can't find purchase. I fall back and try to dig my hands into the soft earth, but he keeps pulling. The leg he's pulling crosses over the edge of the well. I pull my left leg up and away, but I'm still sliding. I cry out. My butt is nearing the edge—I have about one more inch before I go over. Then two sets of hands grab under my arms and yank me back. Damon's grip releases. I land on my ass. Cash and Hailey fall behind me. If they hadn't grabbed me, I would have been at the bottom of the well by now.

I stand and approach the edge again, this time keeping a safe distance. Damon is now holding on to a piece of wood that spans the opening of the hole with both hands. His grip is failing.

"Help me up, help me up. My fucking foot!" he yells.

I look at him and say, "Did you know your fingernails continue to grow after you die?" It's dark, but I swear I see fear in his eyes. Then I hear a snap. The piece of wood he was hanging on breaks, and he falls into the darkness.

"Your fucking eyeballlllllll!" he screams as he drops. It feels like a long time before I hear the splash that ends his descent, but I know it was only two and a half seconds.

BEER'S ON ME! WES YELLS AS HE PASSES one to each of us. "Just a few more minutes, and you can go in, Cash."

We've been sitting around the picnic table in Cash's backyard for the past hour. It's me, Cash, Hailey, Kelly, and Casey. Wheels, and yes, I've started calling him that, is supposed to show up anytime. Wes and Candace have made us wait outside while they "do something" (not that something) inside. We have a pretty good idea what that "something" is, but act like we don't.

"Dude, who are you?" I ask Wes jokingly. He laughs.

"I'm just glad you all are safe," he says, blinking and fighting back tears. Candace walks out the back door and sees it.

"Save that crybaby shit for later when we're fucking," she says, and her smile knocks a couple of years off her.

"It's allergies," Wes says, wiping his eyes.

It's been four days since that fateful night at Palmer Farm. Cash and I got off work an hour ago. Hailey leaves for Europe tomorrow. I'm sitting close enough to Hailey that our bodies touch, but I move closer still. She wraps her arms around me. She says she wakes up several times a night in a cold sweat. So do I. I look at Cash, and he looks back. He sits as close to Kelly as I am to Hailey. She's barely let him out of her sight since we got them back. The cut on his eyelid looks awful. It took several stitches, but the worst part is the bruising. Grapefruit spoons aren't that sharp, it turns out. We've been fielding a pretty insane amount of messages from people we know. Most of them heard about what happened from Maggie. We sat down with her and gave her the whole scoop the morning after the night at Palmer Farm. She put it online before anyone else. She even scooped *Black Forest Breaking News 24/7*. Ha. She says she wants to do a podcast about it. She made mention about a certain someone being a pedophile. She didn't use Cock Mike's name, but it was impossible not to know who she was talking about.

Casey sits at the picnic table opposite me. She seems okay. She's apologized to us profusely. In fact, she's said sorry so many times we told her she had to stop.

She ended up saving us in the end. She blushes every time

I mention that. She was able to find us because she turned on location sharing on my phone. She watched me type in my passcode at one point, and the day she took the ledger, she gave herself permission to track me. A bit stalker-ish, but whatever—it was worth it. She came by Cash's the night we had the showdown, or whatever it was, and found us not there. Candace and Wes were, though. Casey said all at once she got a real bad feeling. She looked up my location and showed it to Wes. He knew exactly where we were. Casey filled them in on Damon having Hailey and Cash. Then they hatched their plan.

My hand still hurts like no one's business. Believe it or not, Kelly did a fantastic job of setting the bones. When they X-rayed, they didn't have to do any repositioning. They put a fiberglass cast on my arm that extends to the two broken fingers. I do my best not to move them because it hurts like hell. But it still happens. A lot.

After Damon fell down the well, we called the cops. Well, after we got our story straight, anyway. We told them that Damon and Buck were the ones that kidnapped Casey. We told them about the DEA agent as well, but not about the part where we thought Kelly shot him. We were at the farm for about three hours being questioned. They let us go home, and then the questioning started all over again the next day at the police station. There were some knowing looks shared between cops when we told them stuff about Damon and Buck. The impression I got was that they weren't all that surprised. It seems the two of them didn't have that many friends in the department. Everyone we have dealt with so far has been super cool. Even Cash seems to have warmed a bit to the police. It sounds like we're going to be doing more interviews before this is over. There isn't going to be a trial since all three of them are dead. Wheels split before they got there, and we failed to mention he played a role in any of this.

Casey and Wheels are going to start out somewhere new. We were able to transfer a chunk of the money from the "slush fund" the person from the cartel had to an account Casey can access. Kelly assured us it was untraceable. So now Casey and Wheels have a nice nest egg to begin again. Maybe he can get a prosthetic finger.

We debated turning Cock Mike into the cops but decided on a different route. We went at Cock Mike's phone again, and wouldn't you know, the passcode was 111111. We were so close. We used his phone to change the info on the original slush fund account. Cash figured out the code on the last sheet of the ledger. It was contact info from a specific encrypted messaging app for someone we assumed was in the cartel. We sent them a note (Cash made assurances it could not be traced back to us) with pics of the ledger, including the last page. Cash left some digital breadcrumbs in the slush account that pointed to Cock Mike. We haven't seen him since. My guess is he skipped town.

We did have a run-in with a handful of Cock Mike's wrestlers at Kum Quick the other day. They were coming out as we were going in. I was expecting some kind of altercation, but one of them actually held the door open for us. And the pink eye kid, who must have gotten antibiotics because his eyes were looking a lot better, stuck his hand out and said he was sorry. Maybe they assumed the pedophile Maggie was referring to was Cock Mike. I shook his hand, and we gave each other *it's cool* nods.

Wes got a message from Wilkinson that said he and Gordon, of Kum Quick fame, were headed to Califronia to find Wilkinson's mom. Man, I hope one of them keeps a journal because, no doubt, if they don't die, that's gonna be an epic story.

My mom has been all over me since she found out what happened. It feels like there's not an hour that goes by without her texting or calling. She's been staying the night at home more and has strongly requested that I do the same. And I have. It's been nice hanging out. In some sense, I think she finally realized how little control she has over the crazy shit that happens in this world. In this town. She still loves her podcasts, but they seem less like research and more like entertainment now. I'm not sure it will last, but we have been closer this last week than we ever have.

Oh, and Candace said that Heath showed up at the front door of Echo Mountain, begging to be let back in. She said he seemed a little disoriented, but other than that, he was fine. When he was allowed back in the laundry, he hugged a giant bag of rags and cried tears of joy. Sounds like that kid is forever institutionalized.

I hear an unbelievably loud car approaching.

"That'd be Reed," Casey says. "Come see his new ride."

We head through the house to the driveway. Parked in front is a dark green muscle car. It has *Shelby* written across the front grill. Wheels hangs out the driver's side window, grinning and patting the side of the car.

"I figured the only way I could stop myself from stealing cars was to get my dream car. She's a beauty, huh? '68 Mustang Shelby GT500," he says and revs the engine a few times. I cover my ears. The backseat is piled high with luggage.

"Now that's a fucking ride," Wes says.

"I don't know how to thank you all," Casey says, making eye contact with each of us one at a time.

"We're even," Cash says. "No thanks necessary."

"Thank you anyway," she says.

"Where to?" Candace asks.

"Not a clue," Casey responds. "I just want to be settled somewhere in time for school."

"You'll keep in touch?" Hailey asks.

"Of course," she says. She gives us hugs and jumps in shotgun. She sticks her head out the open window. "And Hailey, you ever dump that kid, give me a call." Wheels revs it a few more times but, thankfully, doesn't peel out and spray gravel all over us as he drives off.

"So wait," I say. "She wasn't into me?"

Cash laughs and says, "I'm not even sure Hailey is into you."

"He's not wrong," Hailey says with a smirk.

"Funny," I say.

"You ready?" Wes asks, looking at Cash.

Cash looks sheepish but says, "Yeah."

We follow Wes through the front door.

"Close your eyes," he says.

"Seriously?" Cash asks, but he does as he's told.

Wes stands behind Cash and guides him through the living room, down the hall, and into his room. The rest of us follow. Once we're all inside Cash's room, Wes says, "Okay, open them."

When he does, he sees the bunk bed is gone, and in its place is a brand-new queen-sized bed. His room is small, so it takes up most of the space, but the couch and bean bag still fit; it's just tight.

Tears silently stream down Cash's cheeks.

"But wait, here's the best part," Wes says and grabs the sole pillow on the bed. It's red and looks more for decoration than sleeping.

"Candace has a sewing machine. We took the cover from your old mattress and turned it into stuffing. Then we used the stuffing to make this pillow," Wes says and hands it to Cash. Cash grabs it, hugs it, and the tears come down in force. It's contagious. Wes starts crying, then Kelly, then Hailey, and now me. Even fucking Candace is crying.

After a few moments, Cash wipes the tears from his eyes and takes a seat on the bed. He holds the pillow to his chest.

"It's really comfortable," Cash says, pushing down on the mattress.

"It's one of those new kinds, made out of sponge," Wes says.

"Foam," Candace offers. "Memory foam."

"Thank you," Cash says quietly.

The silence turns awkward. Cash looks up at Wes and says, "Okay, the lovefest is over. Get the fuck out of my room."

Wes chuckles, flips Cash off, and he and Candace leave. Kelly sits next to Cash on his new bed and kisses his injured eye.

I take a seat on the couch next to Hailey. It's comfortable, and Hailey is warm. The room is quiet. My heart rate is normal. I close my eyes.

WHEN SOMEONE DIES IN BLACK FOREST, their body is sent to the county coroner's office down the mountain. From the outside, the coroner's office is about as generic as it gets—two stories tall, tan brick, mirrored windows, struggling landscape. Nothing would make you think that more than five hundred bodies wind up there every year. As you walk through the front doors, the most noticeable thing is the smell. Not of death, but of hospital-strength disinfectant. The person at the front desk looks like the person you would find at the front desk of any business that requires a front desk. The current version is slightly overweight, early forties, brown curly hair, business casual. You could pass this person on the street thirty times without recognition.

Behind the front desk, and to the right, are administration offices, where the paperwork of death is handled. To the left, behind a frosted glass door, is a carpeted hallway that ends with a set of locked double doors. Through those doors is where the real work takes place. Fluorescent lights do a manageable job of dispelling the gloom. Two empty stainless steel gurneys are pushed against stainless steel sinks. Stainless steel cabinets and drawers line white walls. Bits of color from red biohazard containers, yellow plastic tubing, and blue latex gloves draw the eye like paint splatter. At the back of the room is yet another door, this one giant and metal; it leads to a walk-in refrigerator. Inside rest more metal gurneys on wheels. There are six in all, four of them currently occupied. The floor is cement with a large drain in the center. The metal grate covering the opening has gone red around the edges. Most likely it's from rust, but it's hard to see anything red in a morgue and not think blood.

The bodies are wrapped in plastic. Not official body-bag-looking plastic, just plain thick opaque plastic. Like something you could buy at a home improvement store. The bodies are secured to the gurneys with thick straps. The very last body in the row belongs to Damon Storey. His autopsy recently concluded. His broken and protruding bones have been pushed back in place. The skin hastily stitched to keep them from poking out again. After falling down a hundred-foot well, he looks as expected.

Contusions and cuts are evident across his body where he skidded and bounced off the rough walls on his way to the bottom. His head lolls slightly to the right; the spine in his neck was mostly eviscerated on impact. His skin is white-gray. His body is not ready for an open casket. Which is fine, because so far he has gone unclaimed. The body has been cleaned somewhat, but there's still dirt and soil stuck deep in the abrasions and cuts. His clothes and personal effects are in a separate room. The person who bagged them, a mousey guy with an underdeveloped brain by the name of Larry Clark, marveled at the utensil with the serrated edge in Damon's pocket. Larry was unfamiliar with the concept of a grapefruit spoon and proceeded to spend a good chunk of the rest of the day thinking about cutting his corn flakes in half.

Not that you would want to look at Damon's hands, because several fingers on both were badly broken in the fall. But if you did, you'd see they were far from clean. If you were to look closely at his nails, you wouldn't say they were long, but you might say they were on the edge of needing a clipping. Jack stated, erroneously as it turns out, that fingernails continue to grow after a person dies. If someone were to inquire about this with Leighton Castor, the coroner who conducted the autopsy on Damon, he would gladly set them straight. He'd say that fingernails, or toenails for that matter, do not continue to grow after someone expires. But it looks like they do, because the skin below the nails shrinks down and back, thus leaving more nail exposed. Even in Damon's current state of being dead, he would be terrified by the length of them. And if Jack Larson were to know this, he'd most assuredly smile. Oh, and during the retrieval of Damon's body, that toe that Jack so mangled with the crowbar ended up getting ripped clean off. It currently sits at the bottom of the well, being eaten by some kind of miniature worms.

Around the same time Jack, Cash, and company were wondering about the whereabouts of Cock Mike, two boys, Greg Connors and Chris Lestig, were messing around in the abandoned sawmill at the southern end of Black Forest. It's a favorite haunt of theirs during the summer months. Chris chased Greg around a decaying stack of unhewn wood, and as Greg swung around the edge of it, he came to a skidding stop when he spotted a neon-green muscle car just sitting there, as if dropped from the heavens. Chris proceeded to slam into Greg's back, but neither barely noticed. For the next minute, they stared in awe. The incongruity of this shiny, bright-colored piece of machinery set against the myriad browns of wood and dirt left them speechless. They looked at one another, then at the car, and then back at each other before smiling.

Without talking, they walked to the car. Chris, the slightly braver of the two eleven-year-olds, tried the driver's door. It opened. Greg ran to the passenger door, which was also unlocked. They took seats inside. Chris noticed the keys hanging in the ignition. If they were a few years older, they might have turned it to see if it started, maybe even gone for a joyride. After rubbing their hands on the warm seats and dash, they peeked into the backseat. Even that looked fast. Chris, sitting in the driver's seat, started exploring near the pedals. He came across the button for the trunk and pushed it. The boys startled at the sound of it popping open. Seconds later, they shared almost identical looks of disgust. The kids grabbed their shirts and pulled them over their noses. Even at eleven years old, they knew they were smelling death. Their excitement at finding the car quickly turned to fear. They stared at the top of the open trunk through the rear window, neither of them wanting to go out and look, but both knowing they would end up doing so.

"I don't want to see what's in there," Greg said with a slight stutter.

"You also don't want to wake up tomorrow knowing you didn't," Chris responded.

"Actually, I might be okay with that."

"On the count of three?" Chris asked.

"I guess," Greg managed.

For some unspoken reason, they counted to three on their hands instead of out loud. When they extended their ring fingers, completing the exercise, they exited the car. Greg's eyes were focused on the ground as he walked to the trunk, so before seeing what was inside, he came upon the license plate that read "COCH-MYK." In his freaked-out state, he wasn't able to make out what it was supposed to spell. Before Greg mustered the courage to look up, he heard Chris gasp. As if pulled by invisible ties, Greg's head lifted, and his eyes turned to the trunk. He was vaguely aware of the sound of Chris puking off to his left.

It was immediately clear to Greg that what he was looking at was a dead body. The smell was so strong it felt as if it should be visible. Greg, in a mild state of dissociation, was able to look upon the scene detached from his emotions. He saw a middle-aged man with some injuries to one arm, a huge bloodstain on the crotch of his pants, and a mortal-looking wound across his neck. Having recently concluded an anatomy unit in life science last year, Greg was able to identify the man's trachea. It was completely severed. Greg's attention was then drawn to the dead man's mouth. A fleshy something hung from it. The object was shriveled and had the appearance of a small, rotten sausage. And for a moment, Greg wondered why the dead man had a sausage in his mouth. But it didn't take long for him to realize it was the man's dick.

Then the license plate flashed in his mind, and he made the connection. And then he thought, *Hmm, is that why his license plate says Cock Mike?* And then almost as quickly, he realized that didn't make sense. Like, he would have had to have gotten the license plate well before he had his own cock in his mouth. And Jesus Christ, who would walk around with their cock in their mouth anyway? That's when Greg came back to the present and rushed to the opposite side of the car, where he joined Chris in puking up the large quantity of Kola Kountry he had chugged earlier.

FUCK, FUCK, FUCK. CASH!" I TURN TO SEE if he heard me, but he doesn't respond. He's slumped in the back seat, bloody, the seatbelt the only thing holding him in place. My shoulder aches and I can feel my own blood slide down my armpit. I hold tight to the steering wheel and urge the crappy Camaro faster. The blown out back window brings the sounds of the outside in, but does little for the smell.

"Cash! Open your eyes man. Just open your eyes, please." Nothing.

I reach a stop sign and blow through it. Luckily it's late. Just a couple more miles. I floor it.

We come to a red light. I flash my brights, pound on the broken horn and fly through the intersection. A car stops just in time and we narrowly avoid colliding.

"Cash, buddy. Cash, look at me. I'm so fucking sorry man." He coughs weakly. A driver pulls into my lane and slows to make a turn, I swerve around the car at the last second. I hear the screech of brakes as I narrowly avoid clipping another car. A hand juts out the open window with middle finger extended as we race past. Yeah, fuck you too.

Finally a road sign with a blue "H" and an arrow to the right. So close, but I take the turn too fast and the car fish tails. The left rear tire slams into the curb and hops on the median. After the side of the car smacks a road sign I manage to right it and keep going. The tire didn't blow, but the car is pulling hard to the left and is almost impossible to keep straight. As we get to the top of a small hill the hospital becomes visible, the only light on this dark stretch of mountain road.

I keep the pedal floored and fly into the parking lot, gravel spitting on the parked cars. The ER sign just a couple hundred yards away. I pull up to the entrance and slam on my brakes. I open my door and tumble out.

I look up at the sound of the automatic doors of the ER opening, but no one is coming. A man stands behind the front desk, cranes his neck to see.

I yell: "Help! I need some fucking help!"

I get Cash's door open and work on the seat belt that's jammed under him. His clothes are squishy and wet with blood.

"Come on Cash, almost there man. Just hold on." At last I unfasten his seatbelt and get him out of the car. I grab him under both shoulders and pull his unconscious body towards the entrance. It's like dragging a dead deer.

I get him halfway across the sidewalk and slip. I'm able to get my body under his before we hit the ground, cushioning his fall. A half dozen nurses and other hospital employees rush to us. Two of them push a stretcher on wheels. Cash's weight is lifted off me and they put him on the bed and place an oxygen mask on his face. They yell things back and forth and I get up and follow them through the doors, trying to keep up. Before I make it to the next set of doors a nurse notices my bloody arm and pulls me to the side and looks for the source. I try to yank myself free. "I need to go with him. I need to be with him."

She grabs my good arm firmly, holding me in place. "He's in good hands. Right now we need to take care of you."

The last thing I see as the doors close is Cash's bloody arm slip off the side of the bed.

I drove as fast as I could, but I don't think it was fast enough.

FOUR WEEKS EARLIER

FOR TWO DAYS I'VE BEEN STARING AT this mugshot of Alex Finn and it still scares the shit out of me. Even without the swastika tattooed across the front of his neck he'd be terrifying. The shaved head, the scar under his right eye. It's not long, but it's deep—more like a stab than a cut. He was twenty-two when this photo was taken. He'd be twenty-four if he was still alive.

My phone rings, I find it buried under the papers scattered across my bed. It's Cash calling on video. He's been on a 'run' with his dad the past two days and got back late last night. Cash's full name is Johnny Cash McDermid, but everyone calls him Cash. His dad wanted to call him Cash from the start, but his mom wasn't having it, so he started life as Johnny. The moment his mom died, Johnny became Cash full time. She overdosed when he was three and he doesn't remember her at all.

I answer and Cash immediately jumps in with: "Dude. Grams didn't kill me. She's losing it, though." He sits on the edge of his bed, a cigarette in his mouth and a book on his lap. He's so tall he needs to bend his head to the side so it doesn't hit the bunk bed above. His red hair covers one eye, but I can tell he's tired.

"About time you got up. I'm coming over. I found something hidden in my dad's study," I tell him.

"Weed?" He jokes holding his cigarette like a joint.

"I think your dad has us covered on that. No, a file. One of his patients. Remember Alex Finn?"

"Duh."

"Well, apparently my dad was his therapist at County."

"Did he try to set your dad on fire too?"

"Thankfully no. But I think the file has something to do with my dad's disappearance."

"You shitting me?"

"I am not. And don't laugh, but get this, in the file Finn said he found the Raubgold."

Cash laughs, doubles over even. Once he gets it under control he says: "Sure he did. I always thought it was Rob's Gold anyway."

"No dumbass, it's German. Raubgold, it means stolen gold."

Most everyone who grows up in this town hears the rumors about the Black Forest Inn having been some kind of secret headquarters for German spies in the 40's. The spies apparently hid a bunch of Nazi gold at the Inn to help finance the eventual German invasion of America. I always thought it was ridiculous. What the fuck would a bunch of Nazis be doing in our tiny mountain town in the middle of America? Most people older than about twelve feel the same. Most, but not all. There's a group of local white supremacists who believe the rumors with a vengeance and they've turned the search for the Raubgold into something like a religion. Alex Finn was the most obsessed of all.

"Finn's been dead for what, two years? He finds the gold and no one's heard about it?"

"He got arrested right after and the only person he told was my dad."

"Okay, so where's all the gold then?"

"According to the file, it's still at the Inn. Hidden in the same place it's been for seventy something years."

"You're high." Cash shakes his head.

"I'm just telling you what I read. There's more, but it'll be easier if I show you."

"Then get your ass over here. I got a gift from Grams."

"Oh, really? What's that?"

"It's a surprise."

"On my way." Without waiting for a reply, I hang up and drop my phone in my pocket. I slide the mugshot, the file and the other papers and maps I've been scouring through for the past two days into my backpack and hop out of bed. I search my room for clothes and grab a clean-enough shirt, a pair of jeans, and my Converse. I run my hands through my hair and decide it's still short enough that I can leave it alone.

I make my way past my mom's room as quietly as I can — she works overnights and sleeps during the day. There's a post-it on the front door of our apartment she must have left before going to bed. It reads: *Jack, my love, have a great day!* The exclamation point has a circle at the bottom instead of a dot, like an unfinished smiley face.

Some people say my mom looks like Jackie O. I just think she looks distant. I feel closer to my dad, who I haven't seen in two years, than I do my mom, who I saw yesterday. Because even when she's here, she's not here.

At first I thought when she would disappear behind her eyes it was because she was on something. Like pills, Xanax probably. I searched through her purse and her medicine cabinet and nightstand and car and everywhere I could think of, but never found anything. So now I don't think so.

Most of the time, I just think she's depressed. Actually, most of the time I don't think about it at all.

My mom and dad got together when I was a year old. I've never met my biological dad, he left the minute he found out my mom was pregnant. I'm told that move was pretty consistent with his personality. My actual dad leaving though, the one that has been here my entire life, that's a whole different story.

I doubt Mom knows anything more than I do about what happened or why. Or where he is. All we know for certain is that he got in his car one morning, drove off and never came back. But I'm convinced she thinks he's dead.

In the beginning, every time I heard a car drive by I'd turn in hopes it was him, but she never did. Same with when I'd hear the chime from a message arriving on my phone, I'd pray it was something from him like, "Hey bud, sorry, finally on my way home, you'll never believe what happened to me." The message never came, but I always scrambled to check. I never saw her do that.

I got my first phone when I was ten, about three years before he went missing. I must have sent him a hundred messages a day back then. Smiley faces. Frowny faces. What are you doing? What are you doing now? Now? How about now? Here's a picture of my hand. Of my foot. Of the grass. And he always wrote back. He never got annoyed, never told me to stop. One night we were at a neighbor's house for dinner and they made this vegetable casserole thing. It was not good. My dad texted me *Gross* right at the dinner table. I busted out laughing. God I miss him.

He'd been suspended from work and things were going on I didn't know about, but they were all still within the range of normal.

The cops came and asked some questions. They looked for a couple of weeks, or said they did. I overheard them tell my mom that sometimes people just leave.

My Uncle Mike gave me some weak-ass talk a week or so after and said, "Adults are complicated. Life gets hard, people fall off the wagon, and all bets are off," and some other shit. Don't get me started on that guy. My dad quit drinking before I was born and minus a three week period when I was nine, he's been sober my entire life.

For most of those three weeks he drank just fine. Then he got drunk one evening before he picked me up from soccer practice. He didn't mean to. He was just gonna have one beer. He walked toward me from the parking lot, not stumbling, but not steady. I smelled the beer on his breath as he helped me pack up my bag. As we walked back to the car he told me to pass him the ball. I did and he took a shot on goal and completely missed. Not just the goal, the ball. He laughed, but I could tell he was embarrassed.

He took back roads home. Just past The Black Forest Inn he turned on Jackpine. It's a dirt road and the first curve is deceiving, the shoulder makes it look more gradual than it is. He took it too fast and we went off the side. Brakes locked and we slid down the embankment into the forest. It's pretty crazy how far we made it before hitting anything.

But all good things must end, and we slammed into a tree. We were going pretty slow by that time, and if we had another twenty feet or so the car might have stopped on its own, but we hit the tree with enough force to shatter the passenger window and send it into the side of my head. It didn't hurt, but blood got in my eye and I saw the world through a red kaleidoscope. I went to the emergency room, no stitches though. Just two small butterfly bandages. My dad managed to avoid his second DUI because by the time he talked to the cops, too much time had passed to give him a breathalyzer.

My dad never drank again. Pretty much devoted his life to staying sober and helping other people get sober after that. On occasion, out of the corner of my eye, I would catch him looking at the two small scars on the right side of my forehead. The few times I made eye contact with him before he turned, I saw his eyes go shiny.

Contrary to Uncle Mike's vast knowledge of all things human nature, I don't think my dad is all that complicated. He likes football. He likes working in the yard. He loves my mom. He's funny. He's never made me feel like shit, or small.

I'm not saying my dad was perfect. He'd lose his patience with me on occasion, and there was the relapse of course, but those are just examples of things that are still him—just further from the usual him.

To me it's like this: let's say you have a dog. And you've had that dog since he was a puppy, nine years now. And sure, that dog might surprise you here and there — he might pee in the house when he didn't usually. He might chew up your baseball mitt. He might even bite your cousin Pete on the arm and break the skin if Pete tripped and fell on top of him while he was sleeping. So no, you can't predict everything, but even the things you can't predict fall into some kind of normal. But my dad just abandoning us? It's like that dog coming up to the table where the family is eating breakfast, going up to your little sister, like he wants a Cheerio or something, like he's done a million times, but instead he attacks her throat. Then, that same dog takes a seat at the table, and with blood and spit and bits of esophagus stuck in his teeth he screams, in actual human words: "I fucking hate all of you!" Then he jumps up and takes off through the dog door.

This is J. Scott Boyd's second novel and the second book in the Black Forest series. He lives in Colorado with his wife Ann, and two children, Lincoln and Hazel. He is a licensed psychotherapist in private practice where he works with clients struggling with addiction, trauma and depression.

@scottboyd
www.jscottboyd.com